Fiancé on Paper

A Billionaire Fake Marriage Romance

Nicole Snow

Description

ON PAPER, IT'S PRETEND. BUT MY HEART KNOWS WHAT'S REAL.

His proposal came in a little black envelope with thirteen unlucky words:

You still owe me that favor, doll, and I'm cashing in.

Marry me.

In a normal life, I'd *never* get hitched to Calvin Randolph. Not with his heart-stopping blue eyes, infamous player reputation, and an ego bigger than the part of his anatomy he loves boasting about the most.

Been there, done that. All except the last part, which he's left to my shameful imagination for seven years apart.

Of course, the fake fiancée contract I just signed is anything *but* normal. Neither was the tragic day our schoolyard romance died, when he made an unspeakable sacrifice.

He saved my life. He paid a terrible price. Now, I owe him big.

He's come to collect in make believe: the blushing lies, the sideways glances leaving me breathless, the teasing kisses every time his teeth grab my bottom lip in front of the world.

It shouldn't be this hard.

It's just pretend. It's just a few weeks. I can *totally* resist the demanding, cold, obscenely handsome man he's become.

We have our rules. But the simple one I kept to myself might be harder: *don't fall in love.*

I already did that once. I know the risks. I won't let it happen.

Because if his charm steals my heart again, if I let him go *all the way* when his lips trace scary promises on mine, this paper engagement becomes real enough to ruin us...

To everyone who ever lived a lie, and still found love. - Nicole

I: Look Who's Back

Something in his makeup made him an utter bastard, but I owed him my life.

It's my heart I refused to give up without a fight. If only I'd known from the very start Calvin Randolph never backs down.

Not in love. Not in business. Not in any corner of his battered existence.

I'll never understand it.

Maybe he's missing the gene that stops a normal man from sinking his hands into the earth and ripping it to messy, screaming shreds until he gets his way.

Perhaps defeat just never made sense in his head.

Or possibly it's because this was just meant to be. There's a natural mischief in every heart that loves bringing together what's complicated, dangerous, and totally incompatible in a blinding impact.

Oh, but I still wish I'd *known,* before our blind collision became love.

We would have prevented so much suffering.

I'm in no mood to pull a jet black envelope out of my mailbox. Not after an exhausting day dealing with corporate legalese and a language barrier that's like a migraine prescription. Especially when said legalese is a hodge-podge of English and Mandarin bullet points outlining bewildering trade concepts that make me want to pop aspirin like Junior Mints.

But the coal colored envelope isn't what ends me. It's a single word, the one and only scrawled on the front in bright pink, without so much as a return address or a stamp to accompany it.

DOLL.

No one's called me that in years. Seven, to be precise.

I have to steady myself against the mailbox when my heartbeat goes into my ears. For a second I'm afraid I'll faint.

It's incredible how the only man who'd ever call me a name I haven't heard since high school still has a freakish ability to reduce me to a knee-shaking, cement lunged mess so many years later.

My fingernail slides across the seal, digs in, and splits it open. I tear gingerly, like I'm expecting a snake or a tarantula to jump out. There isn't enough room for creepy crawlies, I suppose, though I wonder about the hard lump in the corner, rubbing it against my palm.

The constant noise in the hall of my cramped Beijing flat has faded from a roar to a whisper. It's hard to focus on the slim white note I pluck out when I'm trying to remember how to breathe. There's no mistaking the handwriting.

They're his words. I'd recognize them anywhere, even after so long.

Blunt, mysterious, and taunting as ever. He keeps it short and sweet – assuming there's anything sweet about reaching down inside me, and yanking out a dozen painful memories at once.

> *It's been too long.*
> *You still owe me that favor, doll, and I'm cashing in.*
> *Marry me.*
>
> *-Cal*

"Marry me?" I read it again, shaking my head.

If this is a joke, it isn't funny. And I already know it isn't. Cal wouldn't break a seven year silence for a stupid laugh. It's serious, and it's a brand new kind of terrifying.

My eyes trace his three insane sentences four times before my knees give out.

I go down hard, banging my legs on the scuffed tile, dropping the envelope. The object anchored in the corner bounces out with a clatter as loud as a crashing symbol, leaving a haunting echo in my ears.

I look down and mentally start planning my goodbyes. It's a gold ring with a huge rock in the middle, set into a flourish designed to mimic a small rose. I don't need to try it on to know it's probably my size.

I flip the note over in my hands before I lose it. There's a number scrawled on the backside in the same firm, demanding script. CALL ME, says the two words next to it in bold, as if it's the most natural thing in the world to ask for a mail order bride in less than ten words.

As if it hasn't stopped my heart several times over.

I can't believe he's back.

I can't believe he's found me here, on the other side of the Earth, and decided to drag me back to the hell we both left behind.

I really, *really* can't believe what he's asking me to do.

But it's my fault, isn't it? I'm the one who said I'd do *anything,* if he ever needed it.

Without him, I wouldn't have my dream career working trade contracts in China for a prestigious Seattle company. I'd be lucky serving tables with the criminal stain on my record if he hadn't stepped in, and saved me when it seemed hopeless.

There's a lot I don't know.

Like why he's gone emergency bride hunting, for one. Or what he's been doing since the last dark day I saw him, crying while they hauled him off in handcuffs. I don't even know what kind of devils are in the details if I actually agree to this madness – and it's not like I have a choice.

Small town guilt will gnaw at my soul forever if I turn him down.

Oh, but he'll catch up with me again soon, and let me know exactly what new hell awaits. That much, I'm certain.

It won't be long before I'm face-to-face again with the

sharp blue eyes that used to make my blood run hot. Twisted up in knots like a gullible seventeen year old with a bad crush and a blind spot for bad people before I know what's hit me. And yes, revisiting every horrible thing that happened at Maynard Academy in ways I haven't since my therapist discharged me with flying colors.

He's right about one thing, the only thing that matters in any of this: I owe him. Big time.

All the unknowns in the world are worthless stacked up against this simple truth.

So I'll wait, I'll shrivel up inside, and I'll chew on the same nagging question some more.

Jesus, Cal. What the hell have you gotten yourself into?

Seven Years Ago

The beautiful boy with the constant entourage ignored me until my seventh day at the new school.

How my parents thought I'd ever fit into this place, I don't know. They just saw the school's shiny academic track record and absorbed its prestige from Seattle socialites several leagues higher than we'd ever be. A fast track scholarship I won in an essay contest sealed the deal. My old English teacher in Everett submitted it behind my back when I was ready to throw it in the trash, and the rest is history.

Who could blame them for leaping at the chance? They want the absolute best for me. I'm ready to make my family proud, even if it means trading a huge piece of my seventeen year old social life for the best education several states over.

It's not like Maynard Academy has a welcome wagon. The other kids keep their awkward distance since the first day I show up on the seating charts next to them. Almost like they smell the stink of my missing trust fund, or the Mercedes that didn't materialize as soon as I got my license.

I still take the bus. And I'm not sure my parents could ever afford a trust lawyer on their seventy thousand combined income, raising two girls. Their struggle to keep up rent and bills reminds me how lucky I am to get a scholarship to this place.

Turns out the benefactor behind the money at Sterner Corp shares my love for John Steinbeck.

Ever since we moved down to south Seattle, uprooting lives and careers just for this special chance, I'm in another world.

If the black lacquered study desks, the library with the crystal chandeliers and the skylights, or the marble fountain out front hadn't tipped me off the first week, the natural pecking order here certainly does.

My face is stuck in a German textbook when he comes up to me. He doesn't bother with introductions, just pushes his fingers into my book, and rips it out of my hands.

"Do you ever speak?" His voice is smooth as ice, a rogue smirk tugging at his lips.

"Hey!" I stand up, dropping the rest of my small book stack on the floor, arms folded. "I don't know, don't *you* have any manners?"

"There's never been much point," he tells me, sizing me up with his sky blue eyes.

I hate it, but he isn't wrong. It took all of three days here to notice how everyone hangs on his every word. There are always a couple grinning jocks and puppy-eyed cheerleaders at his shoulder. I think the teachers would love to knock 'Mr. Randolph' down a few marks, if only he didn't keep acing all his tests.

He's too good a student and too big a dick to be worth the trouble.

I've seen the summary sheets tacked to the boards. Every time, every class, Calvin Randolph ranks infuriatingly high. I've heard the gossip going around, too. Just because I like to keep my nose buried in my books doesn't mean I'm deaf.

He's a straight A jerk with money, good looks, and brains behind his predictable God complex.

"Seen you around, Maddie, and you haven't said shit. That's a first for me, being ignored like I'm not worth your time." Oh, he also has a filthy mouth, which makes it doubly ridiculous every woman in our class would kill to have it on hers. "I'd love to know why. Everybody, new or old, wants on my good side if they want off Scourge's bad."

For such cool, calming eyes, they burn like the sun. My cheeks go red, flustered and hot when I jerk my eyes off his. "I don't know who that is," I say. "It's only been a week."

"Interesting. Thought a girl who goes for the librarian look would be a lot more observant than that." I stick out my hand, going for my language book, but he jerks it away like I'm a helpless kitten. His smirk blooms into a cruel smile. "It's okay if you're a slow learner, doll. I'd have my eyes glued to this boring crap all the time too if I didn't have a photographic memory."

He's so full of it he's overflowing.

"Give it back," I snap, looking around to see if there are any teachers walking by. I'm not sure I'd have the courage to ask them to step in. This school isn't any different from an ordinary high school when it comes to attitudes, despite the family income level. Nobody wants to be the class runt who goes crying for help, and suffers the outcast consequences.

"Cal, I'm not playing around. I need to get to class."

The second to last bell of the day sounds over the speaker, adding its emphasis to my words. He clucks his tongue once, his strong jaw tightening. "So, you do know my name."

"What do you *want?*" I whine, trying to keep it together. "I don't have time for games."

I try to snatch my book again. Too slow. He lifts it higher, far above my head. I'm barely up to the neck attached to his broad, vast shoulders. He towers over me, one more way his body tells me how small I am next to him. Even physiology rubs in his superiority.

"I want you to crack a damned smile first," he says, laying a patronizing hand on my shoulder. "Show me something human. I've seen two expressions on your face since the day you showed up, doll. Tell me there's more."

"What happens on my face is *my* business, jerk. Not yours." By some miracle, he relents, letting my German book swing down with my hand the next time I grab it. I stumble a few steps back toward the bench to collect my mess of things.

I've got maybe sixty seconds to make it to class before the next bell if I don't want a tardy slip.

"Jerk? You're adorable." He steps closer, swallowing me in his shadow. A few of the kids racing down the halls slow, watching the tension unfolding between us. "On second thought, fuck the smile. I'd love to see those lips say something nasty a whole lot more than I'd like them right-side up. Fact that you're blushing at the mere suggestion tells me I'm on the right track, doll."

His tone is creeping me out. I stuff a few loose books into my backpack, sling it over my shoulder, and start moving down the hall. Sighing, I decide to waste a few more precious seconds asking him the only question that really interests me.

"Why do you keep calling me that – 'doll?'"

"Christ, do I have to explain *everything?*" His smirk is back, and I decide I don't like it, no matter how much light it adds to his gorgeous face. "Button nose, brown eyes, chestnut hair that looks like it's never seen a real salon. You don't fit the Maynard mold. Must be smart if you made it here in the first place without money, but I can't say I'm impressed. Brains don't matter here. It's my job to make sure you find out how this school works the easy way. You don't want hard."

Hard? I have to stop my brain from going into the gutter, especially when he's looking at me like that. I'm also confused. *What in God's name is he talking about?*

I don't remember being so insulted, and never by a man who uses his good looks like a concealed weapon. "I'm perfectly capable of figuring it out myself. Thanks very much, ass," I yell back over my shoulder, moving my feet to put as much distance between us as quickly as I can.

"Thanks for giving me exactly what I want," he growls back, hands on his hips, his strong arms bulging at his sides. They look more like they belong to a weight lifter in his twenties than a boy who's just a year older than me.

The last class of the day, chemistry, is just a blur. It's one of the few I don't share with Cal this semester, thank God.

He's the lucky one, though. Not me. If I had to sit with his smug, searing blue eyes locked on me for more than another minute, I think I'd rush to find the easiest recipe for a test tube stink bomb that would teach him not to stick his nose where it doesn't belong.

Okay, so, maybe he's not the biggest dickweed at Maynard after all. It's a couple more weeks before I find out why everyone dreads Scourge. He's gone for my first weeks thanks to a long suspension. Meanwhile, I've aced my language studies, made a few loose friends, and even settled into a study routine blissfully free from Cal's attention.

That changes when the human storm blows in.

There's a commotion in front of our lockers at noon, near lunch, when the kid in the leather jacket rolls in late. He wears mostly black, just like every other coward in a tough guy shell since time began. Chains hang off his sleeves, looking like they were designed for whipping anyone in his path. I don't understand how he gets away with it at first, seeing how it violates every part of the school dress code.

He's every bad school bully stereotype rolled in a cliché. Shaggy dark hair with a black widow red stripe running through the middle, piercings out the wazoo, and a sour scowl dominating his face that makes Cal's smirk look downright angelic. He also has tattoos peaking out his neckline and crawling along his wrists. Screaming skulls, shooting fire, blood dipped daggers – the scary trifecta for a troubled young man trying his best to look hard.

I've also wondered why there's never anyone using the locker on my left side. I wrongly concluded it might be a spare.

Oh, sweet Jesus, if only I'd been so lucky.

Alex "Scourge" Palkovich Jr. shows me he means business without uttering a word. The boys and girls in front of him who don't clear a path fast enough get pushed out of his way. I get my first shot of panic when he's still ten feet away, after everybody between us slams their lockers shut and scurries across the hall.

"You." He points. I freeze in my tracks. "Where the fuck's Hugo? You his new girl, or what?"

"Hugo?" I don't know that name.

The psycho has his hands on my shoulders, shaking me like a ragdoll, before I'm able to remember why it sounds so familiar.

I inherited my locker from another student. There's a

worn label stuck inside my locker with that name. *Hugo.*

"Don't play dumb with me," he snarls.

"Jeez, look, I don't know him. Honest. I'm not who you're looking –"

"Shut up! Stop covering for his fucking ass, little girl. He put me out for three weeks when his sorry ass got caught smoking what I sold. Nobody does business and then fucks me over, understand? No one!"

My nerves are on needles. His nostrils flare, and the muscular fingers digging into my arms are starting to hurt. "Sorry, I'm new here. I don't think I can help you," I try to tell him, cool as I can manage. "I really don't know Hugo."

He sucks in a long, ragged breath and then shoves me away. He pushes me hard. My shoulder impacts the locker with an *oomph*, and I'm left leaning against it, wide-eyed and staring at the mess of a boy fuming next to me.

Scourge twists the knob on his locker for the combo, nearly rips the door off when he opens it, and slams it with a deafening bang after staring inside for a few breathless seconds. He looks at me. "Consider this your only warning. I find out you lied to me, I'll spend coin getting even, bitch. Already had two suspensions this year. Not afraid of a third, and you look like you're dying for someone to pull up that skirt and throw you against the nearest wall, teach you some fucking respect."

I can't breathe. I can't think. I can't stop my thumping heart from making me light-headed.

"Maddie, come on," Chelle says, tugging at my arm. "Get away from him."

I let her numbly lead me away to the school cafeteria. As soon as we've grabbed lunch and sat down, I start asking questions. It's the best way not to breakdown and cry after one of the scariest encounters of my life.

"What's his deal? Why do they let him stay?" I can't stop thinking how Cal used that name – doll –

as if I'm the misfit at this school. My chicken tenders and chocolate milk comfort me with the slightly-better-than-average charm school cafeteria food has. The academy's selection is nothing amazing, but it's filling and just tasty enough.

"Special protection. Principal Ross wants to run for school council next year, haven't you heard?" Chelle smiles sadly. I shake my head. "Well, guess whose father just happens to be a major shaker in Seattle politics? Ever heard of Alex Palkovich Sr., the councilman?"

"Oh, God." I wrinkle my nose. "You mean *he's* Scourge's dad? He used to show up for fundraisers and inspirational speeches at my dad's company."

"Yep, the apple falls pretty far from the tree this time. It's banged up and rotten."

"Who does he think he's convincing, anyway? I mean, the scary ink, the piercings, the punk bomber jacket…amazing he doesn't get called out for breaking dress code." I look down at my own soft blue blouse and plaid skirt, frowning.

Chelle just laughs. "Girl, you've got a lot to learn about how backs are scratched at Maynard. He's gotten in trouble tons of times. Scourge never gets suspended unless he's done *really* bad. Hugo got caught by his pastor smoking the roaches he bought off that kid. Gave up his source pretty quick, and they had to do something this time because the police were involved."

"Yeah, Hugo, I keep hearing that name. Where the heck is he?"

"You don't get on Scourge's bad side and get away without catching hell," Chelle says, wagging a finger. "Hugo's folks were smart. They pulled him out and transferred to Jackson High the next county over. Heard he *begged* them for it. It's not as good, of course, but it's better than spending the rest of his high school career waiting for the knife in his back."

I'm worried she means it literally. Could it be *that* bad? I knew this boy was bad news, but I didn't know he was a total loon.

"And what's with the name? Scourge?"

Chelle opens her mouth to answer, but another voice cuts her off behind me. "Scourge of God, doll. It's from one of those dumb death metal bands he listens to. He only says it about ten times a week to remind us what hot shit he thinks he is. And don't you know he's got an Uncle in the *fucking Grizzlies?*"

When I spin my chair around, Cal stands there with a twinkle in his blue eyes, his hair tossed in a subtle, delicious mess. He's just come from gym, still wearing his black lacrosse shorts and grey jersey with the school's royal crested M.

"I wasn't asking you." I turn, pointing my nose in the

air. I'm not in any mood for his games after what just went down.

"Heard you had a little run in with our pal. Move over, Emily." He takes her seat without even acknowledging the blonde sophomore next to me who looks like she's just been kissed because he remembers her name.

"I thought the Grizzlies cleaned up their act. That's what mom says, anyway. She used to ride with them sometimes in her wilder days, before she settled down with dad." I'm frowning, trying to figure out why he's decided to give me his precious attention today if it's not for his own amusement.

"They did. The uncle he makes sure everybody knows about has been in jail for years. One of the turds they flushed before the club started making money off clubs and bars from what I hear."

"Always so eloquent," Chelle says, sticking her tongue out.

"Did I invite you to this conversation?" he asks, scorning her with a glance, before turning back to me. "Shame about your mom, though. Good times are underrated. Sure hope the wild streak is hereditary. You look like you could use some fun and take your mind off this crap, doll."

I'm blushing, and I hate it. Especially because it's all too easy to imagine the good times he has in mind.

There's no hope. I'm more like every other girl in my class than I care to admit: smitten, shaken, and yes, completely fascinated by this tactless jerk with an angel's looks. He's bad, thoughtless, and more than a little annoying. But he's safe in a way Scourge isn't, despite how easy his teasing becomes insults.

He also gives everyone on his side a certain amount of protection from what I've gathered. Hugo never got close to Cal, and he became easy prey.

"Seriously, don't be scared of him, doll. *Do* stay out of his way. Tried to warn you when you got here. I can help."

Great. So he's come to impress me by playing hero. No thanks.

I'm also done being a doormat for anyone today. Walking out and giving him the cold shoulder feels like an easy way to replenish the self-esteem I've hemorrhaged with the bully.

"Tell me if you change your mind, doll. We'll work something out." His eyes aren't moving when they lock on, and the flush invading my skin just keeps growing.

I have to get out of here.

It's my turn to do the eye roll. Without saying anything, I pick my tray up, and pause just long enough to share another look with him before the blood rushes to my cheeks. "I'm old enough to take care of myself, thanks. If I ever need your advice, Cal, I'll ask."

He doesn't say a word. But he watches me the entire time as I throw my trash away, drop the tray off, and head out for my evening classes. I resist the urge to turn around until the very end.

Of course, I do. How could I resist?

I'm just in time to see Chelle kick him under the table. He gives her a dirty look, stands, and heads back to his crew of jocks across the cafeteria.

Like I need this weirdo treating me like a damsel in distress, I think to myself, smiling for reasons I can't pin down as I head off to Pre-Calc.

I wish I'd taken more time then to appreciate the smiles we shared, however small. Months later, after the train wreck everyone took to calling 'the incident,' it's a miracle I ever learned to fake smile again.

II: Backup Son (Cal)

If I still had it in me to give a fuck, I'd mourn my father.

I've watched the surly, balls-to-the-walls lion who raised me waste away into a hyena for months. Today, he barely lifts his head when I step into his room, fighting the burning sensation in my nostrils from a hundred medications in the air.

"What do you want?" he snaps, once his dimming eyes focus, and his drug blasted brain remembers who I am.

"Came to keep you company, dad. It's Sunday." I round the space to the front of his bed, taking the chair next to it. I run my fingertips along his nightstand. There's a ghostly dust coating on my hand when I hold it up to the light. "You've been telling the staff to stay the hell out again, I see."

"No point in wasting precious resources on a dead man," he growls, grunting as he lifts himself up with his hands, finding his back support in the headboard. "What'll it be today, Calvin? Hoping for a deathbed confession? The last minute change of heart where I crack, tell you what a good son you are, how it's finally high time we put the bad behind us?"

No. I've stopped expecting miracles a long time ago.

"Or maybe you're just here to taunt me?" he says, giving me a sideways glance.

"Wrong." A wry smile pulls on my lips. "I've met someone, dad. Wanted you to be the first to know. The doctor says you've got a few weeks left, yeah? Should be plenty of time to introduce you to my new fiancée."

His eyes widen, and then he scoffs. "You, married? I'm not going to my grave a fool, kiddo. Forget it. Spare me a meeting with whatever sugar baby escort you've hired to confuse an old man into thinking you give a damn about anything except getting my money."

He's got me there, minus the escort part. Hell, even after all these years, I can't imagine doll fucking anyone else.

My cock is the only one she's ever had in the stroke fantasies sustaining me for years. Naive, sure, but mental masturbation always is.

I didn't mention those thoughts when I sent her the note in the little black envelope last week, but now I wish I had. Just for fun.

That piece of paper and the twenty carat rock had to travel halfway around the globe. Almost a shame I decided to keep it short, sweet, and boring. I can't believe she's in China. Easily the biggest sign yet the Maddie Middleton I'm dealing with today is a far cry from the scared, helpless little girl I took a bullet for seven awful years ago.

I haven't even heard from her yet. I'll be calling the number I dug up with a lot of connections and detective work tonight if I don't get an answer.

I won't be disappointed. Because if there's one thing I know, despite what's changed on her end, she won't let me down. She'll wear the ring, by God, pretending she cares about her loving fiancé every time we make eyes.

A nurse comes in and walks to my dad's IV while the icy silence between us stretches on. The grandmother clock in the corner ticks on. I fold my hands, watching as she adjusts the dose of whatever painkiller keeps him from screaming in mortal agony. We're both quiet until the woman smiles gently, and finds her way out.

I have to try this again. As much as I don't fucking want to.

"I'm a changed man," I say. "It's hard as hell for you to see, I get it. You're too sick to read about the extra billion in revenue my marketing strategy brought the firm, and you don't take calls from Mr. Turnbladt anymore –"

"I don't *care* if Turnbladt thinks you can turn water into wine. I'm out of RET forever," he says, turning over. He stops turning propped on a pillow, his back to me, a human manifestation of the proverbial wall I talk to every time I'm stupid enough to come here. "Keep raking in the money, though. It'll do the charities getting it some good once I'm gone. Or else the partners, whenever they decide to stop fucking around and buy your share out, I suppose."

It's my stake in Randolph-Emerson-Turnbladt he's talking about. Mine, which he controls. He has it set up in his trust to cockblock me from ever truly owning it, the dividends going to feel good groups he hasn't even bothered to vet.

"That's all you really care about, old man? Making sure I get jack squat while working my fingers to the bone, dragging your company kicking and screaming into the twenty-first century?"

He's quiet for several seconds. Then I hear his low, infuriating voice, a poison whisper. "Things don't always go according to plan, Calvin. Make your fortune elsewhere, like your grandfather did, or settle for your measly $200K salary like an ordinary corporate grunt. You're never getting my share. I'll lose it all before I let you become the public face of anything at RET after what you did. The board feels the same way."

I'm ready to spit nails. "Then why include the amendment in the trust at all? Your lawyer slipped over too many drinks at the last Christmas party. Told me everything. He said there's a section for rehabilitation. If I prove myself I'm worthy with good deeds, family, a woman –"

"I had to give you some kind of carrot to shape up, didn't I? The offer stands, son, but we both know the clock is running out fast. You've got a better chance of making a miracle before my eyes than proving me wrong. Show me a woman worth marrying, one you aren't bribing to lie to my face, and anything is possible. Until then, we both know what's in the cards doesn't include you controlling my firm. Not since John –"

My hand shoots up, and I hold it in the air. "We both know what happened. Why waste more words?" I pull out my phone to check the time. It's getting late. "I have to go. Get some rest."

"You always were the backup son after everything that happened. It should've been John filling your shoes, and we both know it." Dad isn't backing down from his parting shot. "This isn't personal anymore, Cal. It's circumstance. Stop thinking I don't care."

Care? The asshole has a funny way of showing it.

He's only stealing my future, killing my career before it goes anywhere. I have to get out of here *now.*

I'm able to resist punching holes through the brittle old walls of the seaside mansion I grew up in until I'm in my car. My fist bangs the steering wheel once before I start the engine.

My black Tesla screeches down the long driveway to the front gate, which the servant in the guard shack has already opened for me. I make it home to my condo in record time, loading my car onto the ferry waiting to take us across the Puget Sound. It's a nice place worth seven figures where downtown Seattle meets the waterfront.

Nice, yeah, but it'll never morph into an unfathomably posh estate surrounded by the mountains, the sea, and centuries old forests. I won't be building any castles I choose while I'm being robbed of my birthright because I'm nothing more than a reluctant Plan B in my father's eyes. A 'backup son' he won't even trust to earn a full partner's stake because that means media, which in turn means reminding every client, fat cat, and blue blood our illustrious company deals with that I have a felony record.

Backup? Where the fuck does he get off?

I don't know, and I try to forget my rage when I'm

home. I head for the balcony, pouring myself a glass of good wine. For a second, I slow when I pass by the photos on the mantle, staring into John's long dead smiling face.

My older brother is still the favorite, despite being gone for almost six years. Paid the ultimate sacrifice for his country somewhere outside Kandahar, where an ambush by the Taliban ended him.

It seems like a lifetime ago.

When I'm in my ivory chair outside, overlooking the evening lights beginning to twinkle on in the hills across the water, I check the calendar on my phone.

It's been six days since I sent my little package to Doll.

She's taking her sweet time getting back to me. I decided when I sent it off I'd give her a few days, roughly a full week after it reached Beijing. It's the least she deserves for the hand grenade I just threw into her life, commanding her in not so many words to bring her sweet ass home to Seattle, and pretend she's my blushing bride.

Desperation does evil things to a man. If I could've let her go without another word, I would.

Hell, I did for all these years, seven and counting. I stayed away.

It was the humane choice. Never forgot how bad she hurt just looking into my eyes the last time I saw her, when she was down on the ground in tears, slapping the pavement like she wanted to drum up mercy for me from God himself.

Her words are branded in my brain.

Wait, wait! Don't take him away. Please, you can't this is wrong.

It's not over, Cal. It can't end like this. I'll be here. I'll do anything *to help.*

Anything!

I close my eyes, stuck on how loaded the last word she ever said to me was when it came out, hoarse and true. Sometimes, the emotional bomb planted in my memory goes off. Everything returns, rushing through me like the lava replacing my blood whenever those memories hit.

The sacrifice, the humiliation, the dirty mistake I made for her because I didn't have a fucking choice. Because it was the right thing to do.

It went further than any act of chivalry ever should.

I'm lost in the past when my phone rings. There's an international area code on the screen. A smile tugs at my lips before I punch the accept button.

"Took you long enough, doll."

"Cal...how are you?" Her voice is soft, slightly huskier than I remember, warm honey to my ears.

"Alive. Making money. Doing whatever and whoever the fuck I want, when I want them," I say, taking a pull off my wine. "All the best in life. What are you doing in Beijing?"

"Contracts for Sterner Corp," she says, ignoring my edgy introduction. "My Mandarin studies paid off, and so did the JD. I never wasted the second chance you gave me – I couldn't. Thank you again."

"You're doing better than eighty percent of our class, and earning it honestly, without special connections. Congratulations." I pause, remembering I'm not here to catch up. This isn't happy hour, or even a sales meeting. It's cold business of the most personal kind. "I won't keep you long, I hope, calling in the favor. Just be here by Thursday, wear my ring, and put on your best act."

"Hope you're right. I kind of have a life now," she says, quiet and unsure. It's like I'm able to hear the guilt sticking on her tongue, thick as chewing gum. Her voice wavers like the fire she readied to hurl my way just had cold water poured over it. "That's why I called. I wanted to talk before pulling up stakes, before we do…well, this."

Marriage. Or at least a pretend engagement.

She can't bring herself to say the unspeakable. Fair enough. It's not like I'd expect the shiest girl I ever met to handle this fake fiancé thing with a laugh and a song.

I only need her to follow through. My brow curls because there's some reasonable doubt creeping into her tone. I never fucking liked second guesses.

Doll better not disappoint. There's no Plan B, short of hiring some clueless broad dad would see through in a heartbeat.

"Are we doing this, or not?" I ask, brusk and pointed.

There's a considerable pause. It's stifling. I'm about to end the call and throw my phone off the balcony when she lets out a slow, soft sigh. "I guess. How long do you need me?"

"Ninety days ought to do it, but probably less," I tell her. "Doubt my father lasts through summer. It's him we really need to convince, before he pushes daisies. If you're able to take a leave of absence and meet me for a month or two, we'll be even. I'll pull every string I've got to make sure there's still a place for you in China, if that's where your heart is anchored these days."

"God, Cal. I'm sorry about your father. Of course I'll be there," she says, sympathy I didn't ask for oozing through my phone. "The company wants me back in the States next week anyway. I think I can be there by Thursday."

"Perfect. There's a charity auction on Friday I'm attending, and I'd like you with. I'll show you off to the movers and shakers, let the tabloids tell the city the disgraced son everybody forgot the last seven years landed a normal woman."

There's an awkward silence. She must remember I have zero tolerance for comforting bullshit, like if she starts telling me the litany: *it's not so bad, I'll find my way, and disgraced? Surely, I'm exaggerating.*

I've heard the same bullshit from my two best friends, Cade and Spencer, a thousand times. I don't need more empathy. It hasn't gotten me anywhere.

"Just tell me one thing," she says nervously. "Why? The details aren't making sense. You mentioned your father, his illness…are you trying to make sure he sees you happy before…you know?"

"Before he croaks? No, this isn't some ego trip, doll. I'm not looking for his sad, selfish approval. There's a condition in his trust before he goes: I need a wife to rehabilitate myself, or I get virtually nothing."

"I see," she whispers. In fact, Maddie doesn't have a fucking clue, but what else can she say? "Well, whatever I can do to help, Cal. Just like I promised."

"Anything," I say, repeating her last haunting word to me after the disaster. "Put on a good enough show for the public, for whoever I ask you to fool. Maybe I'll let you sleep in a separate bed."

She gasps. My tongue slides against my teeth, loving how wickedly close the air escaping her mouth is to a moan.

"Um, I did say anything, but I don't know if I can –"

"Relax. I'm not interested in getting my dick wet where it's not wanted. You're paying your debt with this fake fiancée act. Not with your body."

Honestly? I want her at ease, sure. It won't do either of us any good if she shows up at the auction full of wide-eyed sexual tension, on edge because she doesn't know when I'll push her into the nearest wall and rip off her clothes.

Yet, it's no more than three seconds before I regret those words.

After all these years, I still want to fuck her. Once, I was after her cherry. I'm sure that's long gone, stolen by some other lucky bastard. But I remember the short, sweet taste I had of her lips seven years ago, before I walked out on the schoolyard that day and let fate pull the trigger, blowing my life to pieces.

"I'll see you soon," she says, timid as the old Maddie I remember. "Is there anything else you want?"

"Just you, doll. Friday. Come bright-eyed and madly in love with me, a come fuck me dress on your hips and a pair of heels on your feet. Pick whatever you want online and text me your choice. I don't care how much it costs. I'll put in an order."

She's quiet for a moment. "Really? Is this how it'll be the entire time? I thought we left Maynard behind, Cal. We're in our late twenties for Christ's sake!"

It's finally upsetting her. Don't know why the hell that's so amusing.

"What happened there never left me," I say, picking up my wine glass, letting the dark red sweetness drown my tongue. "Friday, Maddie. We have a lot of catching up to do."

I hear her start to form another word, but I disconnect the call before she gets it out.

If she's still feeling sorry for me, I don't care.

If she's offended, I care even less.

I've protected her enough for one lifetime. I'm done treating her feelings like eggshells.

This artificial engagement is on because I don't have a choice. It's my only shot at convincing dad to hand out more than a few measly million, to open the doors I've earned keys to before it's too late, and to set me up to continue the good work I've done for the firm started by my grandfather.

It's bound to be hell on us both. Maddie doesn't want to be here fawning over my sorry ass any more than I enjoyed the year off my life in jail for her.

That's how this works – *quid pro quo.*

Friday, we do what we need to. She starts paying off her debt. If I decide to have a little fun while this shit show hits the road, then so be it.

"Holy fuck. I know he always said you'd get *nothing*, but you're telling me he means it?" Cade looks at me, running a hand through his thick blond hair. His angular jaw clenches in sympathy. The genes from his Icelandic blue blood father couldn't be more obvious.

I nod once. That's all it takes for him to spin his chair around, breaking out the emergency flask of vodka he keeps under his desk for just these occasions.

"Double shot for me," Spencer says from the corner, looking up from the stock prices scrolling across his phone's screen. "I'm doing time with the boys from New York this evening. Neolithic. You both know what that means."

My brow furrows. "Yeah, absolute ball busters."

The prestigious investment firm from Wall Street doesn't fuck around. Neither does Grant Shaw, the founder, who's sent his boys to the other coast sniffing for new business partners.

"Go easy, Spence. Your miracles always happen sober," Cade says with a frown, passing us both our drinks across the desk, a single shot for everyone. "I'm fucking floored, Cal. How could he just cut you off at the knees? Nobody in Seattle gives a shit what happened seven years ago. Can't believe your old man still thinks it makes you a liability for the firm."

He knows that isn't true. *Plenty* of people care, but I let his lie off with a dark glance.

"I'm not the one he ever wanted sitting here. It was always supposed to be John," I say.

Deep down, when I plow the darkness and come face-to-face with everything I'll never admit, I think my big brother might've done better than me. Hell, I practically *know* it. He had discipline, heart, and a set of brass balls that got him slaughtered protecting his fellow soldiers.

He also didn't have a prison record and a sickening trial that had half the city clucking their tongues, thankful they never raised a 'deeply troubled' kid like me. The other half got to enjoy several weeks of Schadenfreude. Comes with the territory when a billionaire's son lands himself in the deep, perilous shit I did. The poorer, angst types who pegged me for being born with a silver spoon in my mouth loved our misfortune.

"How long does he have?" Spence says coldly, staring at me with his eyes narrowed while he drains his vodka in one swallow.

"Six, seven weeks. Maybe less. Who the hell knows. It's not an exact science when the pancreas burns out and cancer goes everywhere."

"With all due respect, your old man's a prick if he sticks to his guns. He can't fucking cut you out," Cade growls, banging his fists on the desk when he brings them down. "You worked for your share, Cal. Harder than anybody here. We can't let him take it away from you just like *that.*"

His fingers snap loudly, leaving a dull ringing in my ears. "Enough. Forget my crap," I say. "I'll work it out. Told you already, there's a chance I could change his mind if I meet the conditions he set in his trust."

"Oh, up and marry some broad? So reasonable," Spence

rolls his eyes, sarcastic as ever. "What about an escort? They're not all fake tits and one night stands. I've paid plenty for girls who'll suck you off with stars in their eyes. Bet they'd glow brighter if they'd get their money without having to choke on your –"

"You can stop there. Shit, Spence, I didn't come down here to listen to your latest bedroom antics." I shoot him a dirty look.

Spence just grins. He purged his conscience a long time ago, shameless and proud of the high class notches in his belt. I ignore him, look at Cade, and regain my calm. "I have a plan. Might need a few extra days away from the office to get it going. That's what I really came by to ask for."

"Whatever you need, brother." Cade reaches across the desk and slams his fist into mine. He's too good a friend, better than I deserve, especially when I was drunk off my ass those nights after prison, after John died, deep in my rudderless misery while he was halfway through one of the hardest business schools in the country. "We had your leave on the books, anyway. It's no secret he's been closer to death's door. Already had your time blocked off over the next quarter for the inevitable."

"Just give me a few days. You can cancel the rest. If this goes off well, I'll have more reason than ever to hit it hard at the office. Won't need an extended absence."

Spence looks up, surprised. Cade stares through me, nodding slowly.

They know what I've been through over the years, how

everything went haywire with my father after I saved Doll and no one could save John. They've watched me busting my ass for a pittance of a yearly bonus, without the cushy guarantee I'd inherit the stake they've always been entitled to from their dads.

"Cal," Spence calls my name, waiting until I turn around to face him. "Don't let this bullshit make you crazy. We've got your back if daddy dearest fucks you over."

"I know, and one fine day I'll repay it." Standing, I grab his hand, giving it a brotherly squeeze on my way out.

I may have lost the only family I ever had over the last decade to war, booze, and psychosis, but I'm thankful for the men who've stood with me since those days at Maynard.

It won't be the end of me, taking the crazy way out with a fake fiancée in a last ditch effort to fool my asshole father. It's going to work. And it'll be a massive relief when it finally pays off, and I don't need to rely on their support anymore to stave off disaster.

Thursday, Maddie texts me she's home. Same old neighborhood where her folks settled just outside the U of Washington campus. It's summer, and I hope she knows how lucky she is being able to hear herself think without the constant noise and frat parties.

She sent me links to the dress and heels she picked out before leaving Beijing. I vetoed her first two choices – far too plain and far too cheap for a charity ball where the median net worth in the room is right at thirty million –

and told her to choose something that looks like it's suited for a Randolph bride.

She sent back a sleek blue dress with ocean trim, matching heels, and a platinum necklace. Plus four different red-faced emojis I'm sure reflected how abruptly her heart stopped when I told her to stop screwing off, and send me something real.

Everything went on my Centurion charge card instantly. It also made my dick hard, picturing the little doll who always had a gift for making me hot in grown up clothes. I've seen her pictures over the years, and she's filled out nicely. Tomorrow, she'll show me a woman's curves in her classy new outfit, It'll make this job pretending we're on fire easy as sin.

Hell, maybe *too* easy.

I can't shake the curiosity when I'm home from the office that night. Impatient and horny bastard that I am, I break out my phone and pull up her number, typing out a text.

Cal: You've got a dressing mirror, right? Put it on and hit send. Show me everything. I want to make sure it's right for the ball.

It's the better part of an hour before I get a reply.

Maddie: How's this? Not showing too much leg for their crowd, I hope?

The V-cut down the middle rides straight to her bare hip, and I'm a fucking goner. My cock jerks hard in my trousers, its angry tip straining against my belt, ready to ruin everything before it's begun if I give it half a chance.

No. I can't let this do the thinking.

I have to get these pics the hell off my screen before the heat in my balls makes me stupid.

Cal: Perfect. I'll see you there at seven.

I'm glad she isn't looking for a proper date. I'm sending my driver around to pick her up after I show up at the ball half an hour early. It's how it has to be. Knowing what she's wearing, causing my prick to leak heat all over my thigh, I don't think I'd survive the ten minute trip in the back of the car without putting her under me.

I'm doubly grateful she never texts back. Gives me ample time to throw my phone on my nightstand and step into a long, cold shower. It takes the ice forever to soothe my blood, and I've got it cranked to glacial. I'm panting like a bull in rut by the time I step out, toweling off, ignoring the raging hard-on up to my six-pack while it hits me.

This fake fiancée act *won't* be easy.

But the faster it comes, the more I realize how its challenge has *nothing* to do with dad or even our screwed up past. There's a vicious chemistry between us I thought I'd be able to ignore. Thought it'd be dead after so many years apart.

Hour by hour, minute by minute, the march toward Friday evening warns me I'm flat out wrong.

Raw attraction is alive and kicking. It comes at me with

a thousand questions, but only one that's really important.

How the hell do I pretend I'm obsessed with this woman, and keep it professional, without actually fucking her first chance I get?

III: Jitters (Maddie)

I'm no stranger to old money, high class, and self-righteous pricks. Kinda comes with the territory when you're a rising star in a major international company. But glamor and egos aren't the main reason the butterflies in my stomach have teeth, making me woozy when I step into the sleek glassy building downtown for the first time.

"Name or party, madame?" An older man in a tailored suit steps up, swift as a secret service agent, looking me up and down.

At least my chic blue dress and heels pass the first test, and I'm not thrown out on sight. "Randolph," I tell him.

He grins. "Ah, so you're the lucky lady. My congratulations. Mr. Randolph has a table reserved. Right this way."

It's getting very weird, very fast. I follow him through the security line, and we head into a massive ballroom like something out of a fairy tale updated for modern times.

Several dozen well dressed couples mingle, their chatter a steady roil behind the soft piano music coming from the stage. My eyes scan the crowd for Cal. When we near the table with the RANDOLPH sign on it, at first I'm sure there's someone else in his seat.

The man dressed to the nines in his tux and silver tie looks preposterously mature. Gone is the handsome, slender boy I used to crush on, replaced by a tall, dark, and brutally handsome man.

Cal's looks were always good to him. Time has been even kinder.

I shouldn't be surprised. I tried to brace myself for this. Tried, and completely failed.

One good glance at my fake fiancé makes my blood steam down to my knees.

"Hello, doll. It's been a long time. Pull up a chair." The boy's deep voice is a man's now, several octaves lower than I remember. He stands, towering over me at least a foot, and readies my chair for me.

"My God." It's all I'm able to whisper as my butt hits the cushion.

His shoulders are broader. His muscles are bigger, firmer, and sleeker than his eighteen year old bones could've supported. If he's suffered over the years – and I'm certain he has – his body shows no signs. It's like the pain has somehow strengthened his rough beauty, carved more perfection into the jawline covered in a rogue five o'clock shadow, given his neat, dark hair a perfect wave, and deepened his eyes.

Those sky blue gems set in his handsome face are all I recognize of the Calvin I once knew. They're unshakeable. No different from the last day I saw them, full of fury.

Except now there's an added darkness in the blue halo around his pupils. It sends a sharp chill up my spine.

He strokes his chin, quietly studying me, impossible to read behind his gorgeous mask. "What are you thinking?" I try, breaking the eerie silence.

"I think it's too damn quiet. Glad you're happy to see me, doll, but I think you can be happier. Drink?" He waves to the bar in the corner, where there's a man in a vest shaking up a cocktail in a steel tumbler.

"I'd love to," I say, standing. I mean it.

I welcome anything that gives me a few more minutes to decide how I'll deal with telling the world I'm marrying this enigma.

I'm in a daze as I follow him to the bar, struggling to process how I've gotten here, back in the presence of a man I thought I'd lost forever.

I order my usual: a mimosa with extra citrus. He quirks an eyebrow and points it my way after asking for a scotch, more determined than ever to inflame the raw, confused pulse each look kindles deep inside me.

"Still love to play it safe, I see. Can't blame you. It's gotten you far."

"Well, to China, anyway. How are you, Cal? You look good." My cheeks bloom fierce red, transported seven years in the past as soon as the words are out. Why can't I compliment him like a normal adult?

"Miserable," he says under his breath. "Wouldn't have asked you to this shitshow if I didn't have a lot to lose. Let's get on with it, and do some introductions."

Apparently, he's never developed the patience for small talk. His hand drifts to mine a half second after we've picked up our drinks, and soon we're making the rounds.

"Mrs. Vernon, don't you look lovely?" he says to a plump, older woman near the stage, one hand holding her glasses. Yes, *those* glasses, the kind I thought were left behind in the nineteenth century. "This is my fiancée, Maddie."

"Delighted," the woman says in her haughtiest tone. Or maybe it's her normal voice. "My, young man, why didn't I hear you were engaged? Tell me everything!"

"Met on business in China about six months ago. You remember that trip to Beijing, love? Rainstorm caught you outside Mao's tomb, without an umbrella. I was kind enough to share, and you were too beautiful not to. Found out fast we were both Seattle locals." He looks at me and winks when Vernon isn't looking.

"Uh, of course." Not. My head is spinning. I barely remember to nod, before the blush on my cheeks hits my brain, and turns me to stone. Good thing he does most of the talking.

"We fell fast and hard. Real whirlwind romance that'd give old Rhett Butler a run for his wind." Mrs. Vernon laughs when he mentions what I'm sure is an old favorite. "Proposed under a month ago. Can't believe how fast it's coming together, and how ready I am to be a married man."

He grabs my hand. So much for fixing this awkward tension turning my lungs to concrete.

"So charming! You're a lucky young thing, Maddie. I simply can't wait for the wedding photos." Mrs. Vernon goes doe-eyed. Her grin vanishes a second later. "And how's your father, Calvin? Is he close to…forgive me."

She trails off. I expect Cal's warm smile to die, but it barley softens. "He has a month, maybe two at most, or so the doctors say. They've underestimated him before. Dad's always been a fighter. I think he'll go down swinging, and surprise all of us."

"My sympathies, dear boy. If there's anything to settle in the aftermath, rest assured my Charles will be in your corner to put in a good word with your board."

"Thanks. Means a lot." He reaches out, squeezes her hand, and then we're on our way to a few more tittering couples.

He probably introduces me to half a dozen more I can't remember – always as the future *Mrs. Calvin Randolph* – before there's even time to catch my breath.

"Is this helping? Will Mrs. Venison or whatever her name was help you? It sounded good," I say hopefully, looking for any excuse to slow down this bewildering meet and greet with millionaires.

"No. Charles is a thirty year baller and has a lot in our hedge fund, but the board's vote is shackled to dad's will. There's no overriding the pull a founding name has in the company."

There's so much to these delicate politics I don't understand. It's not like he gives me a chance to catch up because we're still moving.

"Cal, Cal, I thought I'd see you here!" A lean man in a grey suit holding a tablet runs up, slowing our approach to the next group of VIPs.

"Turner. Surprised you're taking precious time away from fishing for secrets from tech titans to talk to me. What gives?" Cal eyeballs him suspiciously.

"Actually, I came over to see if you'd have an in for me with Spencer Emerson. Is he here? Heard he'd landed a lucrative deal for your firm to inject new liquidity into ShopUp, and I'd love to have a word."

"He isn't around, and he wouldn't want to talk to you if he was. Nobody at Randolph-Emerson-Turnbladt got where they are with loose lips, especially when it involves multi-billion dollar deals with start ups heading to the moon."

"Ah! So it's *billions,* plural. Got it." Smiling, he holds up his tablet and quickly types his comments into what looks like software for press professionals.

"I can't believe anyone wants luxury brands shoved in their faces when they could buy affordable and efficient, but what do I know?" I say. I can't hold my commentary.

ShopUp is an app designed for rich people, where they can type in any old thing, and receive only recommendations from 'the best of the best.' In practice, it also means the most *expensive,* a reverse bargain approach suited for the ones who hang their lives on having the most bling.

Turner's eyes go wide, and he gives me a soft smile. "Forget ShopUp, Cal. Who's the fox with the mouth?"

"This is my lovely fiancée, Madeline Middleton. Soon to be Mrs. Randolph after we have our wedding in Tokyo in a few months. She can't wait for the honeymoon. I hope you'll forgive her snideness. I'm quite looking forward to our sixty day cruise around the South Pacific. Her uncle did a lot of missionary work on a lot of islands. This woman knows them all like the back of her hand. Isn't that right, doll?"

I didn't know a nod could be so heavy. The white lies are getting much darker.

"Tokyo? fiancée?" Turner looks like he's struggling to keep his jaw off the floor.

Honestly, so am I, because the improv stories Cal keeps making up about us just keep getting crazier. What's next? Telling them I'm already pregnant with the twins he's probably written into his script for a perfect life?

"Don't look so stunned, my man. I just handed you an exclusive." Cal slaps him on the shoulder and gives it a squeeze that rocks the skinny young man roughly our age. "We've got a lot of people to see, though, so why don't you get cracking and send me a link to the story in the morning? Good way to announce our engagement for free."

"Hold up, hold up! I've got questions…can't I at least have a picture?!"

Turner chases us like a hopeless puppy. Cal leans in with a heavy sigh, whispering in my ear. "Play along. It'll be good practice for dad soon."

"Fine, one good picture to go with your article. As for the details, you fill them in. What's fit to print isn't always honest. Here, I'll get you started: we met in Hong Kong doing charity, we're both Seattle natives, and I love the hell out of this girl. You've got five seconds to get your camera going."

Under five seconds warning before I'm in his arms. Cal seizes me, locks his powerful hands around my waist, brings me to his chest, dipping his face toward mine.

Oh, God. Isn't it a little soon for –

Our lips collide, destroying my thoughts. It's more explosive than I dared imagine.

The big bang happens all over again in our ten second kiss.

Whole worlds are born in a shower of sparks. They glow, they burn, fading into the molten shock flowing through my blood. So sudden, so unexpected, and so relentless my body reacts on pure instinct.

My brain hasn't caught up to what's happening.

But my heartbeat, my pulse, and the shameful fire building between my legs…*mother mercy.* They're as hot and bothered as a ShopUp user laying eyes on a five figure toaster, and my tongue melts against his far more naturally than I'd like.

Resistance? Restraint? Common sense?

Gone.

My brain may be screaming *no, no, no*, but the moan that slips out of me, and into him when my nipples turn to hard peaks through my dress is a simple, unmistakable *yes.*

This kiss is living memory. It takes me back through time, retraces all seven years to the first and only night he first laid his lips on mine, a carnal promise we never had a chance to act on.

Maddie, what the hell are you doing? My senses return, and I'm pushing hard against his chest with both palms before he eases up a second later.

"Was it as good for you as it was for us?" Cal asks, an eyebrow quirked at the blogger. I'm catching my breath, surprised Turner's glasses haven't fogged over from the scene he just witnessed.

He never gets a chance to answer. Cal leads me away, leaving him speechless.

I guess that makes two of us.

We're done making the rounds and in our seats when my thudding pulse finally lets me speak. "Okay, what *was* that? I thought we were keeping it professional, retaining certain boundaries, just like you said…"

"Practice, doll. Professional doesn't mean ice. This has to be believable. If we're never physical, no one will buy it. Besides, Turner's got a good track record making this crap viral." Cal looks at me and smiles like we're talking about nothing. "Would you rather he show us off in a series of Tweets, or should I march you up on the stage for a repeat performance?"

God, no. On so many levels. If kissing him is practice for this farce we're putting on, I never want to see the grand finale.

I'm saved from a retort by the first speaker stepping up to the microphone, announcing the charity auction underway. Turner isn't the only person fixated on us. Low, hushed jabber flies around the room, impossible to ignore, more than a few middle aged couples pointing our way, and smiling.

At least they're happy. The gossip mill is a lot less pleasant when you're steering it. It's hard to even look at him as the bidding starts on a priceless sculpture by some wonderfully weird and gifted artist. I'm reeling in silence, frozen in disbelief that I gave in.

It doesn't matter that there wasn't a chance to put up my guard when I didn't know what was happening until he'd taken a nice, long sip of me. I caved, went weak in the knees for this crass, strange man I owe my life to.

It's terrifying how little the distance the years have put between us means. My body responds the same way it did when I was young and clueless. I'm in grave danger.

Three priceless art pieces sell for six figures each before Cal says anything. "Watch this," he tells me in a hushed voice, holding up his sign.

It's hard not to gasp. Bidding for the huge white urn with the soft pink roses brushed by hand up its sides starts at a hundred thousand dollars.

Not even a year's salary for me. And he's the one roping me into this stupid fake fiancé thing, worried about *money?*

"Two fifty," he says simply, holding up his sign.

"Two hundred and fifty thousand dollars! Do I hear two seventy five?" The auction hawker beams, scanning the room for fresh competition.

Another sign goes up across the aisle, several seats down. "Three fifty," a portly man in a vest says, giving us a quick glance with his beady eyes.

Just because the money is going to a good cause doesn't take the sport out of it. My heart leaps into my chest as I realize what I'm really seeing: a dick waving contest for rich people. And I'm seriously afraid Cal is going to get his slapped hard before it's over.

"Four hundred even," Cal says, his deep voice louder.

The auctioneer at the microphone blinks. He never expected a bidding war over the most boring item yet. Low whispers roll through the crowd. I hear several cries of "really?" and "they're crazy!"

Whatever the Victorian vase is worth, it's already smashed through its ceiling. I lean in, hand halfway over my mouth. "Cal! I don't know what you're trying to prove, but –"

"I've got this, doll. Keep watching." He cuts me off, a wicked smile pulling at his lips, waiting for his competition to up the ante, or else slink away with his tail between his legs.

"Four fifty," the man a few feet over growls. I see his wife clutching his shoulder from the corner of my eye. We share a brief look of solidarity. Saving men from themselves is harder than breaking up dog fights sometimes.

"Do I hear –"

"Four seventy," Cal says, his jaw subtly clenched. The bidding slowdown to smaller increments means they're both nearing their limit.

"Five hundred even!" A new voice says. Half the audience gasps.

The portly man looks defeated, red in the face, and suddenly goes quiet. Cal, he's ice next to me, revealing very little of the tension pulling him apart inside.

He *needs* to win. I sense it in every wolfish glance from his eyes.

"Five hundred thousand for this marvelous hand-painted relic from a nobler time!" The auctioneer squawks.

"Do I hear five ten, ladies and gentleman? Five ten for this glorious, one-of-a-kind piece with roses sure to make your own gardener jealous?"

There isn't a sound. Just swift, crushing silence.

Cal's fingers twitch once on his sign, wedged against his thigh. I wrap my fingers gently around his rock hard bicep, squeezing it through his suit. "Let it go. You did your best."

He pushes me away softly, and stands. "Five fifty."

The floor drops out. I'm hanging my head, wondering how I was ever so stupid to believe this brash, crazy man would've sobered up with age. He's just as reckless and determined when he senses a fight as he was when it all went to pieces.

My heartbeat swallows my ears, making me dizzy. I feel like I'm reliving the incident all over again.

"Five hundred and fifty thousand!" The auctioneer sings, his smile becoming a grin. "Do I hear five seventy five? Five seventy five?"

I'm shaking, counting the seconds. He can't go higher than this. Five slip by before I hear the final countdown.

Going once!

Going twice!

"Sold, to the handsome young man from Randolph-Emerson-Turnbladt with the heart of iron!" Auctioneer man sings. "My lovely assistant will be in touch to wrap it up and find out how you'd like to bring this beauty home."

Cal drops into his seat, a thin halo of sweat on his brow. He wipes it quickly with his sleeve as the vase is wheeled off the stage, and they start setting up the next piece.

47

"I sure *hope* you know what you're doing," I mutter, leaning into him and whispering it as softly as I can, without surrendering the sharp worry in my gaze. "Over half a million dollars for art? Are you *sure* you need me to do this? Seems like you're kinda loaded."

"This thing just cost me a decent chunk of my cash reserve, Maddie," he says, calmer than ever while his words make my heartbeat ten times faster. "You'll help me make half a million a drop in the bucket after this marriage gets me what I'm owed. Also, what kind of loving fiancé would I be if I let that piece of history go? Didn't you recognize the cream background? The roses?"

"Obviously not!"

He's lost his mind. I'm still shaking my head when it hits me.

When I look up, a nervous wreck, he's smiling. His lips close in, leaving a peck on my cheek, and then I feel his hot breath oozing into my ear. "Now, you remember, yeah? Those roses on white...exact same pattern you wore on your dress the day I went on the field with Scourge. I'd be a fool to *ever* let us forget."

He asks me to hang onto the huge vase wrapped up in thick newspaper as we crawl into the back of his limo. I clutch it like a kitten hanging onto a tree, so jittery over accidentally banging it against the car I'm about to explode. The nerves he's soaked in kerosene and lit on fire for a dozen other reasons aren't helping either.

We're halfway to his penthouse downtown before I finally find my courage "I can't do this if it's going to be crazy. We need ground rules," I say, meeting his blue eyes in the darkness.

"What did you think we'd discuss tonight at home? What kind of lingerie I'd like you to wear when you parade around the house?" His smart slays every part of me his words don't reach. "I never operate in chaos, doll. I'd have never gotten my life halfway back on track if I did. Of course we'll have a plan."

There he goes again. Making me feel small, restless, stupid.

That's the Calvin Randolph I remember. If that weren't so infuriating, it might be charming because it's familiar, a ghost from a simpler time when I didn't have a life complete with an impending fake marriage to worry about.

"Why did you really kiss me so hard in front of the reporter? I don't believe that was just 'practice.'" I let loose the other question eating me. "Something softer would've worked. You didn't have to put so much into it."

"It's called passion, Maddie. You should try it sometime. Real emotion makes people excellent liars. No, you're not truly my blushing bride, doll. You just taste fucking good to me. I don't need to lie about that. If you're asking my permission to half-ass this arrangement, don't. I need you here, all the way."

I can't hold his eyes. *Ass.*

I'm forced to look away, staring sadly out the window. A thick Seattle rain hits the glass and forms rivulets. It's pouring by the time we pull into his heated private garage. He tells me to leave the vase on the seat – the driver will take care of it – and I do.

The icy tension between us doesn't get any better on the elevator ride up his tower. When it reaches the top and I hear the ding accompanying the door sliding open, my hands are trembling on the gold banister behind me.

Sighing, he steps forward, and punches the button to close the door, giving us some privacy. "What's wrong?"

"What does it look like, Cal? It's too much." No lie. It's overload. "I can't believe I'm back here, doing this, with *you*. I should be in Beijing for another week, working contracts in English and Mandarin. Not taking a leave of absence from my career to settle our old score from half a lifetime ago."

"I know this is hard." He steps in front of me, slides his strong hands on my shoulders, his fingertips pushing gently into my skin. "Believe it or not, I appreciate you, Maddie. Even if I have a twisted way of showing it sometimes. Stay strong, and we'll be even. You'll never hear from me again."

That isn't what I want! I'm prepared to scream it after him, torn because he wounds me so easily, but always does just enough to remind me there's a soul somewhere behind his freezing looks.

He takes me by the wrist and leads me out, down the hall to a tall, ornately carved door, one and only entryway to his million dollar condo.

If he hurt his finances tonight dropping over half a million on charity art, it won't hurt his standard of living.

FIANCÉ ON PAPER

His place looks like the kind I've only seen in platinum card traveler's magazines, and sometimes among the new desperate-to-impress money in China's business elite.

His world is lush.

Overstuffed leather chairs next to windows oversee the city's best view, towering over Pike's Market, stretching out to a picturesque shot of Bainbridge Island and the mountains beyond. An obscene mantle attaches to a fireplace probably able to produce enough heat in the winter for a small army. And a sleek glass liquor cabinet yawns full with wine, fine spirits, and imported beer, most of it totally out of reach without using the library ladder on the shelves.

I sit while he walks to a long fancy table. When he returns, there's a thin stack of papers in his hand. He pushes them into my lap and hands me a black pen. "Read it and sign, doll. Had my lawyer cook up something to protect us legally."

"Fake fiancée, defined here as Ms. Madeline Middleton, agrees to pursue the duties outlined below in the strict spirit of non-disclosure…" I read the words slowly, letting each one slide down my throat and pool in my stomach like ice water.

My fingers page through it, and the dread only grows. There are so many clauses in cold legalese. Nothing seems unreasonable. But that doesn't make it any better.

When I look up, he's smiling, sitting in the chair next to me with another God forsaken smirk on his lips. "Is this *really* necessary? There's so much here."

"It's for your protection as much as mine. Here, look at the last page," he says, reaching over, pulling the last sheet out and putting it on top. "I knew we'd be pressed for time, so I asked my guy to spell out all the rules in a neat little list."

My eyes skim more. He's not kidding about the little part. It's three short phrases that could mean anything if they weren't backed up by longer parts:

No sex. Both parties agree to keep their relationship strictly professional.

No money. Fake fiancée understands this arrangement guarantees no compensation, beyond what Mr. Randolph decides to spend on gifts, expenses, or direct rewards.

No disclosure. Fake fiancée agrees to keep this agreement strictly secret, until such time it's terminated, and further agrees any disclosures to the media without prior approval by Mr. Randolph are prohibited.

I'm shaking my head. He grabs the pen, pushes it into my hand, and holds it up in a writing positioning. "What's wrong, beautiful? Anything you'd like to add?"

My eyes bleed fire when I look at him. I seriously contemplate asking him to add *no teasing* to this stupid agreement, if it wouldn't sound so ridiculous.

"No. Let's get this over with," I say, sighing as my wrist glides over the paper. I scrawl my name and initials on several pages, drawing on my legal experience to take one last quick look to make sure there's nothing buried that can bite me.

When it's done, he grabs the papers, and throws them

into a leather case on the table. "Perfect. I'd say 'pleasure doing business,' but then that's a given when I'm dealing with you, doll."

It still doesn't sit right. I press my hands together, looking away, staring at the city's winking skyline through his windows. "I know what we need to do. I signed it. Tell me what else you need."

"So thoughtfully boring. How about a drink to celebrate?" he asks, helping me sit on one of the posh chairs next to a massive window.

"No," I whisper, blinking back my tears, wiping them beneath his unrelenting gaze with my wrist. "I just need a moment."

For half a minute, he's quiet. Then he sits down across from me, takes both my hands, and gives them a reassuring squeeze. "How do I make this easier?"

Easier? No such thing. There's nothing *in the world that will make this faux engagement with a man who has his kind of history a breeze.*

"Let me in," I tell him. It's the one concession that might give this a shred of normalcy. "Treat me like a friend if I supposedly want to be your wife. Talk to me about life, where you're going, what you really want to achieve after this madness."

He looks away, dropping my hands. "We're actors, Maddie. Just like the contract says. We aren't old friends, and certainly not lovers. We were classmates who got in too deep, and on the wrong asshole's worst side. We did some stupid shit it's taking years to undo. Why do you want to complicate this?"

"Because it *isn't* simple. Not when you shove me into your arms and kiss me for the first time in years! God, Cal. I know it can't be easy, everything that's happened, but do you have to be so heartless?"

He reaches up, scratching his clenched jaw. His sky blue eyes pierce mine, angry and electric, like it's almost as hard for him to sit here with me, and re-live the past.

I'm a fool for asking him to step back with me into the pain, I know. But honesty never hurt anyone, and right now, it's the only thing that'll let me process this screwed up arrangement without feeling like a plastic accessory.

"I picked you because we have a certain history, doll. That's undeniable. I need it to fool the world, and make sure my father coughs up what belongs to me before he's gone. Don't see any sense in this burning need you have to rehash hell at the academy. Let's put it behind us, and keep it the fuck there. Let's play our parts. You're here to be my fiancée. Not my therapist."

His harsh look threatens to set me off all over again. The tears stinging my eyes worsen because I haven't even had a chance to sleep off the jet lag.

I hate this. I hide the tears behind my palms, turning my face, willing him to shut up and disappear.

"It's been a long day for us both. Let me show you to your room."

"No!" I'm on my feet, clearing my eyes one more time to give him a harsh look. "Just point me to the right place. I'll find it myself."

With a savage glance, he points down the long hallway

starting under a crystal chandelier. "Last room at the end. Sleep in tomorrow. I'll be out all day. Won't need you again until Sunday, when it's time to visit my father."

I storm away, resisting the urge to head for the front door instead, and find my way out.

By the time I clean up and lay down in the Egyptian cotton sheets, my new headache is worse. It's shocking how much the four hours I've spent with him are like staring into a mirror, expecting familiarity, and seeing only distortions.

He's the same. It's the Cal Randolph I remember in all his arrogance, his wit, his ruthless good looks with the ocean eyes able to melt any panties he desires, whether the women wearing them like it or not. The boy who teased me, who turned out to be my savior, always showed the same smirk, same poise, same bottomless energy and focus as I see in this man.

But there's also something different; a dark, cold, and very adult aloofness in his character. The old Cal wouldn't have shuffled me off to bed if he'd seen me cry like this. He would've swept me into his arms, kissed away my tears, and carried me off to join him in bed after making certain I wore a smile again.

This new man, who I've agreed to marry, and pray it won't ever go that far, I don't know. He confirms my biggest fear I've carried around for seven years: our tragedy changed Cal forever, and not for the better.

IV: Schoolyard Crush (Cal)

I'm pissed off the next day, and grateful I have business elsewhere.

Don't know how I could spend it in the condo with her moping around, hidden in her room, greeting my calls to breakfast with an icy silence. Before I left, I grabbed a pen, scrawling an angry note I slipped underneath the door, giving her my driver's number if and when she's ready for food. My kitchen is also well stocked, but I can't imagine Doll cooking for anything.

Sure, she's grown up. She's developed talents I'm sure I haven't seen. Hell, for all I know, she's become a master chef in her spare time, and maybe one day when I'm not making her miserable, she'll whip up something that makes me lean back and say, "wow."

Yet, I can't stop seeing the Maddie I knew. She's there, staring me in the face, daring me to live like the gullible kid I swore I'd killed. I see the innocent girl who never came to school with lipstick, wearing a uniform blouse a size too big for her, those thick black lenses framing her eyes, still bringing her lunch to school every day in a Power Puff Girls lunchbox well into her Junior year.

The marketing campaign I'm working for Spence and Cade can't distract me from the past. Nothing makes a Saturday afternoon stuck at the office fly by faster than letting my mind wander.

Seven Years Ago

I never met a girl so dense. Doll must think I'm teasing her for some sick pleasure, and not because I'm dying to get in her pants. She's never so much as cast a wanting glance my way, and let me hold it. But I see how her eyes study me when she thinks I'm not looking.

Those looks get me hard. They're the same eyes I've seen on the other girls in the small harem I've boned since I lost my virginity to a cougar at a Phoenix resort a few years back. Lust is always familiar, yet so fucking different in her soft hazel eyes. I wish I could figure out why.

Curiosity killed the cat, they say, and I think it's trying to claim Cal Randolph, too. This crazy need to get under her skin, or at least between her legs, sends my thoughts in dumb directions. Like deciding to ask her to the winter dance, rather than the cheerleading captain, Tina, who's been choking on my cock for several weeks.

Thanksgiving is over, and Christmas is coming fast for the Academy. That means a two week break, more freezing rains hammering Seattle non-stop, and – what else? – presents.

My old man probably has my new Mercedes lined up, just like I want. He's been ignoring me a lot between business and John coming home last week. It's good to see my older brother again, and my parents love having their hero home for the holidays.

I find him in my room one evening, after I come home early from German. My plans to ask Tina over here or take my fist to the hard-on raging between my legs go up in smoke as soon as I see him reclining on my bed, cigarette tucked between his lips.

"John, what the fuck?"

"Can't sleep in my old bed anymore. It's too damned soft. Yours is a lot firmer."

"So, you think you can take over my room whenever?"

He looks at me, pulls the smoke from his lips, and flicks the ashes into the silver waste bin next to my bed. "I think you're all grown up, and maybe you can handle letting your big brother crash for a few hours on a mattress that doesn't want to eat him alive. Also thought I'd come by and make sure you're not into any stupid shit."

"Fuck you, if you've been looking through my things. I'm not fourteen anymore," I growl, marching over to my closet, scanning it to see if anything is out of order.

"Oh, I already did my inspection. What kind of sorry fuck would I be hunting IEDs and mines for Uncle Sam if I couldn't cover my little bro's room in five minutes? You've got nothing to worry about. Just a couple crushed beer cans, a few dried up joints, oh, and porn. Didn't know you kids even whacked it to magazines anymore. Isn't it all digital now?"

I see red. He's found the vintage European collection Cade swiped from his attic last week, and passed off to me and a couple other guys.

"None of your business! Don't make me say it again, John – stay the hell out!" Anger sticks in my throat like thorns. I swear, I'll stare down Scourge and his crew of idiots all day, but my brother has a real knack for pushing just the right buttons to turn me into a kid throwing a tantrum all over again.

"Saw the trophies you've got in your dresser drawer, too," he says, sitting up and flicking his depleted cigarette into the trash. "At least, I'm hoping they're trophies. Don't tell me you're into wearing lace now?"

The blood drains from my face. This is worse than finding my porn stash. *Goddamn.*

I look him dead in the eye. "Had to take something from the girls I already fucked. I'm not the kind to kiss and tell, so that's all your getting. Go ask your army pals for jerk stories, if that's what you're after."

He chuckles, pointing and laughing at the red damage carved on my face. "You're a good kid," he says, finally standing up. Hope like hell he's ready to give me some much needed privacy.

He heads for the door, stopping when he's got one foot in the hall. He's still wearing his army boots, huge rubber beasts that seem out of place for the Brazilian wood on our floors. "Nah, on second thought, you've changed my mind. You're not a kid anymore, Cal. You're a man. Think you'll go better places than I did at eighteen, screwing off a year in Florida and drinking my brains out, before I decided to enlist. Had to stop dad from getting *really* pissed. All I'm saying, I guess, is sorry for treating you like the same little shit who used to bug me."

"Whatever," I mutter, before I let out a sigh. "Thanks, asshole."

He's a dick, but in his own way, John's an okay guy.

We briefly shake hands before he leaves me alone with my deepest secret, the one he couldn't find because there's no physical evidence except empty air. Last week, I shoved aside my trophies from the fucks I've had, and cleared an empty space.

In my brain, it's got Maddie's name on it. I'm going to stuff her soaked, torn panties there sometime in the next few months, or I *will* lose my shit.

I can't let this weird fascination go on without finding out what's underneath her prim and proper skirt. Bigger and better things are waiting after I screw this out of my system.

I'm so fucking *over* Scourge today. The bully clanks when he walks with his stupid chains, always the same two lapdogs at his side who think they're hard because they're willing to run errands for the school's prize pig.

This morning, he pushed Cade out of the breakfast line so hard my buddy lost his food on the floor. Both him and Spence are calmer, cooler than me. They're lucky, and so is fuck-face.

I wouldn't have held back giving him the business end of my fists if he did it to me, discipline and detention be damned.

I'll never understand why they let him share classes with us. What job could possibly be worth it to make Principal Ross kiss so much ass?

By mid-morning, he's mouthing off to Mr. Gregorson, our European history teacher. He's senior faculty, silver haired, and he's just as done as the rest of us with this kid's shit.

Scourge tells him he doesn't give a rat's ass about flunking yesterday's quiz on the Borgias. Gregorson orders him back in his seat, placing a call to the front desk, informing them he'll be down in the office shortly.

He sounds defeated. That gets to me today, makes my guts churn.

It's always the same: Principal Ross doesn't want to do shit. Even if Gregorson pressed the issue, he'd suspend Scourge for a day to get his slap on the wrist. Asshole would return tomorrow, more determined than ever to give the rest of us a hostile learning environment.

We're in gym near the end of the day when I catch him circling Maddie. She has like two friends in the whole school. They're all slow runners, lagging behind everybody else while we're doing laps on the track.

Scourge picks up speed, racing behind Chelle on Maddie's left, and knocks the poor girl over. I'm not close enough to do shit.

She goes down hard on one knee. Him and his assholes

laugh, all three shooting the girls the middle finger as they race past them, buying five minutes worth of cruel, simple entertainment.

"What's up?" Spence asks, running at my side, a knowing flicker in his eyes. "Looks like you're about to do something stupid."

"No, but you keep pace with Cade. I'm going on ahead." I pump my legs as hard as they can go.

The bullies have slowed, fallen behind the girls again, who are moving at a crawl as Maddie and her other friend, Elizabeth, help Chelle walk on her banged up knee.

When I'm closing the last ten feet, I'm moving like a maniac, watching Scourge's wingman, Reed, try to repeat the tipping prank with Doll. I never give him a chance.

My shoulder impacts his at a furious speed, throwing him into Scourge. The three idiots fall like bowling pins, swearing the whole time.

I don't slow down until the girls are well ahead of me. Then I turn, giving the bastards behind me the stink eye. If they want to catch up with the trio again, including Maddie, they'll have to go through me.

"What the fuck's your problem, Randolph? You got a crush on them bitches?" Scourge stumbles up to me, spitting raw hate. "Fuck you, if you do. No joke, I'll find out who she is, and make her life a living *hell* if you think about swinging your dick at me again. Shit, maybe I'll go after all three. Just because."

"You'll do nothing," I growl, my voice so deep and feral it surprises me. Clearing my throat, I see Spence and Cade appear at my side. Perfect timing. If this gets uglier than it is, I'll need backup. "Just leave them alone, Alex. Save your bullshit for someone else."

His whole body bristles when I use his real name, instead of that stupid moniker. "Getting awful tired of you trying to play Sheriff around here, Randolph. Your daddy ain't the only one who's got money and connections. None of you assholes have an in at this school like my old man and my uncle."

"Yeah, yeah, we know how you've got Ross on a leash," Spence says, flashing his teeth.

"Can I?" Reed steps up, his dumb face turned to his leader, quietly asking Scourge's permission to break my friend's nose.

"Leave it," I tell Spence, putting my arm across his chest. I don't need to do it with Cade.

They're usually calmer, but they're also more trusting. The assholes in front of me are unpredictable. There's a decent chance we'll have a fight on our hands as soon as our backs are turned. We don't need to go starting it.

"You don't want to fuck with us, kid. Stand down. Last and only warning I hand out. Next time, you'll be dealing with Uncle Match."

"Whatever. Glad you've got someone in prison, at least. You'll wind up there yourself one day, asshole," I say.

I hold my boys back, wishing I could roll my eyes harder without touching off a fight. Surprisingly, Scourge doesn't bother doing more than mumbling a parting *fuck you.* We wait, watching them slink away.

"Ever think he means his uncle's so tired of his crap he'll bring us brownies for knocking his shit in?" Cade says, a rough grin peeking through his lips.

"Getting our hands dirty is no joke. Let him have his space, long as he isn't up in ours."

"Funny, doesn't seem like *ours* he was getting in." Spence and his damned knowing looks.

"What? You wanted me to stand here with my thumb up my ass while he put those girls in stitches?"

"Nah, obviously," Spence grunts. I grab my friend by the collar, giving him a firm shake. "Course not. Just thought you were awful quick to stick your nose in his business. But the asshole had it coming."

"Yeah. Sorry," I snarl, releasing his jersey. I jog several paces ahead of my friends.

Need the space to clear my head. Several yards away, the school's outside bell rings, letting us know it's time to get our asses back in the locker room, and change.

On my way in, I see Maddie with her friends, stopping to check Chelle's knee. She looks up, catches my eyes, and there's a moment.

For some ungodly reason, this obsession isn't purely sexual. Sure, I want her wrapped around me so I can finally stop jerking it to fantasy, but it's more than young lust.

I'm starting to *care*.

It's the pinpoint moment when I should've known I was officially fucked.

A week later, I'm standing by her locker. There's no Scourge to worry about, thank Christ, because he's been skipping out the last few days.

I see Maddie trot up, punch in her code, and pull the silver handle until the door pops open. She ignores me standing behind her, leaning casually against the wall. Clearing my throat gets her attention.

"Yes?" She turns, her eyes wide and anxious behind her thick black frames.

"You got a date yet for winter dance, or what?" I ask, stepping up with an arrogant smirk overtaking my lips.

Christmas has come early for her, and it feels good to play Santa. She ought to thank me, maybe be a good girl and sit on my lap. *The* Cal Randolph is asking her to be his date, and I'm confident my competition is nil. She's too damned shy to catch any other guy's interest.

Doll stays quiet. Looking down. Blushing. I've given her such a dream-come-true shock she can't even answer me. It's adorable at first. I appreciate her as she really is.

So innocent and pensive. So ready to be corrupted. So fucking mine.

I want to grab her face, push her hair over her shoulder, and then bite her lip while I find out what it takes to steam her lenses.

"Answer me, Doll. It's next week, and I need a date." I move in, bringing my fingers to her chin. Gently lifting her head, I wait for her eyes, lock them down in my gaze. "I want it to be you."

"Cal, what happened last week…with Scourge…" her

voice is so hush I have to lean in to make anything out.

Can't believe she's still worried. "Forget it. He pesters you again, just say the word, and it's done. Anything else, ignore the idiot. If he's leaving you alone, we're all better off letting bygones be bygones, right?"

I've never seen a girl's cheeks so red. She doesn't answer me, just shuffles her feet, kicking my toe lightly with hers. "I'm sorry, but I can't. I'm not going," she blurts out.

"What?" *Are my ears fucking lying?*

Her eyes break from mine in a panic, and she steps out of my grasp, bumping her locker shut behind her. "My parents don't want me to go. It's too close to Christmas, and we're heading to Oregon to visit my grandma. That's it. I'm sorry I can't come. Have a good time."

No, it's not my ears. It's her. Feeding me the biggest load of crap I've ever imagined in such a reluctant, mousy tone.

I don't chase after her. I watch her practically run, race to the bus, where she clambers into her seat and looks back at the school through the window. I think I see tears in her eyes.

It doesn't make sense, whatever's gotten into her.

Frankly, it doesn't fucking matter.

No one says no to me, and walks away with a second chance. I don't pursue ice queens. My big brother always said the worst mistake a man can make is chasing pussy that isn't interested, and I believe him.

Fine, Doll. We'll do it your way.

Fuck the winter dance. Stay home with your crayons and cartoons. I'll have fun like a grownup. I'm done. Won't even wonder why the hell you're so scared to claim the prize every other girl here would die for.

I resist the urge to slam my fist into somebody's locker, either hers or Scourge's, and head straight for the boy's locker room downstairs. It's the off season for lacrosse, my last one before college, and I'm already over-training. One more dark winter evening won't hurt.

It's the better alternative to ripping this school apart with my bare hands in rage, one rotten brick at a time.

Present Day

Silence follows Maddie like a shadow.

She's barely said a word all morning. We're having our chicken and waffles at an upscale seafood place across town specializing in low country food from the Carolinas for Sunday brunch.

I try to enjoy my meal, knowing I'll need the sustenance before we catch the ferry to Bainbridge. It'll be our first meeting with my old man at the big, empty hospice I used to call home.

Selling this engagement needs to hit *hard.*

Halfway through the meal, her fork clatters and slaps the plate. She looks at me, arms folded. "So, are you ever going to apologize for being a dick the other night?"

"Depends. If I do, are you willing to talk boundaries, and then pull the stick out of your sweet ass and start acting like you're happy to be my wife?"

Wrong words. I see her eye twitch, a signal she's a heartbeat away from getting up and storming off.

I'm not getting anywhere without an apology.

"Look, my tact might have been better, I'll give you that. Never meant to put you in tears, Maddie. Honest," I say, looking left and right in my peripheral vision to make sure there's no one around for what comes next. "I owe you an apology for that. There are no excuses, but this whole arrangement isn't any easier on me. I haven't handled the stress as well as I should, and that's on me. I won't take it out on you again."

If she's satisfied, her expression doesn't show it. At least she hasn't fled. "You've always been a *jerk* to me, Cal. I can think of two, maybe three times when you weren't. One being the day you saved me from those bullies when we were running laps, next time when we kissed, and the other –"

"Don't say it," I hold up my hand, before she takes us down the darkest part of memory lane. "We can't go there. No fucking point."

"Fine. I'll give you the benefit of the doubt because it sounds like you mean it. Christ, I *want* to believe that. One more chance, Cal. But it's probably the last if there's another evening like Friday."

"Fair enough. You respect my boundaries, I'll respect yours, and we won't have issues."

"Showing a little humility works wonders. I could have used that at Maynard, after you asked Tina out in front of me and rammed your tongue down her throat…"

Oh, she's still bitter about that? I suppose she ought to be, but it doesn't stop the fire spiking in my blood.

"It was seven years ago, doll. You said no to the winter dance for reasons I'll never understand. We were clueless fucking kids, everyone."

How the hell could I forget that day? I waited like a snake in the grass for her to come out of the locker room before I laid the heat on Tina. Made sure she had her lips all over me, halfway moaning my name, before I popped the question about the dance, and she gave me an emphatic yes.

Maddie looked crucified. Don't think she ever forgave me until I came to her rescue for the very last time.

Even now, she looks indignant, like my excuse does zero for her pride. "I tried telling you how I felt several times. Did you really never get my notes in jail? Not a single one?" she asks coldly. "I couldn't do the dance. I was worried about *both* of us, Cal, after you and your friends got into it with Scourge and his guys that day over Chelle. Turns out I was right. My friends told me what he said, how they vowed to make life hard for you, and any girl you were with. I couldn't let that be me. I couldn't be responsible for pulling you in deeper."

I don't say anything, stabbing at the last of my food. "Who cares? Never helped in the end, did it?"

She shakes her head reluctantly. We know exactly what happened next, how evil life can be.

"It was seven years ago, Maddie. Time to start living in the present."

She's quiet for a few seconds before a soft sigh escapes her lips. "Whatever. You're right."

We clear our plates, enjoying the relieved atmosphere. One more cup of black coffee for me and an orange juice for her later, and we settle our bill, heading out into the quiet morning.

It's almost half an hour to Bainbridge. I take my own car onto the ferry, as I do every Sunday, dispensing with the driver for local, private hops like these. It's a good thing, too, after I dropped half a million on that damned vase. My budget is going to face corrections soon if I can't win my father over, before he screws me beyond the grave.

"Any last minute questions?" I ask her as we roll through the illustrious family gates, the Randolph name formed in wrought iron overhead like a greeting, or a warning, to all who enter.

"No. I'll follow your lead. It's probably good that I don't say much, and let you do the talking, considering how things are…" She stops herself just short of getting into the crap between my dad and me. Wise choice.

"Wrong, Maddie. I need your tongue. Charm him. Please." I give her a look while I park the car on the long driveway, witnessing her surprise. "He's heard the same old shit from me every Sunday for the last three months since he got in that bed, and they told him he was never coming out. You're fresh. New. A wild card, even if he thinks you're just a Joker."

"That's…kind of a lot of pressure," she says, looking down at her lap.

"You'll pass the test. You always do. Never saw you fail one even once at the academy. Your record in contracts speaks for itself, too. Cade knows a guy in Seoul who said you were instrumental to opening up the Great Firewall of China and letting Sterner code apps into their market. Think you made every other sorry bastard after the same thing turn green with envy."

Her mouth drops slightly. "Those details were never public! I'm not sure why you'd take any interest in what happened months ago, either, unless of course you were –"

"Keeping tabs? Of course I did, doll. I never forgot you." I stop, knowing I've said too much and it's coming out wrong. "Always figured the day would come when I'd need to make good on that favor. I had to know where to find you. Now, come on."

I want to get this over with, and I'm done sparing minutes for chit-chat.

Nothing good will come from too much talk, too much honesty. She can't find out how much dust she's kicking up in every corner of my soul that should stay abandoned.

I want to keep this professional. As much as this fake fiancé thing can be without invisible strings tangling us up like spiderwebs. There's a billion of those and counting thanks to the past.

Still, I don't give up easy. I know what I need to do.

No emotions, no sex, and no second guesses.

Two out of three, I'm failing miserably. It has to stop. And doll absolutely, positively can't find out how much strain she's putting on the careful walls I've built.

Because if they ever crumble, our protection is gone. There's no telling what happens then.

V: Over the Pit (Maddie)

The elder Randolph is a shell of a man, slow to sit up when we find our way into his room. It's disconcerting for such a fine room to smell so strongly of heavy medications and decay. I expected this, true, everything except the hateful energy in his eyes.

"What is it today?" Cal's father grunts after we take our seats.

I put on my best smile, trying hard to keep the girlfriend act up for this critical moment.

"Dad, how are you today?" Cal practically beams.

"Dying, the same as yesterday," the old man snaps. "Who's she?"

Cal turns to me with a soft smile on his face. There's a clear tension behind it, a cruel apology that says, *I'm sorry we have to sit through this shit.*

"Madeline Middleton," I say, reaching for his frail hand, without skipping a beat. "Soon to be Mrs. Calvin Randolph."

His grip is firmer than I imagined. He squeezes hard, like he's testing to make sure I'm really here, and it's not some ghastly trick of his mind. "She doesn't look like an escort, at least. I'll give you that."

"My fiancée is *not* a damned escort, dad. Please, just give her a chance. I wanted you two to meet before the end." Cal sounds angrier than he should.

Almost like he's eager to defend my honor, but I really know it's about the trust, the severe risk this charade could fall apart here and now.

I release the old man's hand and replace it with Cal's. His fingers lace through mine, pinching so much harder than his father. He brings my hand to his lips and kisses the back. I don't know why it brings me instant goosebumps everywhere.

"We met in Beijing, Mr. Randolph. It happened like it was always meant to be. I've loved your son ever since," I chirp, smiling so hard it hurts. It certainly isn't easy with the constant scowl on his thin, pale lips. "It's an honor to meet you. Really. I've heard so much. Everything about how you raised him, and took the firm to heights nobody ever imagined."

"You heard lies, girl, no different than what you're feeding me." He sits up straighter, closing his eyes for a couple seconds. My heart jumps into my throat, pounding much faster, before he looks at me again with extra disdain dripping from his eyes. They're eerily identical baby blues to Cal's. "I remember who you are. I still have a pulse and my memory, despite this withering flesh. I read the police reports."

I turn my head, giving Cal a panicked look, pretending

I'm not ready to jump out of my skin. *Jesus. Now, what?*

"Sometimes I think you're more forgetful than I am on my IV cocktail, boy." He looks at Cal and sneers. "Did you really think you had a chance? Bringing *this* one here, thinking I'd magically forgotten the years our lives went to hell in a hand basket? Did you think I wouldn't remember her, you little idiot?"

"Had to do something to test your faculties, *dad,*" Cal spits the last word like it's rotten fruit. "Of course, we didn't meet in China. We stayed in touch all these years, and reconnected a few months ago."

"Typical. I'm glad you showed me how much bunk your desperate cries about how much you've changed are, Calvin. You're a terrible liar. You always were. It's a small miracle you've gotten anywhere at RET at all, rather than collecting your accolades off the name I built with your grandfather."

The two men stare, saying nothing, contempt in their eyes.

Hello, disaster. I sit for a second in the frigid silence, head spinning, wracking my brain for some unreachable combination of words that will salvage this.

"I knew you wouldn't approve," Cal says quietly, moving his chair an inch closer to his father's bedside. "That's why I brought Maddie here anyway. I wanted you to see I'm building my life with the woman I love, the way I want, whether you leave me a fucking penny or not."

"You're marrying your stupid little crush who brought us to the brink of *ruin,*" Mr. Randolph barks, giving me a furious look. "No more of this. You've come here with her to rub it in my face. Leave now, or I'll call the nurse and end this sickening joke myself."

"Mr. Randolph, please!" I stand up, flustered. His hand stops, halfway to the red button for the intercom on his nightstand. "We were wrong to make up stories. It was my idea, and I'm sorry. I thought it'd go down easier that way. I was wrong. Truth is, Cal's about to make me the happiest woman in the world. I could care less about the fortune you two are playing tug-of-war with. As long as he's mine, I'm richer than I ever imagined. I'll just miss the fact that we could never win your approval."

I don't know what comes over me, but it's making me shake. I plop back down in my seat before my own mouth runs me over, clueless why I'm so emotional. It's a bad situation, yes, probably the end of this whole stupid thing if he's already convinced Cal deserves squat. But it shouldn't be like *this,* cold ink running in my blood, vicious tears stinging the corners of my eyes.

"She's telling the truth, old man," Cal says coldly. "This isn't a game. It's honesty. We fell in love because we learned how to deal with our pain, something you never did. Who the hell do you think kept my spirits up that year I spent in prison? And then when I couldn't find a job, couldn't find my way, couldn't find *anything?* Wasn't you, or even mom. Not after John. You never gave me a second chance, even when my brother begged you."

Hearing his dead son's name makes the old man blink. "Don't you *dare* drag him into his. Watch your greedy, forked tongue."

"Greedy? Oh, you ought to know a thing or two about it, dad. You earned the best money of your life after the funeral, when you stuffed yourself away in your booze and women, while mom cried herself to sleep alone. Maybe her heart wouldn't have given out if you'd been around to help mend it."

"Like you'd know, Cal," the old man says. "Spare me the high and mighty scorn from the good son who wasn't. If you ever gave a damn about this family, you'd have never broken her heart in the first place, before losing John killed what was left."

I cover my mouth to hold in the gasp trying to slip out. When the elder Randolph turns to me, it's brutal. Cal sits quietly, bowed up like he wants more than anything to resolve this with more than words. Too bad force isn't an option.

"Watch out for him, girl. I don't know what you see, but don't let it blind you. He's a screw up, a liar, and a hideous excuse for a backup son." He cranes his head, slowly rolling over, punching the call button on his intercom. Our signal to leave.

Thank God. I'm too stunned by the train wreck that's just happened to contemplate where we go from here.

But before Cal can grab the door, I hear his father's voice one more time, a hoarse whisper from the sheets. "If it could've been you, instead of John, we'd all be better off. I wish sometimes it was the Taliban who missed, and not that sick bastard's son."

His reference to the worst of the past feels like a bullet slicing through my chest.

Oh, God. I look to my fiancé, searching for the shot to the heart I expect to see written all over his face.

There's nothing. Just a cold, blank tension he wears from the time he slams the door shut behind us, leads me through the mansion by the wrist, and climbs into the car without one word.

"I'm sorry, Cal. I didn't know what to do. Nothing could've prepared me for that." Well, maybe if he'd given me a heads up about what a dying sourpuss his father really is, it would've been better than flying blind. But I can't blame him for the disaster.

"Forget it. You tried." The wind sweeps through his short dark hair, casting a rugged edge to his chiseled good looks.

We're standing on the upper deck of the ferry as it churns toward it's Seattle terminal, putting the island and its secret money behind us. What do I even say to numb the hurt? It seems like it's so pointless now. If we can't convince his father, he's out of luck.

I might as well talk to my boss about coming back early. I'm mapping the conversation in my head, wondering if I'll be sent straight back to Beijing, when he turns away from me, beginning a slow walk across the ship.

Apparently, even my presence at his shoulder is too much. I don't know if he wants to be alone today, or forever.

I give him a few minutes alone before I step up,

sheepishly whispering behind him. "If it's over, and you'd like me to go, I can."

"Go? What the hell do you mean?" he turns, his eyes blue fire.

"I mean, it's over, isn't it? We lost. He couldn't have been more unimpressed with me if I'd spat in his face for the nasty things he said to you."

Cal smiles, small and tenuous, but it brings such a delicious glow to his gorgeous face. "I miss your glasses, doll. You're beautiful without them, too, but you used to wear your innocence on your sleeve."

"I got Lasik a few years ago," I say, puzzled. "What have my glasses got to do with anything?"

"You're the same woman without them, aren't you? Older and wiser, sure, but same heart. Same spirit. Don't believe you'd be standing here with me right now participating in this facade if you'd changed for the worse."

"Of course. I did what I had to."

He lays a hand on my shoulder, an instant signal to my heart to quicken. "Then you should know I'm not so different, either. Not at my core. Would the Cal you knew at Maynard ever give up this fucking easy?"

He makes me smile. Shaking my head, I whisper one word, slipping into a chill that goes up my spine having nothing to do with the windy ride across the sea. "No."

"Exactly. Come here, beautiful." He doesn't give me a chance to pull away. No time to second guess what happens a second later.

His kiss is fierce, hot, and oh-so-nice. Cal attacks my

mouth like it's natural, like we're more than frauds, sinking his tongue into mine, owning me from the inside out. His fingertips dig into my skin, too hard to be a proper peck. Too long to even be a normal kiss between lovers.

This is want. It's a living symbol of the desire flickering in my nerves, alive and magnetic, surrendering me to him for the next few seconds without the slightest protest.

It's plenty wrong, but I allow it because I hope it helps him feel better after the disaster an hour ago.

Heck, maybe I allow it because I want it, too. His hands, his lips, and his five o'clock shadow are a comfort. A very dangerous one, but a kindness nonetheless. It's the first time I really notice the black petals and vines with their tangled thorns stamped across the back of his hand as it slides down my cheek, returning to my side.

It takes me a long, terse breath to recover. "And what was that?"

"More practice. We aren't done, Maddie. If we can't convince my old man directly, we'll get to him through the senior partners and the board. Spence and Cade's dads have been good to me over the years, but they never forgot the bad. They're too afraid it isn't all behind me to go against dad. If I ever wind up with my share in the company and its money, they only see dire consequences."

"If you think it's worth it, we'll try," I say, giving him a nod. I owe him another shot, as long as he's treating me like a decent human being. Jesus, maybe more than decent, if I'm being honest. "When did you get this?"

I grab his hand, holding it up, marveling at how heavy

and strong it is. He looks down, new ice in his eyes, reminding me I'd better not get too comfortable or ask too many questions.

"Jail. Black rose. Has to do with something private that went down there."

Message read, loud and clear. He doesn't want to go further. Rather than probe more, I walk with him to parking on the lower level, hand-in-hand, seeing how we're only minutes away from docking.

Maybe the worst is over. If we're able to avoid another ferocious confrontation with his dad, then I think there's a chance I'll survive this fake fiancée thing without losing my mind, or my heart.

I'm in our old neighborhood the next morning, preparing to say hello to my parents before I get back to the condo and prep for our next chance to shine with the senior partners at Cal's firm.

It's always a little weird coming home. The old houses and rental duplexes haven't changed a bit since my college days. My parents live on the lazy side of the university, pockmarked with ramshackle houses and quirky businesses too forgotten to be gentrified by the city's housing boom.

I try to quell my nerves when I knock at the door, expecting to see my mother's soft, pleasantly plump face appear through the glass before she lets me in. Instead, I see a girl in her early twenties, just a couple years younger than me, sticking her tongue out like a twelve year old.

"Home already, Kat? Lucky me. Thought you had to work afternoons?"

"Boss gave me the evening off to say hello to my big sis. Come the hell here." She opens the door and sweeps me into a hug. "I'll make us some coffee."

My little sister is grown up, but clearly no less a brat. We embrace just the same as close kin who haven't seen each other for the better part of a year.

She leads me into our old kitchen. The little stools at the breakfast bar are the same as I remember. I take my old spot at the one with a rickety leg, tapping my fingers impatiently on the peeling counter as I watch her fix our coffee. While a silver gooseneck kettle heats on the stove, she measures several spoons of coffee grounds into a glass chemex lined with a filter. Then slowly, lovingly, she pours the water across the grounds.

"Smells heavenly," I say, inhaling the coffee-infused air. "If there's one thing I miss about home, it's the coffee. The stuff they're serving in Beijing just doesn't cut it. If you ever have a chance to go overseas, I bet you'll teach them a thing or two."

Katrina rolls her eyes, watching as the last boiling water sifts through the grounds, draining dark brown goodness into the glass. "Oh, sure. I'll be on the first plane the second Mr. Kolaris opens his first international store. Sorry, Maddie, we can't *all* be international hotshot wunderkids."

I smile sadly. There's more than a little jealousy in her voice, but she's usually supportive. For now, Kat has accepted the same fate I once seemed destined to, working at the small Greek coffee shop a few blocks away. It's close enough to bike to, even in the heavy rain. A major plus because that's the only vehicle she can afford on her tips and minimum wage.

"So, what really brings you back here?" she asks, sliding over my coffee. I take a few seconds to answer, savoring the rich flavors on my tongue. "Can't believe you'd take a leave of absence from paradise just a couple months after they finally sent you abroad like you always wanted."

"Business doesn't care what I want," I say, narrowing my eyes. I wonder how much my father passed along from the story I concocted when I told my parents I was coming home for several weeks. If they'd kept it on the down low like I asked, Kat wouldn't know it's a leave of absence at all.

"And what business is that?" she says, chugging her coffee like it's water. "Sterner doesn't do much here in Mandarin, I suppose. You're lucky they didn't drag you up to their new headquarters in Anchorage to freeze your nipples off."

I laugh at the notion. The company's strongman CEO, Ty, spends most of the year in Alaska, the official base of operations every employee in Seattle and beyond contends with. Once upon a time, he rocked the boat quite a bit when he married his stepsister, a scandalous slice of drama making me all too aware why I'm really here, and what I need to keep hiding from my nosy little sister.

"I'll keep my nipples as long as I'm home, thanks. If you must know, I'm doing some side work with an old friend." The last word tastes hard and bitter in my mouth. Whatever the hell Calvin is, he isn't my friend, as he recently made painfully clear.

"Boyfriend, huh? I always knew you were hiding something from us." Kat says it so nonchalantly I almost spit out my delicious coffee.

"I'm *not* here for a boyfriend, sis. Don't know where you got that idea. I'm happily single and way too busy to pick over the expats, co-workers, and digital nomads who make up my options in Beijing."

"Duh. That's why you came back here to land a man. Who is he?"

She just doesn't quit, does she? Rolling my eyes, I drain half my cup before I set it down, rolling over a few different options in my head.

There's a decent chance someone will find out the truth about my fake engagement sooner or later. If it's inevitable, I'll still welcome a delay. I can't put a price on time, however long I have to concoct a story about why I'm getting married, and then again when it falls through.

My little game with Cal has an expiration date. It's the only saving grace from getting too deep in drama or too attached.

"Madds, hello?" Kat waves her hand over my face, reminding me I haven't answered.

"Katrina, why do you even care? I want to have a good time here. I don't want drama," I say, hoping my eyes are sufficiently patronizing for a big sis. "I get it. You're frustrated because you're stuck here, putting in your hours, trying to entertain yourself in this expensive, crazy town.

I've seen the cost for a few drinks and a round of oysters –
one night in Seattle is two week's worth in China. Admit it
– you'd love to show mom and dad the daughter they
banked on isn't as perfect as they think."

"You think this is jealousy talking?" she snaps, snatching
my cup for a refill. "Truth is, I'm worried. I'm just curious
why you're lying to everyone instead of just fucking telling
us you're engaged."

"Engaged?" My heart almost stops. She slides my cup
back slowly, a satisfied 'gotcha' spark in her eyes. "Where
did you hear that?"

"Every hipster who's on his laptop at Roasted reads
Seattle Widgets. Techies everywhere. Don't think I'd have
missed their local gossip page today if I tried." Smiling, she
pulls out her phone, and taps it a few times. When she turns
it toward me, I see myself on the screen.

At the charity auction.

In Cal's arms.

Completely swept away in his sudden, shocking,
infuriating kiss.

FORGET THE PAST. CALVIN RANDOLPH MAKES
IT OFFICIAL, AND YOU WON'T BELIEVE HOW HOT
IT IS!

The cringe-worthy clickbait headline alone would burn
my cheeks down, but the fact that it's accompanied by a
banner sized pic of us locking lips, his bright blue eyes
drilling through my soul, makes every drop of blood in my
veins lava.

"Please, just let me break the news to mom and dad," I

say, my voice cratering to a whisper.

"Maddie, you don't even sound happy. What's really going on?" She props her face up, elbows on the counter, giving me a more concerned look than I've seen for years. "I can't believe you're marrying him...but the thing that really surprises me is, you sound like you can't believe it either."

"It's not like that. Things happened really fast. Cal, he kept in touch after everything that went down at the academy. I wrote him for years. Found out we were on the same page about a lot of things. We decided to meet and..." It's hard to continue. Her eyes are huge, accusing, disbelieving. "Aw, screw it. I owe him one, Kat. I don't know if you were too young to understand everything that happened at Maynard years ago, but if he hadn't gotten between me and a disaster, I'd be nowhere. Now, he needs my help."

"Of course I remember the news. It was all over," Kat says, folding her arms and sticking out her nose, as if I owe her an immediate apology for questioning her crystal clear memory. She quickly gets over it and sends me a baffled look. "Wait, so...are you engaged to him, or not?"

I furrow my brow, wondering if there's even an answer to her question. "We are. But it's only temporary. He needs a fiancée, a wife, a woman to get his father to change his trust so he doesn't lose everything before he passes. Two, maybe three months tops – that's all the time his father's got – we'll know the outcome. We'll dissolve it. Pretend it never happened. I'll go on my merry way, and I'll never have to think about actually marrying Cal again."

Why does saying that basic cold fact feel like a blow to my stomach?

At first, Kat looks stunned. She sets her coffee cup on the counter quickly, like she's seconds away from dropping it, and then flattens herself against the old fridge with its rust spots, releasing the world's longest sigh.

"Whew. And mom thought *I* sold out when I skipped community college to stay with my crappy indie band."

"Hey, I'm *not* doing this for money." It isn't that simple. She doesn't understand.

I should stop expecting anything different.

It's obvious, isn't it? No one will ever get the tragic connection between us. They weren't there for the heartbreak, the gnawing guilt, the years spent wondering where he'd gone when he never wrote back, and how badly I'd mucked up his life.

"Sis, I don't even want to know," she says, holding out a hand, feigning to push me away. "You can keep your secrets to yourself, as long as you tell our parents. They deserve a run down, before they hear it from everybody else. Dad takes heart medication now, as you know."

I do. He doesn't need more surprises, certainly not any rude, bizarre ones thanks to me.

Cup in hand, she marches out of the kitchen. I hear her clomp upstairs and slam the weathered door to her room.

Just like old times. I'm left alone to stew in my stress.

As unbearable as Kat can be, she has a point. I can't let mom and dad find out I'm engaged to the boy who became the talk of every hushed whisper Maynard parents uttered that year on some stupid blog, or through the local gossip mill.

Of course, that means there's a new dimension in this insane game of pretend we're playing. We're not just convincing his straight-buttoned business associates and screwed up father anymore.

We have to convince my freaking parents. And every time I imagine how that's bound to go, I wish to holy heaven sis' coffee came with a nice splash of hemlock creamer.

Cal makes himself scarce the next few days leading up to dinner with the partners. I've always been adaptable, able to conform to morning birds and night owls alike, but when he's in full work mode, I barely see him.

He's gone before sunup, when I roll out of bed and pad into the kitchen. I spend the daytime more alone and confused in the vast Emerald City than I've ever been. A dense summer rain brings a fog through the streets for the better part of the next two days. I visit the art museum and spend time under an umbrella near the Great Wheel next to the water, biting my lip the whole time, hoping my phone doesn't ping with a voicemail or worried texts from my parents.

I'm not sure whether they'll be angry or just confused. They don't like secrets.

I haven't even had a chance to talk to him about the

introduction yet, and I still don't have a clue how I'll make it remotely normal.

It's one thing to kiss, hold hands, and put on these sweet lies in front of rich strangers. Quite another to do it to mom and dad – especially when Kat knows the truth, and made me crack like a walnut the second she gave me her scornful eyes.

The evening before dinner, I'm moping next to the window at his condo, waiting for my Chinese takeout to arrive. My phone vibrates next to me, and I hold my breath as I flick the button to see the screen.

> **Cal:** Coming home early, doll. Show me what you're wearing tomorrow. I'd go with something sleek and sexy, considering the occasion.

Ridiculous. It's the first time I've heard from him in days, and a laughable *what are you wearing* text is what I get? I wouldn't have gotten it quicker on Tinder.

> **Maddie:** I don't know. Seems like I'm engaged to a ghost. And I don't know if I believe in them.

> **Cal:** Stop fucking around.

> **Cal:** Ghosts don't make their fake fiancées wet. You're also the only one I'll ever imagine moaning.

His last text sends a vicious adrenaline shot through my heart before I even see what's attached. It's a pic of Cal, sitting at his desk in his best selfie pose, half the buttons on his shirt unclasped, revealing a hint of the dark tattoos framing his chest. It hangs open too far to be considered business casual.

Even from the screen, his blue eyes pierce me, and the wild, tempting smirk on his lips settles like a drug. I cross my legs a couple times, resisting the damp heat pooling near my thighs, outrageous as it is uncontrollable.

Unfortunately, this marvelous bastard has a divine gift for doing everything he threatens, and more.

I slam my phone against the chair's armrest with a huff, wondering how I'll ever snap out of it before he shows up tonight. I'm already starting to miss the days when he was no more than a mysterious afterthought. My fingers punch the screen and I chew my lips, tapping a quick response, hopefully my last before I plot my escape.

Maddie: You're crazy if you think we're playing games.

Then my phone pings again. I resist the urge to look for all of thirty seconds, before I snatch it in my palm, defusing a hateful smile.

Cal: Doll, I'm serious. Play dress up for me before I'm home in the next hour, or I'll drag you down the hall and consider showing you games are the last thing on my mind.

I don't know what's gotten into him.

I don't care.

All that's certain is, I wait about five more minutes without replying before I stand up, stuff my phone into my purse, and retreat to my bedroom. That's where I crash for a nap to shake this wicked flame he's sparked in my pussy, but not before I peel off my old outfit, and slip into the jade green evening dress, black heels with gold bow-ties, and matching gold necklace with ruby tips I still don't feel grown up enough to wear.

I can't believe what I'm doing for this impossible man.

Maybe it's because this is the first fun I've had since this started, without being intimidated by the ferocious spark between us.

Fine. I'll give his push just enough pull to stay on his good side.

For now.

"Evening, doll. You're lovely when you sleep, but I think I prefer you bright-eyed and bushy tailed." He wakes me with a kiss.

In my half-conscious state, it's easy to indulge the Snow White fantasies I've had since I was a little girl, being brought to life again by the handsome, noble prince. But the rest of my brain switches on, and I remember who he *really* is.

I jerk up, pushing him away, instantly angry as I see the amusement twinkling in his eyes. "Jesus, don't you ever knock?"

"Why should a man knock when it's his place?"

"Nice. I'm lucky you're so respectful of a woman's privacy, jerk."

His smirk turns into a full grin, and he comes closer, sitting next to me at the edge of my bed. "And I'm very fortunate you never learned how to swear like an adult. Stand the fuck up."

Annoyed, I obey. I think I set a new record for the time it takes to feel familiar fire in my cheeks. My blood goes from lukewarm to molten in less than ten seconds, about the time it takes for him to put his hands on my waist, and slowly maneuver them to my hips, where he stops and cups my rear through the silky fabric.

"Ass out. Legs apart." He pauses, moving his hands lower. When he slides several stiff fingers between my thighs and eases my legs apart, I whimper, holding in a harsh breath. "Good girl."

"Excuse me?" I'm stunned. He says nothing.

Okay, a woman can put up with a lot, but he's just hit my limit. Whirling around, I shove his hands off me, freeing myself from his invasive and horribly sexy grasp.

"Last I checked, you're my fiancé, Cal. Not my personal valet. I'm old enough to dress myself. I've given you more than I ever should've, now get out of my room!" I hold out a finger, pointing to the door.

Still wearing the same awful smile, he stands, grabs my wrist, and brings it to his lips. "Maddie, you're trembling. We've got to get better at this. I need you to touch me without looking like you're about to either keel over or drown in your own lust if we're going to close the deal."

"Deal? What deal?"

"Us," he growls in my ear, making sure I'm able to feel his heat. Goosebumps line my neck, every sensitive inch of my flesh rising to meet their unwanted master. "The dress works. You'll be a knockout tomorrow. My fucking knockout, and only mine."

No matter how many times his fingers glide across my body, they still make me jump. I fall back against him, deeper into his grip. My ass brushes his hard-on, tenting through his trousers, leaving no doubt whatsoever what he wants behind the sarcasm, the teasing, the thrill he gets drowning my panties in a heat I can't cool.

Yep, it's bad, I think to myself, as soon as I see us in the mirror, his face hovering over my shoulder, brilliant blue eyes pointed at my cleavage. *From ice cube to hot mess, just like that. And I don't even know how to do it in reverse.*

I'm worried this pretender freak knows how to push buttons on my own body I didn't know were there. When I try to pull away, ever so slightly, my knees moving like quicksand, he curls a big arm around my waist and pulls me backward, into his throbbing erection.

When I feel it, I gasp. He growls, low like thunder, an animal glint in his eye.

"Cal…" I whisper, running my tongue over my lips, too afraid to say the rest for several seconds. Oh, and if only I could keep it in. "What are you doing? I thought we weren't…weren't supposed to…*holy hell.*"

It falls out when his free hand snakes up my side, rolling

my nipple. One simple motion, no more than several seconds, and somehow able to make my thighs shake on command.

"Of course I *want* to, doll. Hell, I'd love nothing better than to throw you down face first, shred the dress you're supposed to be wearing for my rich friends tomorrow night, and fuck you like I should've years ago."

Oh. My. God.

I don't realize how rough I'm breathing until his hard-on grazes me again. That's when I moan, and the soft sound moving through my body resonates in my lungs, which can't produce more than a couple shallow breaths every few seconds.

Not when this want, this need, this confusing, relentless urge keeps calling me to do the worst with him, consequences be damned.

But he isn't done toying with me yet. My fingers go to his huge tattooed wrist, digging into the black rose inked on his skin. Its make believe thorns could prick me, and still I wouldn't care, falling deeper and deeper into this wall of muscle and divine, masculine scent surrounding me, cutting me off from my own better judgment.

"Obviously, we can't really do this, Maddie." And just like that, he untangles himself, and walks away, heading for the door. He acts like nothing happened when he stops, adjusting his collar, looking at me as if we're almost about to head out for a night on the town instead of rip each other's clothes off. "It's wrong, you know. You could never handle it."

He can't be serious. I'm speechless, jamming my thumb into my chest. "What? *Me?*"

"You're too good for casual. Some things never change. If you could open your legs, enjoy the dozen Os I fuck into you tonight, and then wake up tomorrow like it never happened, we'd be on, so on, in just a heartbeat. But I'd have better luck asking for my asshole father to have a magic change of heart tomorrow morning, making this whole thing pointless. Sorry, my mistake. I won't be teasing you again."

There's no time to answer, to quip back, to drop the nice girl act stamped into me since I was raised by a woman who directed the Sunday choir at our church, and curse Calvin Randolph to the darkest F'd up parts of hell.

Because by the time I'm able to move my tongue without tasting the foul taste he's left in my mouth, he's already gone. I'm left in front of the tall mirror, looking like a fool, wondering how hard I'll lie tomorrow to make sure everybody doesn't see the brutal truth written on my face.

I'm starting to *hate* this man.

He saved me once, but he's no hero. He's a pushy, screwed up, arrogant alpha-hole joke who takes every liberty I never agreed to when I came running back to the States to bail him out. I knew I should have amended that stupid contract to say *no teasing allowed.*

I won't even mention the complete lack of gratitude.

As soon as my ninety days are up, I'll be out of here on the first flight to Asia, without caring whether or not Sterner has more work lined up for me or not. Or faster, if I can't hold the urge to slap him across his callous face. I can't share the same continent with this reckless idiot who loves winding me up for amusement.

The sad part is, if he'd just drop the pretenses and apologize, or at least open up, then I might be able to forgive the teasing, the wit, the frantic push to places that aren't even on the same map as any of my comfort zones.

I might remember the horror he's lived for the ten thousandth time, and forget his wild infractions.

I might be able to wrap my head around his heart, and figure out where it comes from.

I might stop the hate sprouting like a bad seed in my heart, nourished by the desire, the disdain, and the incredible, conflicted emotions he stirs up like a tsunami.

And yes, I might be able to deal with the sick, sick feelings for him I've been ignoring since the second I got here. Everything he preys upon, and everything guaranteed to be my undoing if I ever loosen up, let them out, and come to terms with my seven year attraction to this unfathomable creature.

When he texted me earlier and touched off the latest round of crap, he was right.

Ghosts can't make me wet.

Demons, on the other hand, have uncanny powers. And there's no way Cal's demented hold over me is anything less than pure evil.

VI: To the Charade (Cal)

Mistakes always take their toll, and I have to pay *big* if I want to fix last night's wreckage.

It's almost lunch before I've decided what to say. I'm ready for my evening off, wrapping up my last marketing campaign when I call her. The phone's ring echoes in my ear. I've already decided to swallow my pride for the next two minutes so her second thoughts don't fuck me over.

Click. "Maddie?" I say her name, expecting the silent treatment.

It's her voice, but there's no anger. No, wait.

What the fuck? She says something in Chinese I have no hope of understanding, and then switches to English.

"…you heard me, and you've come to the right place. That's Mandarin for 'sorry I can't come to the phone.' Wait for the tone and I'll call you back!" Voicemail. I should've known.

"Doll, look, about last night…I'm sorry. I got carried away, and I know it. I meant to reinforce boundaries, and I went at it a stupid way. Won't happen again. I'm coming home soon, hoping you're ready for tonight. Give me a chance this weekend, and I'll find some way to make it up to you. Promise."

Promise? I wonder who's saying these words.

Cal Randolph never apologized to any woman for flaunting his package. Hell, I've left repeat fucks in tears over the years, the long chain of club girls and phone dates I've had trying to bleach her from my head.

Sure, she left her mark on me, even in prison and the hell that followed.

Fuck no, I'm not a monk.

I've had my women, hand-picked honeys looking at me with their big doe eyes and all too eager lips night after night. Bedding them never took Maddie too far from my brain, but a casual fuck does momentarily calm the lust beating in my balls like an incessant war drum.

These women were basic bread, my sustenance, plain and fuckable enough to silence the feral urges running in my blood. To them, I was an Olympian god. Rare, perfect, untouchable. I gave them one night with me in heaven.

Surprise, surprise, they always wanted more.

I never did. Stopped doing repeats three or four years ago, whenever the first few chicks laid the drama on thick after they got my dick inside them for two or three nights, instead of the usual one.

They thought sharing my bed more than once meant something. They were dead wrong, and they always wanted to leave damage when they figured it out.

Word gets around in this town fast, especially when Cade, Spence, and the rest of the single boys at the firm poach pussy from the same downtown hunting grounds.

It's incredible how boring the high class bar scene becomes with each passing year.

True, it could be stress clouding my head, this single-minded focus I have on restoring my name and preserving everything I've built over the last five years on the backs of sixteen hour days. I won't be cock blocked by any girl with what I'm really after. Without my chance at dragging RET into this century, outshining dad's dimming star, I've got nothing.

I know what's important.

I don't have time to chase meaningless pussy, and I definitely don't apologize to the ones I've scorned.

Why, then, is there a black ache I don't recognize in my gut when I think about Maddie?

It's because she isn't any old lay. Nothing casual ever left the hole in my life saving her did. She's my fiancée on paper, and it sends me into an annoyed fugue when I stop, think, and recognize the wicked hold she already has over my soul.

"Doll?" I call her nickname, pushing into my condo.

Predictably, she's nowhere to be found. I start heading for the bedroom when I come to an abrupt stop. Standing in the hall, decked in her dick-teasing jade green, black heels, and gold accents, she looks at me without moving, her suitcase at her side.

"Where do you think you're going?" I ask, narrowing my eyes. A nasty doubt in the pit of my stomach tells me I shouldn't ask questions with obvious answers.

"That depends. I got your message. It kept me from leaving the letter I wrote on your kitchen counter, and heading straight for the airport. So, congratulations on keeping me here a few more hours, I guess."

"Shit, you can't just up and go," I take several steps toward her, but she throws out her hands, telling me I'd better not come closer. "Maddie, please. Everything I said on the phone, I meant. I'm about making this work."

"Serious enough to start treating me like a woman who's supposedly in love with you, and looking forward to our wedding day?" She narrows the gap between us until we're only inches apart.

So close it's easy to see the anguish and disappointment in her eyes.

What the fuck did you do? I wonder. *It isn't fair.*

I never meant to hurt her. How the hell did I know treating her the only way I know would cut so deep? She doesn't need an apology. She needs me to rip my heart out, and admit I did *wrong*.

"Doll, listen –"

"No, *you* listen to me for a change, Calvin. I'm trying to help you, and I'm giving up a lot to pay you back. I want to do right for everything you gave me years ago. But you're making that so freaking hard. Let's step back. Put any feelings aside for a minute, and see what this really is: a glorified *quid pro quo*. Nothing more. Do you know what that means?"

"Of course." I pretend it's obvious.

"It's spelled out in the paperwork we signed. I'm not your accessory. I'm not your sex toy. And I am most certainly *not* the next notch in your million dollar bedpost." She lays a hand on my chest, tapping my collar with her pointer finger. I don't even recognize her anymore.

Where the hell is my shy, sultry girl with the quiet spark in her dark eyes? She's gone, replaced by this wildcat who wants my balls on a silver platter. "Do you remember the months at Maynard, before everything got ugly? You were desperate to get my attention. I ignored you as much as I could. Swore I'd never admit to the stupid little crush we shared, knowing it would be the end of us."

"End? Love, it might've been the beginning, if things hadn't gotten so fucked up."

My words give her pause. I'm just as shocked at what's exiting my mouth.

I'm annoyed this little heart-to-heart has bled into the abandoned places, awakening things I want to keep buried. Maddie's hand slides off me. She backs against the wall, and sighs, averting her eyes.

"Stop toying with me. I'm done riding this emotional seesaw," she says, angrily flicking her dark hair over her shoulder. "Let me do the job you brought me here for. That's it. I'll be whatever you want in public, as long as you're giving me respect."

Her curt, business-like words ought to be music to my ears.

Yet, somehow, I can't shake the unease in my bones when I lean in, study her sad face, and see the number my antics did on her. "Doesn't have to be all work and no fun, doll."

"We're *not* having sex. Even if you weren't totally right about me last night, I'm not interested. We're not really a couple. I'm a paper fiancée, remember? Do what you want without me. I won't hold it against you if there's a need to go out, have your fun, and come home like it never happened. Just don't do it in front of my face."

She thinks I want...what, exactly? A goddamned hall pass to get my rocks off with whoever?

"Shit, Maddie, it isn't like that. I wasn't asking for..." I stop, swallowing a lie I didn't know I was about to tell her until now. If there wasn't something very sexual happening subconsciously, I wouldn't need to struggle to keep my eyes from roaming her body like a lion's on its prey. "Fine. No sex. To be fair, we were on the same page yesterday. We knew it was a bad idea, even though I made my point in a fucked up way."

"You did. At least there's one thing we agree on," she says, turning her eyes to the floor. "I wish it weren't like this. I'd love this to be easier. I don't know what to do with you, Cal."

"You're not perfect. You worry too much. Look at me," I say, coming forward, slapping my palms down on both sides of her head against the wall. I box her in until she gives me those hazel eyes that seem to go on forever. "I've lived a fucked up life since our high school days. That's no excuse for last night. I hear you, doll. I really do. I'm listening, and I'm sorry. Can't we press reset?"

Maddie's eyes soften slowly. She breaks eye contact to glance at the suitcase just a couple feet away. "Let me put this away, and then I'll be ready to go."

My sad apology works. Thank fuck because I don't have another second of therapy hour left in me.

"Tell me what will make this square first," I say. "Believe it or not, I want to do this right. No more fuck ups. I'm grateful for what you're doing, sidestepping your own life to repair mine."

For a second, she pauses, teething her bottom lip in thought. It's sexier than she intends, drawing my eyes like bees on honey. Another temptation I don't need, threatening to blow everything I've just fixed to kingdom come.

"Treat me like a lady, for one. Prove you're serious about everything you just said. After this dinner, I want a night out. Not just because I'm looking to be wined and dined in a way I can never afford – and honestly, maybe part of me does, simply because I'm all about new experiences."

"Done." I smile, nodding. Typical Maddie, chasing bucket lists instead of wealth and prestige for their own sake.

"Well, I'm not. I'm also asking because it's still *insanely* difficult to keep up this charade, and we're only a week in." She walks past me, picks up her bag by the handle, and looks over her shoulder. "I'm going to mess this up if I don't believe we're in love. Nobody will buy it. And honestly, Cal, I can't believe it enough to lie well unless you're able to treat me like a normal girlfriend for one stupid night, instead of a free ticket to get your dick wet. If you want that, do it without me, I don't care. I'm happy to let you have your hall pass with whoever, if hall passes are even a thing in a fake relationship."

My eyebrows go up. She turns, rolling the suitcase back to her room, before I'm able to see more than a hint of the cherry red blossoms blazing on her cheeks.

They're several shades hotter than the new half a million dollar decoration I won at the auction. I watch her walk by the vase, and I remember her dress lined with roses on white, a style I'll always associate with tragedy.

But she isn't that girl anymore, and I'm not the scared, angry kid who let a pissing contest over her go much too far.

This is a whole new game, dealing with this strange woman, who looks like my doll with a freshly sharpened tongue.

The old Maddie never would've so much as gotten the d-word out of her mouth. The new one leaves me standing against the wall, a new hard-on raging in my trousers, forcing me to think how good it'd be to put every fucking inch down her throat.

Everything just got harder, including this fake engagement.

Proving I'm a man of my word and taking her out on a date without putting the emergency magnum condom in my pocket to good use? That's guaranteed to be harder still, like chewing gravel, which just might be the only thing with any chance at getting my mind off fucking Maddie's newfound sass straight out of her.

I was wrong about the gravel.

Dinner at the long table in the elegant board room situated at the very top of the RET tower reminds me there are nastier things in this world able to smother my libido than breaking rock with my teeth.

Wilford Zephmyer, for one, the board's current President. The old, bloated bastard can't keep his eyes off my wife. I should just be thankful he approves with his quiet, hungry stare, but a possessive part of me wants to grab his long grey beard and manually twist his head, point his greedy eyes elsewhere.

Maddie barely notices herself. Probably for the best. She's busy making the rounds, talking to the wives and handful of women in our firm's upper echelon.

"Cal, how is our Thomas doing? Barely hear from him anymore." I turn around and see Stefan, Cade's old man, looking like a retired professor in his tweed suit. He speaks with the faint foreign accent he never lost after leaving Iceland in his early teens. He's also our senior partner in marketing, and effectively my boss.

"Hanging in there," I say, about the only words that keep me from biting my tongue when I have to mention my dying father. "Have you met my lovely fiancée yet?"

I wave my hand, catching Maddie's attention. She pulls herself away from Mrs. Bruninks and trots over, extending a friendly hand to the older gentleman.

"Maddie, meet Stefan Turnbladt. Friend, boss, and senior partner."

"Lucky dog," Stefan mutters under his breath, smiling at my woman. "Wherever did you find her?"

Maddie and I share a look. We haven't decided if we're sticking to the Beijing story we used at the auction last week, or telling them the honest truth. I stay quiet, letting her decide.

"Old friends, actually. We both went to Maynard and kept in touch," she says, searching for my approval with her eyes. "A few love letters later – or emails, I guess – and here we are."

"Ah, yes, the Maynard days," Stefan says darkly. He's careful to avoid the sensitive landmine that could easily blow me up before I've gotten anywhere. I appreciate him always being good about that. "Did you know my Cade?"

She shrugs, shaking her head. "Saw him around a lot. Mostly when he hung out with Cal. We never interacted much."

She's right, thank God. The only thing worse than the bomb blowing a hole in my life would've been watching it tear through Cade and Spence, too.

"It's a sincere pleasure. Calvin, we'll catch up later. I'd like to find my seat and text Joe again. His naps, you know, always make him late." Before Stefan walks away, I smile and nod, knowing how Spencer's father can be. The two founding men left standing do the big picture stuff when they have to, but they're both nearing retirement more with each passing month.

"*Pssst.* How do you think it's going?" Maddie leans over, whispering in my ear.

"Too early to say. Just keep showing off your pretty smile and let them do the talking," I tell her, running my fingers through hers, and then closing my hand around them tight.

I'm about to pull out her chair when a high, shrill voice explodes behind us. "Madeline Middleton! It's been *far* too long."

"Oh my God!" Maddie sings her prayer in disbelief.

"And how are you, my dear? Immersion paying hefty dividends in China, I hear?"

By the time I whip my neck around, my woman's laughing, embracing Mrs. Anders. Maddie talks a mile a minute, all about her job doing deals in three languages, teleporting the three of us back to the days we shared the same German class together.

The sixty year old woman with her cinnamon bun hair is the board's newest permanent voting member, inheriting it from her husband who passed away last year.

She also knows exactly who I am and hates my fucking guts. Easy, when she knew me first as the arrogant, self-absorbed little shit I used to be at the academy because she taught there.

It takes forever waiting for the two women to peel away from each other. When Maddie steps back into my arms, the widow's smile wilts. "Hello, Calvin. I heard we were honoring your engagement tonight, but it's rather shocking to find out it's to one of my best pupils."

"Guilty as charged, Mrs. Anders. I love surprises." The old woman isn't amused, her lips curled in a permanent frown. "Excuse me. Think I'll fetch some drinks and let you two catch up for a few more minutes." I have to get the hell away. Seeing the disgusted look on her face isn't doing any favors for my short fuse. It's all too likely to ignite the words sticking in my throat, everything I've wanted to say to the old bat since she wound up installed on the board last year.

What's your fucking problem, ma'am?

What did I ever do to you?

It wasn't my fault, you know. I didn't have a choice.

There's a makeshift bar set up in the corner. I order a scotch, dry, and say a few words to Wilford about our new crypto-currency investing ventures. It's bound to make a lot of people a shit ton of money in a few years, or else it'll be the biggest bust of all time. I do love a calculated gamble.

While the old man prattles on, my ears are tuned to the conversation going on behind us, the one carried on Mrs. Anders' low sing-song disappointment.

"How, if I may ask, did you ever end up with *him?* Forgive me, dear, but after everything that happened…"

"I stood by Cal when he got into trouble, Mrs. Anders. I'm happy I did. There's a wonderful man with a big heart behind the rumors. I'd hate to think where I'd be today without him. You should've seen how kind and supportive he was when my company sent me overseas. Literal angel. I couldn't ask for a better man if I tried."

"No, but perhaps a boy without a criminal blot on his record?"

Silence.

My fingers pinch the glass in my hand so fucking hard I

think it'll crack. Good thing Wilford has shuffled back to his seat, giving me some privacy. Just in time for the waiters to start making the rounds with shrimp and sashimi appetizers.

"I wish you'd open your mind, ma'am. Give him a second chance," Maddie whispers, so low and sad I'm just able to hear her. "You were there after the incident happened, just like me. I get why it's made so many people uncomfortable. But there's more to this man than a horrible mistake. I've never been more sure. I love him, and I'll never stop believing there'll be a day when the rest of the world sees the same person who's stolen my heart."

Mrs. Anders sighs. "Love is a fickle thing, I'll grant you. Calvin is a competent employee, at least. If he weren't, I might have insisted the company take *other* measures after I first saw his name on the marketing department's roster. I'm thankful you're happy. It's been a pleasure seeing you again."

Is this shit over?

Turning, I look their way. The older woman nods, giving my girl one last uneasy smile before finding her seat. My gaze keeps returning to the hateful crone as I find mine, waiting for my pretend love to join me.

Normally, when she attends other meetings, Mrs. Anders can't stop gossiping with anybody next to her. This time, she's quiet, studying the ice in her cocktail, like everything Maddie said actually got through her defenses.

Maddie lays her head on my shoulder while we wait for our order, and smiles. "It's so good to see her again.

Whether you're on the best terms or not, I like being in touch with the past. It grounds me."

I pause before answering. "Heard everything you said, doll. Very heartfelt. You're not as terrible an actress as you think."

Underneath the table, her hand brushes mine. There's nothing pretend about the way I take her wrist, close my hand around it, and hold it against her thigh.

Yes, for once in my adult life, I'm fucking satisfied. Someone stuck up for me, went above and beyond when they didn't have to. Hasn't happened since John exited this hellish world.

Mrs. Anders is the biggest holdout on the board. After today, there's a chance it could change.

How do I thank Maddie for laying on the sugar where it counts? The needy current electrifying my blood has a few ideas. But I can't exactly shove her hand aside, run mine down her thigh, and squeeze with a promise of what's coming later without demolishing our new understanding.

I'll live. And that tells me something much scarier: there's a chance we'll get through this and make progress without missing her hand on my cock.

We're five or ten minutes from our dessert wine and the decadent chocolate ganache RET's chef has whipped up. It's time to close this deal.

"Ladies and gentleman, I'd like to say a few words," I say loudly, giving Maddie's hand one last squeeze before I stand. Lifting my fresh drink, I look over the two dozen ballers in the room and smile. "I've never had it easy, and it's pointless to go into why. I'm not here to make excuses. I came out tonight, to thank you for your patience, your kindness, and your generosity over the years. You've been mentors, many like extended family to me, even the ones I've had my disagreements with." I'm careful to avoid Mrs. Anders, but I see her in my peripheral vision, her eyes fixed on mine like she's just waiting for me to slip.

"Come on, Cal! No need to sugarcoat it for us." A very drunken Joseph Emerson laughs, elbowing Stefan. Right this second, I wish he had more in common with Spence. His son knows how to handle his liquor like a champ in public.

Forcing a smile, I point to him, pushing my free hand into Maddie's. "All right, all right, patience has never been this firm's virtue anyway, right? Eighty percent of the reason I'm here tonight is thanks to this lovely lady. Maddie Middleton, soon to be the next Mrs. Randolph."

I tug on her arm, signaling her to stand. Several people slap their drunken hands together. I wait for the applause to continue before I stroke their heartstrings one more time.

"We've had our ups and downs. Every last person in this room, including yours truly. There'll be more ahead with this girl hanging off my shoulder, too, no doubt. Marriage isn't meant to be as easy as pulling money from thin air." I wink, and the seniors laugh at the reminder how much money I made for this biz in the last two years. "Still, I wouldn't trade it for anything. This woman's the best thing that's happened to me in years. I know she always will be. Most of you know about my father.

I lower my voice. "He gave his life to this firm. He won't be with us much longer, I'm sorry to say, but rest assured he wanted the absolute *best* for every person at this table. Whatever happens next, know I'll be trying my damnedest to continue his legacy. So, one last time, thank you, beautiful people. Thank you for your faith, your open minds, and your everlasting support at my worst. Maddie, I love you like I didn't know I could. While I make these guys and gals a whole lot richer in the years to come, let me make a special pledge to you."

The room goes quiet. The tense, adoring looks from everyone around us threatens my focus, makes it hard to stare into the beaming, melting pools spreading through her eyes.

Christ, I've branded this speech into my brain since morning. I can't fathom why the last words are so hard to get out.

Oh, but fuck, they are. Like dislodging a tumor in my chest.

I've put on my salesman face for high class associates a thousand times before, ever since I started selling risky assets to glorified gamblers who called themselves investors the year after I left prison.

It's supposed to be easy. Second nature.

But the look in Maddie's eyes makes her, hands down, the toughest client I've ever faced. Let's do this. "I'll be everything you wanted, and so much more, until the day I die. It's not enough to be your loving husband. I want to reach into the night sky, pull it apart, and bring down every dream that's ever been written in our stars. I love you, doll. Always have. Always will. Love you more than there's room above."

My eyes flit past hers to the summer night sky appearing through the window. There's a break in the rain tonight. It's eerily clear, a placid atmosphere stretching to Mount Rainier. That's what I see when they start clapping, and when her hands go around my neck.

Doll pulls me in with a ferocity I didn't think she had.

Certainly not when we're lying to a gaggle of strangers she's never met before tonight.

Certainly not when I swallowed my ego before we got here, told her how it'd be, and tried to draw new boundaries.

They're fucking vaporized the instant her lips meet mine. This kiss calls something mad, dark, and primal up from my belly.

My hands sweep down her spine, hugging her hips through the jungle tinted dress, pulling her in. I take her tongue with mine and own it. She moans into my mouth, subtle and sweet. My teeth find her lower lip, the same she's always chewing in her nervous little fits, and they take their hostage.

I've never had a kiss like this. I'm still leading her mouth with mine, but fuck if I haven't lost control. My heartbeat drums louder in my temples, drowning out the happy words flying around the room, sending fire straight to my dick.

Doll.

Fuck.

Stop.

My brain remembers the high stakes we're gambling with just in time. If we carried on a second longer, it'd be improper. Recovering my willpower at the last brutal second, I push her away, remembering to smile to my peers and bosses, knowing full well I probably look like a jackass.

When I tear myself away and we drop back into our seats, she doesn't even look at me, hiding half her rose red face behind her glass of port. She's as embarrassed as I am. Likely just as confused at the sudden, devastating loss of control.

I stab at my dessert for the next few minutes, making small talk with my best friends' dads across the table. They ask me a dozen questions about our wedding, and I come up with answers on the fly. Maddie helps a little, but she's been rendered speechless. I don't blame her.

This can't continue, I think, swallowing the paralyzing truth with every bite of chocolate and port. It's a culinary masterpiece, like everything our four star personal chef turns out, but I don't even taste it.

It's Maddie's kiss hanging on my tongue.

Her taste lingers in my veins.

Her heat.

Her aura next to me, magnetic as pollen to a butterfly, and just as fucking dangerous when the bug isn't able to see the mower bearing down on it.

There's no doubt anymore. I have to get her out of my

head, and I definitely can't be alone with her tonight, or the impending catastrophe will leave us both in pieces.

"We did good," she chirps, as soon as we're in the backseat of my limo, and the privacy visor between us and the driver is up. "We turned heads, and I think we changed some minds, too. Your toast, oh my God, it –"

"Don't mention it again." It comes out more cold than I intend. "Look, doll, let's both be happy we're doing what we came here to do. That's it. Those words I threw at you, I came up with last night. Wrote them down and burned them into my head all morning. Like being back in Anders' German class, just practicing new words and reading a script."

"Oh. Impressive speech, I guess." Her face sinks. I knew she'd be disappointed, but it isn't any easier bracing for it. "I wish you'd told me Mrs. Anders was on the board sooner. I'd have gotten her on our side for sure if I'd had just a little more time, a little more prep."

"You did plenty, Maddie. Everything I asked, and then some. Keep it up, and we'll be going our merry ways soon."

She's quiet the rest of the ride home. Fine by me.

We ride the elevator up together, and I walk her into the apartment, stepping into the kitchen to fetch us water while she crashes on the plush couch just outside the balcony doors.

"It really is a beautiful night," she purrs, sitting up as soon as I take my seat next to her, passing her some water.

"Been too long since we've had a clear night."

"Too good to waste," I agree, refusing to stare at the flicker in her pretty eyes too long.

It'll consume me if I let it. There's no escaping the fire once it begins, and after what happened tonight, there's zero doubt I'll be able to stop myself breaking my promise, taking this straight to the bedroom, if I even so much as feel her fingers laced with mine.

"What should we do?" Hope springs eternal in her voice. She nods through the glass behind us, a smile forming on her lips. "I saw the gold telescope you keep by the window. There's a lot of city lights, but it's clear, and the moon is out. Want to give it a try?"

"I'm not a big enough nerd," I lie, hating how fucking good she is at tapping into my not-so-secret amateur hobby. "Sorry, doll. I've got somewhere to be tonight."

"What, you're going out?" She gulps her water, trying to hide her surprise. "Work again or…"

"Close enough. Help yourself to whatever from the wine cellar, if you'd like. I'll leave a credit card on the counter in case you want to use my account to order a midnight snack." I dig out my wallet, find my black Centurion card, and grip it between my fingers, before meeting her eyes for the last time. "Enjoy yourself, Maddie. You've earned it tonight. Think about where you want to go for our night out, and let me know tomorrow."

I don't slow down. She never stops staring until I'm out, banging the front door behind me.

It's too bad it has to be this way. If only she knew what

happens next is for her own good.

It's to keep my sanity intact.

Putting the hallway pass she gave me earlier to good use, and fucking everything that happened out of my system, is the one and only sensible choice I have.

"Holy shit, baby. This place is gorgeous!" Hearing baby on that tongue makes me cringe.

I need her lips, her pussy, not her goddamned pet names.

It's over two hours since I left the condo, and I'm staring at another wide-eyed blast from the past. We haven't fucked yet and I'm already bored. Tina steps into my unlocked high end hotel room, where I'm sprawled out on the bed, reclining against the leather headboard with my shirt unbuttoned and a fresh scotch in my hand.

I met her at a bar on the same block about an hour ago, chatted her up, and told her to meet me here after she made a condom run. If it wasn't for running low on rubbers, except for the lonely backup I always keep, I would have taken her sooner. Probably in the bar's bathroom, where I could've let her suck me off or hate fuck her from behind, drop a couple loads, and forget the fling.

Quick and easy as peeling off a used sheath.

"Duh, Tina. Money buys class. That never changes. Speaking of which, I'm willing to bet you're just as big a slut as you were in the old days." I wonder why my veins feel dull ash instead of fire when I growl the words.

"Guilty." She smiles, giggles, and steps up, giving me a shake of her ass in the low cut cocktail dress. "How long has it been, anyway? Four, maybe five years?"

"Almost five. Told you earlier tonight," I say, surprised her memory seems so shitty after watching her hang on my every word. Of course, the girl has a few martinis in her system, and that's the most dangerous cocktail of all when it's blended with high school crushes.

I think back to the dark day we last hooked up. Wasn't too long after the first anniversary of John's funeral. Feeling low, disgusted, and nostalgic drives a man to strange places, and stranger pussy.

And what does that say about where you're at tonight, asshole? I ask myself.

Doll keeps popping into my head, alone where I left her, sipping on a half-empty wine glass if she hasn't just gone to bed. I fucking hate it.

Tina purses her bubblegum pink painted lips, leaning into me, hungry for our opening kiss. I push her back with one hand, unsure what's come over me. She laughs again, thinking I'm just being playful.

"Talk to me. What the hell have you been up to?" I ask. I'm not sure why I need this small talk before I'm inside her.

"Me?" She taps her bountiful cleavage with her thumb, like she can't believe I'm interested in anything except the panties under that dress. "Oh, you know. The usual. Makin' money, going back to school for pharmacy tech, spending summers with my little girl…"

"Little girl? Fuck, you're married?"

"Um, not exactly. More like a few bad hookups and a broken condom. I wouldn't trade her for anything, though." Tina shrugs sheepishly, her blonde locks hanging like tarnished gold. "Does the mommy thing appeal to you?"

She recovers, slipping back into the eager succubus mode I remember. There's nothing sexy about it.

I nod weakly, lying, growing more sick of the pretense by the millisecond.

Her words are a brutal reminder just how much can change in half a decade. Last time we fucked, she still had the same light pink highlights in her hair she wore through senior year at Maynard. She wore ripped tights like something out of Seattle's old grunge scene, and pulled me into her body with the same young enthusiasm most girls had when Kurt Cobain was all the rage.

I certainly used her passion to drain *my* rage against the world that night. She gave everything. I gave her nothing more than angry, hot thrusts back. She was so tight there's no way a kid ever dropped out of her.

She's always been a vacant shadow since the days she blew me as a cheerleader, but tonight, her gritty aura is paper thin. Honestly, it's hideous.

No, the mommy thing doesn't appeal to me. But it's not because it's made her older or uglier, even if she's looking tired and more worn than I remember.

It's a reminder she's as pathetic as I am, hopelessly chasing the ghost of a chance she thinks she has with me just to have my cock one more time.

She shouldn't be here tonight, desperate to get filled with a cock fixated on another woman. She should be home with her kid, who presumably loves her, hoping there'll come a day when mommy can find her jollies on more than cold hookups.

Shit, at least she's got someone, though.

Deep down, I wonder if I'm more pathetic because I can't pin down what I'm after. My whole life runs on money, work, and an obsessed cat-and-mouse chase with a woman who's been nothing but bad for me.

My stomach churns sicker by the second. I try to look at Tina like a woman I need to fuck one more time, but it doesn't work. There's no desire for what's in front of me anymore.

I want Maddie, abandoned at home, alone and disappointed and sorely missing my touch.

"What's wrong, Cal? You're so quiet tonight. Ever since the bar..." She's on the bed now, crawling toward my lap. Her bright red fingernails reach out, hovering over my lap underneath the blanket.

Grabbing her wrist, I hold it away, keeping the soft, unfuckable mess I've become mercifully hidden. I can't even get hard for this chick when her tits are hanging out in front of me.

Not when she doesn't belong here, and neither do I.

Lord knows she won't give up easy. Tina scoots closer, straddling me, wrapping an arm around my neck. Her lips come close, too fucking close for comfort, and that's when I snap.

"Get the fuck off," I growl, giving her a firm shove. "This was a mistake. Tell you what…" I pause, reach for my wallet on the nightstand, and dig out a wad of cash. "Call yourself a taxi, an Uber, whatever the fuck, and go. Here's more than enough for wasting your time, bringing you out here. If you can't put it to good use yourself, then buy your little girl something nice. We're through. You'll never hear from me again."

At first, she stands there stunned, her fingers limp as I push the bills into her hand. I stare at her over the rim of my glass, draining my scotch.

"There's…Jesus…like eight hundred dollars here." She flicks through her stash, counting, more haunted than I am by what's happening. "I don't understand. What is this, Cal? Are you on drugs, or something?"

I ponder her question for a few seconds before I wave my hand like I'm shooing a pesky dog. "None of your damn business. Go. Don't make me get up and throw you out." I use my coldest voice. I want this bitch gone.

She stares a few seconds longer in disbelief, trying to process what's happening. Finally, with a sigh, she grabs her purse off the chair, stuffs the money into it, and clicks her hooker height heels to the door.

"Shame. We could've had *so much* fun tonight," she coos, a last desperate attempt to make me change my mind.

I won't even look at her. Laying like a zombie, I stare at the wall, waiting for the door to fall shut.

It does ten seconds later, and I'm alone.

So fucking alone.

Grabbing the half-empty scotch bottle off the nightstand, I don't bother pouring more in my glass. I raise the neck to my lips and drink my fill, every gulp more fiery and bitter than the last.

It wasn't supposed to be this way, dammit.

That's what I get for thinking I could stick my dick in a paradox, and come home to Maddie tomorrow without bleeding guilt all over her.

I wanted nostalgia as much as amnesia tonight.

Sought a quick fuck pretending it'd take me away from the mounting storm in my blood.

Fooled myself into believing I'd forget doll, when she's all that's been on my mind since the instant I left my condo, checked into the hotel, and texted Tina, planning to have her fluffed up dick-sucker lips pull every last woe from my balls.

Tipping the bottle up to the dark white ceiling, I make another toast. "Here's to the charade. Not just this engagement, but my whole damned circus of a life."

Draining another fourth of the bottle, I look at the remnants in disgust. I throw my legs over the bed, beginning to put my clothes on. Before I make my call, I scan through my contacts one more time, and delete Tina's number forever.

"Emilio? Bring the car around, and have some water ready for me." I say, as soon as my driver picks up. "I want to go home."

It takes twenty minutes to get to my place. Three or four hours total since I left, abandoning her to the night. I wanted to shut her out so bad after dinner. Instead, all I've succeeded in doing is wasting my time with a whore I couldn't even get hard for.

I drag myself in the condo. All the lights are off, and it's quiet. It's times like this I wish I had a cat or a parrot or something. Anything to break up the dead, cold stillness when I shuffle down the hall to my master bedroom, chugging my second water of the night.

When I walk past Maddie's room, I slow. I can't help it.

My hand goes to the doorknob, and I turn it gently, peering inside through the crack. She's left the soft lamp on next to her bed.

The fine booze in my system overrides propriety, giving me the liquid courage to violate her privacy. I tip-toe next to her, staring down at my sleeping angel. She's snoozing gently, dark hair tossed to the side, her little lips twitching when I bring my fingers to the switch and turn off the lamp she's left on.

There's a book next to her. *Grimm's Fairy Tales,* no less, written in its original German.

I smile because it takes me back to the class we shared years ago with Mrs. Anders. Our grades were always at the top of the roster, leading the handful of As. I teased her like mad over the fairy tale translation shit she used to do, mocking her for sticking to children's crap, and not the oh-so-grown-up passages I pretended to understand when I butchered translating Nietzsche and Goethe.

The years have been so much kinder to doll than Tina, apparently. She's matured, but underneath her world class business act, she's the same old girl. There's something endearing as hell about that, and it's impossible for me not to reach out, brushing her cheek.

"Huh? Cal?" Her eyelids flutter, soft and half-awake.

"*Shhh*. I'm not really here. Go to sleep, darling, and get ready for our big day tomorrow."

A second later, she closes her eyes. My cue to walk into the bathroom, pull off my shirt, and hang it up over the sink. I can still smell the scotch I sweated out all over it on the way home.

Then I walk to the bed, crashing down next to her, throwing my arm around the woman I can't get out of my head. I'm gone less than a couple minutes after my head hits the pillow.

It's easy to drift off when you're right where you belong.

As fucked up and confusing as this is, there's no place I'd rather be.

Laying next to her like this and basking in her warmth tells me I've made the right choice. Before, I never thought I'd see the day when I'd forgo rowdy pussy just to spoon with a girl I've sworn up and down I'll never, ever fuck because I don't want to ruin her.

But the day is here. The unbelievable keeps happening.

And it's sterling proof there's a growing chance other rules may wind up broken, too.

VII: Hard Truths (Maddie)

When I open my eyes, at first it's hard to figure out why I'm so warm and refreshed after the glacial send off to bed he gave me last night.

Then I realize I'm not alone.

"Cal?" I whisper his name, rolling over.

Groaning in his sleep, he twists in the sheets, a sweat halo on his brow. He's had a hard night. There's no question, judging by the strong liquor on his breath and the pallor in his face.

Very slowly, he opens his eyes. "Shit. I fell asleep."

"Yeah, in my bed." I give him an accusing look. "Hope there's a good reason you decided to come and lay down next to me."

He sits up, rubbing his face, not answering for several seconds. "You left a light on. I was drunk. What else is there to say?" He sighs, and then turns to look at me, still not satisfied with his answer. "You looked so peaceful, doll. I couldn't resist. Told myself I'd just have a nap and head to my own bed before you noticed anything. Didn't quite pan out that way."

"Whatever. At least you're over the cold shoulder last night. But next time, I'd appreciate a little notice if you want this fake engagement thing to drag us to the same bed."

"Sure, I'll send it certified." He smirks, but only for a second, because I'm sure the headache from his hangover is making itself known.

God, he looks so pathetic. Infuriating as ever, yet fully able to tug on my sympathies. Short notes for my whole existence with this man.

"Can I make breakfast and bring you some aspirin?" I stand, closing my robe, grateful I slept in it so at least he wouldn't find me in my underwear.

"Please," he murmurs, reaching for the last of the water bottle next to him. "Should be duck eggs, bacon, and bread in the fridge for toast. Pancake mix, too, if you're feeling adventurous. Surprise me."

My eye rolling turns into a stare. "Oh, and anything else you'd like, sir? Maybe a nice glass of fresh squeezed orange juice and an avocado spread for your toast?"

"Nah. Aspirin and whatever you'd like to make will do. Better to keep it simple so we can get ready. Soon as I unfuck my head, I'm taking you out. Hope you decided where you want to go for our date." His scathing blue eyes are almost normal when he looks at me.

There's that familiar heat in my blood again. I turn away before it has a chance to consume me, heading for the door, ready to get into the kitchen and pretend I'm cooking a lovely breakfast for my equally lovely (ha!) fiancé.

"Oh, and when did you stop talking in your sleep, doll?" he says, when I've got one hand on the door. "Because if you did, I was too out of it to notice. Sleeping through the night real still, real quiet…that's new."

I pretend I don't hear him. There's no need to start a weird day with more memories, but it seems he isn't giving me much choice.

Twenty minutes later, I'm cooking up omelets and toast. I've kept it simple like he said, lining up the coffee and orange juice in fancy glass bottles on the counter before he comes in. I put another water and two aspirins at the empty space on the breakfast bar.

Of course, I'm cooking, hopelessly lost in the past.

His sleep comment brings me to Chelle's party, the first and only place he ever saw me sleeping before last night. It was late, it was wild, and completely overwhelming for a girl who'd never so much as seen two people get hot and heavy outside a TV screen before.

Her parents beers flowed freely, and so did contraband joints, passed around by the older kids like candy. The night wore on with my friends and acquaintances disappearing one by one, retreating with their boys into the corners, the closets, wherever they could find a little privacy. And when they couldn't, they had their fun in front of whoever might be watching.

I tried to look away at the clumsy pseudo-sex happening around me. But I was no angel, despite my inexperience.

My curiosity kept my eyes on everything until they grew way too heavy sometime after midnight.

"What the fuck are you doing out here alone, doll?" I remember how he woke me up.

Cal's face was just a few inches from mine as he sat next to me, thinner and more innocent in those days. I jumped when I opened my eyes after hearing his words, folding my arms.

"You first. Something weird must definitely be up if the great Cal Randolph isn't necking upstairs with Tina Reynolds, and maybe a couple of her friends, too." Yes, I was scorned. It was just a few weeks after I'd missed the winter dance, and several months before the disastrous incident made our petty high school quarrels over who's kissing who seem so benign.

"Tina and me were never a thing. Just a date for the dance and some simple-minded fun. Pay more attention to what's going on outside your books, Maddie. There's a whole world out there, you know." He smiles like he's giving real advice.

It doubles my urge to slap his smug face off. "Sorry, not interested. I think I'll just study hard now so I can save my chastity for college. It's supposed to be a lot more exciting there. People get dorm rooms so they can actually do things in peace."

"Hmm, very interesting. I thought professors just talked all the time and sent people to the library for research papers. Didn't know people actually had fun, got drunk, or fucked like rabbits. Tell me more." Swallowing what little was left in his beer can, he crushes it in his fingers for emphasis.

"Ew. I can't stand how that stuff tastes," I whimper, wrinkling my nose. "Don't know how you do either."

"It's pretty bad, this cheap ass swill. Think I'll always be a whiskey or scotch man when I'm old enough to cruise the bars. Need something more refined."

Such a snob That 'swill' is my father's favorite.

His blue gaze falls on me with a curious pull. I'm trying to look away, but my eyes crawl back to his, more frustrated than before. "Don't you wonder what you're missing, doll?"

"Missing? No – especially not with you."

"Come the fuck on. One kiss won't turn you into a pumpkin. I'll even walk you home after I get some of that sugar under your glasses. Pretty fucking boring around here, anyway."

Before I can answer, his hand lands on mine. Every impulse in my head screams fight, resist, throw him off, then stand up, and show myself the door.

But nothing is ever easy or obvious with him around.

"Come on. Our little secret," he whispers, leaning in, his handsome face closer than ever. "There's no one to see us. No one to tell the rest of the school. Scourge and his assholes will never find out."

I'm silent. His young cheek touches mine, making me feel the faint stubble on his skin. Instant lightning up my spine. I tense, the pressure in my muscles building.

"Kiss me," he growls again, straight into my ear, nipping at my lobe with his teeth. "Just this once, doll. I know you fucking want to."

I hate how he rips me open, sees everything underneath so easy. What's the point in hiding your want from a man who smells it coming off you in waves?

I've had enough. I give in. Let him have what he wants, what I want to get over with, because I foolishly think he'll finally leave me alone once it's done.

Oh, but his kiss comes like the morning sun. Bright, invigorating, with just the right golden warmth. My hot breath spills into him, and he takes what he needs with his tongue, melting me against the floor with his fingers tangled in mine, my hips searching his, our mouths fused together in all kinds of wrong.

I can't remember how long we lay tangled together like that. But there were more kisses, more confusion, and a much later walk home when I finally tore myself off him, shaking because my fingers needled their way up his back, desperate to rip away his shirt.

Back in the present, his chair scrapes the floor behind me, and I jump. It's hard to turn around, pretending to look normal, when I'd started getting wet over my first kiss with this reckless man. "You're just in time. It's ready," I say, throwing the toast onto our plates and sliding his over.

"Smells fantastic, doll. It's nice having a wife worth waking up to." He pops his aspirin and we eat our food in happy silence, only making small talk about the day ahead.

I tell him I want to see the city like it's my first time here. At first, he rolls his eyes, telling me Beijing made me more predictable than ever. But it's honestly been years since I've had fun in this city. He tells me to have a second coffee before I shower and we head out because we're going to the best spots, and then some.

Once I'm cleaned up, we're off.

First stop is Pike's Market, where we browse around the kitsch and share a couple pastries, braving the long lines packed with tourists. Then it's the art museum, where he teases me over how long I spend looking at the naked people, paintings and reliefs from so many times and places. He buys me a mug with a rose watercolor on it from the gift shop.

Neither of us comment on the meaning, and risk letting old venom screw up our time together. We're enjoying the moment too much to share our secret any way but silently.

It's also nice to blend in for a change like normal people. The constant gold necklaces, evening dresses, and foodie dinners are nice, sure, but it's just as lovely spending the day melting into the sweet average happening around us.

It's early evening when he reminds me he's rich again. We take his yacht out from the public marina, him at the steering wheel, me hanging onto his shoulders as guides my hands, and says it's high time I learned to handle his pride and joy.

I laugh, resisting a comment on the ego trip. Or any choice words about penis size involving this very big ship.

We're lucky the weather stays beautiful. There's barely a cloud in the sky as we maneuver around the coast, heading out to some of the nearer islands before we find our way back, watching whales blow jets of water on the horizon. I notice we keep our distance from Bainbridge, where there's nothing but sadness and his sick father wasting away. He won't even look in its direction.

"Scratched your tourist itch yet, or what?" Cal asks, steering us back toward the docks.

"Not until we've seen the Space Needle," I say, smiling at the Seattle icon on the skyline.

"Whatever, doll. You're lucky it just so happens I have dinner reservations at the best seat in their restaurant tonight."

"Oh, honey. You're the best fake fiancé a woman could hope for!" I throw my hands around his neck and cling to him, trying not to make it totally obvious how much I enjoy inhaling his scent.

"Best on paper," he says, enveloping my fingers in his.

Our situation is no less crazy and screwed up than before, this lie we've decided to live for the next few weeks. But it's nice to see he's able to stop being a jackass for a full day, long enough to forget it's only pretend, and only temporary.

I don't care how touristy or overpriced it is. Up here, at the top of the Space Needle, you can see *everything*.

We've finished dinner, and we're standing outside on the deck, taking turns with the binoculars peering through the safety wires. I focus on the little cars and people below, each miniature life happening in the night. It's easy to wonder if there's ever someone looking back at just the right moment, sharing my curiosity.

"Planning to stand here all night and people watch?" Cal's rich voice floods my ears, and his hand saunters down my spine, low to the edge of my shorts.

Standing up, I turn around, shooting him a repressed smile. God, even when his fingertips aren't actually on my skin, he triggers desire. One glance at his eyes makes it seethe, a constant rushing thunder in my blood, calling tension, heat, and need between my legs.

"Your turn." I clear a path to the binoculars. Also put myself further from his reach, before he makes me wetter.

"I think you're confused, doll. Unlike you, I haven't left this city since Maynard. Didn't do my time in Beijing, London, or Bumfuck, Egypt. I've seen Seattle thousands of times. Only scenery I'm really interested in tonight is right in front of me." He steps forward, taking my cheek in his hand, folding an arm around my waist.

"Cal, no." It's hard to speak. Even harder to breathe through the heat in my lungs and the flutter in my heart, without letting him hear the fire crackling in my body. "Isn't this what we're trying to avoid?'

His intense blue eyes narrow, clear as day. "Things change all the time. Look where you're at today: high society, international businesswoman, soon to be hitched to a world class marketing billionaire."

"*If* it's mission accomplished, you mean." I don't really need to remind him of the high stakes we're playing for with this lie that's starting to feel like blatant truth.

But I'm glad I do because it sends his fingers through my hair. His hand glides up my neck, cradles the back of my head, and twines my dark locks. When he tips my head up, moving his face closer, his eyes are more beautiful and bewildering than the city's own nightscape.

"I'll win what's mine, Maddie. Everything. Never met a challenge I couldn't own." His fierce stare tells me we're not just talking about his father's company or the family fortune anymore. "We've already broken so many fucking rules. Tell me again, what's one more?"

He *knows* the dangers like I do, what we stand to lose if we cross the ultimate line.

Doesn't stop his lips from coming down on mine a hot second later like an avalanche. Nothing stops me from loving it.

Our lips dance, drunk on mutual hunger. One hand pulls my hair harder, sending new thrills down my shoulders, and the other slides to my ass. He pushes me against the wall while his hand cups, searches, and squeezes, perfectly timed to his tongue on mine.

Everything goes from zero to a hundred on the heat scale. I've never done anything like this, kissing my dark desire so wild and freely in the open. Several tourists walk by, slowing to gawk when they see us, and it still doesn't slow me down.

I fall into him, shame and blush and all. Sinking into his enigma quickens my lust, turns my pussy into one more Randolph property. I'm ashamed to admit how much I want him, but God, I can't control this.

So we kiss, the only thing we can do, tangling our bodies, minds, and lips tighter. The lightning seconds flash by, lust incarnate at six hundred feet over the Emerald City.

Nothing will tear me away, or disrupt this beautiful moment until it's over. If Mount Rainier split open and showered us in gold, I'd still be buried in his lips, his fingers maneuvering around my thigh, devilishly close to everything we've tried so hard to ignore.

"Do you have any fucking clue how many nights you were my wet dream before everything went to shit?" he growls, tearing himself away. His fingers pinch my chin, keeping my face up, a hostage for his blistering blue eyes. "Even after it, when I spent my year in juvey, and came out desperate to make up for lost time, I never forgot how good you tasted that night at Chelle's party. I would have fucked you senseless a long time ago if it hadn't gone bad, Maddie. I never stopped dreaming, imagining, wanting like I was losing my mind...and now I'm done with all that. I don't want to see you naked in my head anymore if it's nothing but a goddamned tease."

Holy mother. What do I even say?

I've never had a man proclaim love for me before. This isn't that.

It's a declaration of lust, primal and panty-soaking hot. It's an invitation to wonders with incomprehensible strings attached. I wish just for one night I could shut off my brain.

Stop thinking. Pull him in. Open my legs and my mouth for another kiss after I breathe the only word blazing a fire through my core, threatening to burn me to cinders if I don't let it out.

"Tell me I'm not crazy, doll," he breathes, touching his forehead to mine, holding his delicious lips just out of reach until I give him what he needs. "Tell me we're able to break the rules, muddle through what happens when we do, and not fuck it all up. I want this. I want you. Want you so bad I'll spend the next thousand nights regretting this one if I can't bring you home, to my bed, and take what I should've laid claim to seven fucking years ago. You feel it, too, don't you? Maddie, I know you do. We share the same torture, wanting like this."

Again, that word. *Wanting.*

It drips in me like poison, seethes when it touches my resistance, and ignites it like napalm.

How can I say no?

In what bland, rational, sexless universe can I control the ache between my legs, the wanton need to find out what's through that last forbidden door together?

"Answer me, beautiful," he whispers, harsher than before. His forehead presses mine, sending those blue eyes everywhere.

"Yes." So simple, so powerful, it comes out in a whimper. "Yes, Cal. It's worth a chance."

He breaks into the world's biggest grin. I haven't seen that kind of smile on his lips since we were kids, when our time at Maynard shielded us. Before we imagined the darkness we're dealing with now.

"I'm calling the car," he says, devouring me in another kiss as he reaches for his phone.

"I need to find the ladies room," I tell him, reluctantly

tearing myself away. "Then we'll go. I'm so ready."

My body is, at any rate. My brain still won't shut up, thinking through everything that could go wrong, but its protests are dying by the kiss. I walk away, shooting him one last sultry look over my shoulder, heading for the bathroom.

I need water. My palm collects a splash of coolness I throw across my face. It calms me enough to straighten my hair, which is messier than I'd imagined from our very public make out session minutes ago.

I'd might as well enjoy its shape for the next hour or so. Because once he's done with me, I'm certain it won't be the same.

Jesus, I don't even know how easy it is to fix sex hair. I've never had it before.

In all my years since him, I've never gone all the way with a man. Not even once.

Maybe it was the guilt over everything that happened. Maybe just my single-minded focus, finishing college and working to make a dent in my loans, then launching a career. Or maybe it's because I know that if I ever gave my V-card to anyone else, rather than the man who was always meant to have it, it'd wipe away a piece of me forever.

Tonight, it's his. Not just pieces, but *everything.*

Yes, it's a contradiction. Harrowing and enthralling, sensual and scary, so many kinds of right and wrong twisted in knots I won't unravel in ten lifetimes. Calvin Randolph is my life's gravity, always holding me in his orbit, and now I'm about to dive straight to his core, while he drives himself to mine.

Hard. Deep. Breathless. Irrevocable.

Those eyes of his, fixed on mine, on top of me or however else he'd like…*mercy.*

Every time I think about having him to myself tonight, it's hard to move. Everything he said about the dreams, the fantasy…it's been my reality since the day he disappeared through a fog of my tears.

It's the buildup I've waited years for, soon to be complete in its sweet crescendo. But now that I hear it coming, feel it in my very bones, it's as terrifying as it is wondrous.

I'm just thankful I'm alone to regain my wits. Practicing my breathing, I stare into the mirror, reapplying the subtle red lipstick worn down by his feral lips.

You can do this, Maddie. Without destroying yourself. Go out there, enjoy it, and rock his freaking world.

I'm as pumped as I'll ever be, and ready to move again, when the loudest sound I've ever heard goes off. I almost hit the ceiling.

It's just my phone. I slap the skin over my rampaging heart, digging in my purse with a crease in my brow. Someone's sending texts. A lot of them.

I see Kat's name on the screen and groan, scrolling through the 'sis, are you there?' messages until I get to the end.

Kat: You need to see something, and we need to talk. Like now.

I tap out a one word reply and press send. I'm annoyed to keep him waiting, but something's up. She rarely reaches out to me like this and blows up my inbox.

Maddie: WHAT?

Kat: I saw him at the bar last night. Couldn't put my finger on why this man looked so familiar until I looked online. You'd better ask your pretender about these pics.

My heart leaps into my throat. I'm waiting, impatiently tapping my foot on the tiled floor, while the four pictures she's sent over load.

The first two are bad. It's such dark lighting and there are so many people in the way I can't make out anything.

The other angles are better. So good, it's easy to make out that face. Those firm blue eyes. Glowing with delight as he holds another woman's hand, a familiar face drooling all over him, flanked by dirty blonde hair.

Tina. I'd remember her wretched smile anywhere. It hasn't changed a day since he asked her to the winter dance, pushed her against the wall in front of me, and took her lips with what I'd always believed was just an exaggerated heat.

My lust takes a shot through the heart. My blood pressure hurtles into the danger zone. Kat texts me again, feeding the urge to march this phone back to the main deck, and hurl it into the park below. Knowing I'd see him is the only thing that stops me.

Kat: Is it really him?

I can't bring myself to answer. It's bad enough admitting when your little sister is right. Worse when you know she'll be eager to enjoy her smug satisfaction, saving me from something I should've seen coming.

Maddie: Tell mom and dad I'll be home soon. I want the guest room tonight.

It's all I can bring myself to say. She texts me a few more times, and I ignore them all. I'm too busy finding my way out, skirting the exit to the bullet elevator, which takes me down to the main level without having to face him again.

I sidestep our car, hoping his driver, Emilio, won't notice me, speed walking another block to put as much distance as I can between heartbreak. By the time my Uber pulls up on the curb, I have tears in my eyes. I'm able to hold them in until I pull up his number, fire off a message, and toss my phone into my purse after switching it off, wishing it'd never been invented to make torture only a few easy taps away.

Don't wait up for me, I told him. *I know about Tina. I saw the pics at the bar, and I can't see you tonight.*

The night's only mercy is the fact that my driver minds his own business while I blot my eyes with a tissue, desperate to thwart this sadness before it becomes an ugly cry.

It's a hell ride and a half home. Worse when I crawl through the backdoor, hoping to avoid my sister or my parents, and find everybody relaxing by the windows next to the kitchen.

Of course. What else would they be doing on a cool summer night?

I have exactly ten seconds to find a way to keep it together before I break down in front of everyone, especially when mom stands up, Kat smirking behind her.

"Madeline, what's wrong?"

It's probably a minute before I'm able to answer. "Nothing, nothing. I need some water. Be right out."

I can't face them again without purging this pain. I rip the ring with the disgustingly huge diamond set in rose carved gold off my finger, stuff it in my purse, and head to the sink for a cool drink.

Evidently, It's easier to clear the heartache lodged in my throat than the sudden emptiness I feel on my finger.

I feel like a fool for not realizing it sooner, three simple truths collapsing on a soul under a siege.

Can't go on trusting him.

Can't keep pretending it'll ever be different.

Can't forget those hideous pictures.

I. Can't. Do. This.

Admitting it will gut me later, but right now I'm just numb. I never should've trusted him.

It's hard to sit down with my family and make small talk like a normal human being, ignoring knowing glances from my sis while I make up a story about bad oysters and cramps.

What's one more lie when the big one killing me is over?

This fake engagement is done.

VIII: Game Off (Cal)

She leaves me in the world's worst position: waiting six hundred feet in the air like a worried, blue balled fuck while the summer breeze turns into a frigid wind.

I don't get her message until I'm going down, taking the very last elevator of the night, heading for my car waiting on the curb. The tower shuts itself down fast, becoming one more deserted sentinel watching over the city, and all its unlucky, condemned, damned citizens.

Population: me.

Home is worse than ever. I sit in my penthouse all night, waiting for her to respond to my texts, wishing I could punch out my idiot self from twenty-four hours before, when I thought I'd put my dick in Tina to soothe the tension.

There's no excuse.

I fucked up big time, despite her hall pass. I almost acted on it, until I saw I couldn't get hard with anyone else. I don't even know how she found out, where she got those pics, but I'm certain it involves a malignant twist of fate.

At some point, I crash out in my living room. It's light

again when my phone goes off, its volume waking me like an air raid siren.

No text, but an email. It's from her. I open it in a frenzy, clenching my jaw as the words drift across the screen.

Cal,

It's over. Whatever big mistake we almost made last night, it isn't happening again.

I won't let it.

It's not all your fault. I don't know why I expected you to behave like an angel when we agreed no sex, no complications, no craziness. I even told you to do whatever, without knowing you'd already gone and done it.

I'm sorry. It shouldn't hurt so much. But it does.

Finding out where you went really messed with my head.

I still owe you the favor, and I'm not bailing over this. We just can't be joined at the hip when there's no good reason to be.

We're not actually engaged. We're not in love. We're not even friends — exactly like you said.

It's taken me a long time to realize how much sense the first rules we laid down make.

Do your thing. Call me when you need me. I'll be there.

Otherwise, I'm staying at my parent's house.

If your dad or anybody else questions it, tell them it's sick family I'm taking care of. Tell them whatever. I don't care anymore.

I'll be in touch. Not for a couple days, though, unless it's urgent.

Fuck.

I haven't eaten since dinner last night, and digesting her words on an empty stomach tastes like bile. Pacing my marble floors, I turn over the options in my mind, one hand on my phone, ready to call her and explain everything.

Trouble is, I have no proof.

She won't say it to my face, but she's disgusted with me, and why the hell shouldn't she be? Sure, it's a two way screw up, but we'd both be in an infinitely happier place if I hadn't gone after easy pussy in my weakness. If I'd just stayed home, taken her a night earlier like she wanted when I saw those bedroom eyes, I wouldn't have built my own prison. At the very least, I'd be able to think, without my desire rotting in every angry, denied inch of me, degrading into rage.

There's a wisdom in her words I can't deny, despite how furious it makes me.

My crime is doing a one eighty when I should've stopped her from ever getting her hooks in.

Hers is dissolving my discipline, my strength, everything that's gone to pieces ever since the day I reached out and dragged her into my life because there wasn't another choice.

I hate my stupidity, my loss of control. Hate it so fucking much I run for the bathroom, where I think I'll vomit, but I can't even expel the poison twisting my guts in agony.

She hates me.

I hate Maddie, too.

Hate her like mad for the effect she has on me. She's put me on the edge of ruin, knotted my heart and soul. They're gradually strangling me like a noose she crafted with the black cords of the past, and I'm the fucking moron pulling it around my own neck.

My fist goes into the silver wall, leaving a heavy dent. Blood seeps from my scrapped knuckles. I wash my hands, splashing water over my face, desperate to cool the red hot insanity bleeding out my pores. I stare at myself in the mirror like a maniac for the next few minutes.

Goddammit, no. It isn't hate.

It's something much worse.

Love, with a capital L. So heavy it'll break every bone in my body.

I don't know how to get her back. I can't wipe yesterday from existence.

But if I don't find a way, I'm all kinds of fucked.

I probably already am. Because if I'm brutally honest, maintaining the charade for my old man is the last thing on my mind when I stare, and plot, letting the fireball exploding in my heart torch through me.

There's no mercy in its flames. They touch everything I thought I ever knew, and turn them to cinders.

I give her two days for space, the max I can tolerate.

Day three, after work, I take my Tesla straight from the office into the university district.

There's no hesitation, no creeping up to the house as soon as I'm parked. I've been rehearsing what's coming in my head for forty-eight hours. It'd take a bus screaming down on me with its brakes cut to stop it.

I bang on the door and drop my fists to my sides. I expect doll to appear for about a second before I sweep her up in my arms, but the face behind the door when it opens is younger and way too relaxed.

"Well, if it isn't Mr. Millionaire Player himself. Come to kiss and make up with your fake bride?" Kat Middleton is possibly the only woman on the planet with half her sister's good looks, and ten times her sass.

"No. I'm here to talk with the whole family. Is Maddie home? How about your folks?"

She twists her lips sourly, giving me a look. I hear the TV behind her, leaving little room to lie to my face. "Did you not get her note? We don't need your games around here, Calvin. It was hard enough for her to sweep your stupid engagement under the table for mom and dad's sake…"'

"I got the email, and I don't care," I growl, filling the doorway, pushing past her. "Where's a good place to talk?"

I'm not taking more delays. I head for the kitchen, leaving her racing after me.

"Kat? Who's that?" Mrs. Middleton pops up from her living room recliner as soon as I enter the kitchen next to it.

Her lazier half, Maddie's dad, stays glued to the TV, too caught up in his thriller explosions on the screen to care. It's a few more seconds before I see doll. She's just come downstairs, dressed more casually than I've ever seen, jean shorts and a tank top hiding her little body.

If I didn't have the whole world's weight on my shoulders, begging to be dropped with precision, I think the instant hard-on raging in my pants would put me on my knees. "Doll," I say softly before I cross the room, ignoring her wide-eyed look.

There's nothing soft at all about how I throw her over my shoulder, put her against the counter, and give her the hottest mouth-to-mouth this home has probably seen in decades.

Fuck, she tastes good. Sweeter than usual because she tries to fight me. Tries, and completely fails. Surrender comes roughly ten seconds after my lips smother hers, re-taking what's always been mine.

What the fuck were you thinking, doll? I ask her silently, grunting when her sharp nails go into my neck. *Did you really think I'd quit over lies? Misunderstandings? A note by Google pigeon?*

"Kat!" Her mother calls again, no longer a question. "Someone want to tell me why your sister's necking with a complete stranger in the middle of my lasagna prep?"

Kat just shrugs. "Not my problem, ma. Why does everybody always look at me? He's here to have a heart-to-heart with the whole family, or so he says."

Shit. I notice, too late, that when I threw Maddie on the counter, her thigh crushed a pack of flat noodles. Cheese is on the floor. An open can of crushed tomatoes teeters on the edge, saved by my fingers at the last second when I lift her up, shooting her mother a sympathetic look.

Finally, her old man is on his feet too, arms crossed as sternly as his eyebrows while he surveys the damage to tonight's dinner.

"Sorry for the intrusion, people. It's a little messy, yeah, but that's how it's always been, hasn't it, Maddie?" I look her in the eyes and see the hurt, the confusion, the shame because I've forced my way back without more than an ugly word.

"Put me down, Calvin. Now!" Her tone tells me she isn't playing around.

Neither am I. It's not until a couple seconds later, when I haven't so much as let her toes touch the floor, that she adds some teeth to her threat. Her palm crashes across my face. Pain blossoms up my jaw, into my temple. She lands gracefully, released from my arms, and I smile like a fool as I touch the burn I thought I'd avoided.

"Madeline, just what the hell's going on?" Her dad booms. "Tell me. I'll throw this idiot out if you don't want him around."

"No, Mr. Middleton. I deserved it," I say, stepping closer to the living room, where the entire family has lined up, watching me like the crazy intruder I've become. "I'll tell you guys the truth because I'm done screwing off. A few weeks back, Maddie and I got engaged. We fell in love longer ago than that. If you're wondering where she's been since she came back from China, why she hasn't stayed at home, well, she's been at my place," I say, watching her mother's head whip toward Maddie, surprise stretching her face. "Everything was perfect. We planned to do this the easy way, make the announcement over a normal dinner or something, but that's out the window now, it seems."

Her dad looks past me at the ruined lasagna ingredients strewn around the counter, seething. I'll make it right soon, once I know he won't clock me out cold for upsetting his eldest daughter, and his eats.

"Calvin?" Deep lines criss-cross her mother's thoughtful face. She studies me, creeping closer, the dark eyes she shares with Maddie going wide when it hits her. "Calvin Randolph? From Maynard? Sweet Jesus. And after so much drama, too...nobody knew you stayed in Seattle."

"Oh, he's here, all right," Kat says, a smirk on her face. She scurries aside a second later when her father approaches, rolling up one sleeve, officially at his limit with the tornado I've brought into their house.

"Not for long. Calvin, Randolph, whoever the hell you are, I want you *out*. Go. I'm not asking twice."

He's dead serious. I give Maddie a look, caught in a twist I never planned for. A physical confrontation with her old man wasn't a scenario I imagined. Guess I'll have to stand my ground and loose a few teeth to his fist. I'm not moving until I get what I came for.

I stand there, feet anchored to the floor, unmoving.

For a few precious seconds, I think she'll let nature take its course, or at least her father's rage, weaponizing the muscles he hasn't lost from years working the loading docks. Then, when he's close, ready to shove me through the stove, she jumps up, reaching for his shoulders.

"Daddy, please. Just wait. Listen. This isn't all his fault." She talks like the words disgust her.

I'm heartened, and also the luckiest SOB in the world. Shaking my head, I step closer, trusting her hands on his shoulders will keep his cannonball sized hands from splintering my ribs. "No, beautiful. I'm not letting you take the fall. You folks want the truth? I'm the *only* reason things are so screwed up here. I was an idiot. Kat told Maddie what I did, and she was right to run. I played with the heart she promised me. I took it for granted. That's a mistake I'm never making again."

"Finally!" Kat says, throwing up her hands, smiling at her mom. "Dad, Maddie's right. Let him talk. I'm just sorry there's no popcorn."

I don't bother glaring. Kat's snark, her parent's confusion and anger, plus the volcanic tension fades. It's background noise.

It's doll in front of me, and only her.

My woman, my claim, my charade and my reality, standing there in her casual wear looking more beat down, humiliated, and vulnerable than ever.

She's in this situation because I took a fall for her years ago. I tangled us in chains we could've avoided.

Now, maybe it's her turn to bear the weight. Difference is, I can't fucking stand it.

Walking past her father in full gorilla-mode, I put my arms around her, and hold on until she slides into me, relaxes, sobbing against my shoulder. "This is my fault. Nobody else's. What happened at the bar – or should I say what *didn't* happen because I couldn't bring myself to do it – was a hell of a blunder. Last error I swear I'll ever make with this angel."

Fuck it, I'm going off script. Can't even remember the words I spent the evening practicing in my office between conference calls with the marketing team and new whale investors for RET.

"Maddie, look at me. You deserve better, and sure as I'm standing here in front of you like a goddamned fool, I swear you'll get it. I'll bring it." I wait a small eternity for her eyes. When she digs herself out of my shoulder, and finally looks at me, seeing the pain on her face is like staring at the sun.

If I wasn't deadly serious before, I feel like I'm taking a vow in front of God himself now. My heart threatens to beat itself out of my ribs. Squeezing her tighter, I pause to reassure her with my lips, laying them on hers softly, honestly, more real than they've ever been since I had my soul ripped away seven years ago.

"It's insane, but I love you. I still want to do this. Give me one chance to treat you like the diamond you are, keep you hanging on my heart through the good, the bad, and every ugly fucking thing that's bound to come. You'll see this fool can learn, and I'll make you stop regretting the day I sent you the ring." I close my eyes, pressing my forehead to hers, no longer giving a damn about the audience gathered around us, if I ever did at all. "I'm not asking for more favors. Just a second chance. You owe me nothing, doll, but if you'll give me another chance to prove everything I'm saying – this time for real – you'll see. I'll go to hell before I ever let you down. If I don't make you the happiest woman on earth like you deserve, that's too good a place for me."

"Shut up, Cal. One more," she whispers, her faint voice trembling. It's a miracle she's able to get out at all after I've brought shock and awe to her entire family.

I don't care if she's speechless. I don't care that their suspicious eyes stab us repeatedly like daggers. Her lips tell me plenty more than words ever will when they collide with mine a second later.

We kiss like stars branding their light on the Seattle sky.

We kiss for our own heartbeats, slowly merging, becoming one as our lips find peace.

We kiss through her parents swapping soft, hurried whispers I can't make out, through Kat sighing, shaking her head, muttering just loudly enough to pick up her words.

"It's your funeral, sis. But I'd probably give the asshole another chance, too."

Her family never congratulates us on the bizarre engagement announcement, but I don't think they're horrified by the idea by the time we're leaving. It'll take time, and I'll win them over.

Slipping Mr. Middleton a five hundred dollar apology

with a tip about the best pizza place in town helps. I listen to Maddie gathering her things upstairs, her mother hovering, hitting her with a thousand questions.

What little I catch from the conversation tells me I've patched the worst damage.

Miracles do happen.

Mrs. Middleton's questions echo in my head several times over on the drive home.

Are you really sure, Madeline? I mean, spending your life with him?

After everything *that happened ?*

I stayed on the sidelines while they talked, resisting the urge to jump in. Glad I did, too, because Maddie's response would've thawed the coldest heart.

Mom...it's my choice. Love doesn't choose. Frankly, we should've been together years ago. He's different now. The things they said about him were wrong. There's more than neighborhood gossip, bad press, a police report the bully's father paid to have altered.

Give it a little time. Give us a chance. You'll see it, too.

There's no one else I'd rather marry than the boy I thought I'd lost forever.

Touching. Honest. Everything except the part about me being different.

To her, different means *better*. I'm not the same clueless kid who stumbled into disaster, true, but there's no sane argument it ever helped me mature, made me a better man, or taught me an important lesson.

I learned nothing. Only how random, cruel, and

unforgiving this world can be. And how fucking rare second chances are.

Sure, I love her spirited defense, but her ignorance about what happened scares me. Doesn't she know I'd trade it all to go back in time to the day everything went up in flames for a chance to un-fuck my life?

In the slow, rainy commute to my condo, I don't know what to believe.

But it's progress. I've got her in my car.

"So, when do you want to tell me what the heck that was back there?" she finally says, giving me a disbelieving look.

"You don't know? It's the only way we'll ever make this work without blowing ourselves up," I say. "I can't lie anymore, Maddie. Neither can you. We tried to strip this down to its base essentials: cashing in a favor. We played our parts, and failed every time. It's more than that, doll. We both know it. It's a whole fucking mountain of more."

"You seem serious this time, at least," she says quietly. "That's the only reason I'm going home with you."

Rain patters my black hood as we ride through the dark city streets. I say nothing until we're a few miles from home.

"Doll, I'm being honest when I say *nothing* happened with Tina. You gave me that hall pass, and yeah, I thought about using it. But I never did. What your sis, Kat, saw in the bar is where it ended." I pause, studying the jealousy tensing her lips into a thin line. "I brought her upstairs to my room, and almost got sick to my stomach. I couldn't go through with it. Not with you on my mind, knowing you were at home, sleeping off my bullshit after I walked out.

Gave me a lot of questions, and one right answer. I came home. Crashed down next to you where I belong. Forgot her, and it's never felt so good."

The anger on her face dissipates. Slowly, she reaches for my hand, gripping it loosely with her fingers over the console. "I believe you."

Her ring is back where it belongs, its gold warmth glowing against my knuckle. Christ, I'd kill to see it wrapped around my cock.

"All I needed to hear."

"No. No, it's not," she whispers. "You do have a heart in there somewhere, I think. Hard to believe at times. But then you let it out in front of everyone back there. I just wish you'd do it more often. Maybe this wouldn't be so hard."

She's fucking right. A little honesty would've saved us a ton of heartbreak.

I told myself before I brought her back I had no interest in ever revisiting those dark, painful chasms in my life I left behind. Too bad it took so much hell to realize how stupid that was.

I can't escape it. Can't ignore it either.

Just having her around every day picks at old scars. And I've realized I'd rather open them up and bleed my heart out if the alternative is losing her thanks to the time bomb ticking in my head, leading me to self-destruction.

By the time I pull the car into the garage, I'm hanging onto her fingers so hard it hurts.

I can't lose my doll again.

I swear I fucking won't.

My sanity, my fortune, and the life I thought I wanted will go up in flames before I ever fuck up with her again.

She thought this was pretend a few weeks ago. So did I when it started.

Truth is, we tried to fool ourselves harder than the rest of the world after seven years apart. It was always real – *always* – and I'm done dancing around her thinking this is anything less than serious.

Upstairs, I bring us some wine. She looks out of place, sitting on my plush leather sofa in the same worn summer clothes she brought from home. Misplaced or not, the outfit gives her curves a dangerous, wholesome, cock-teasing quality that calls me next to her, and makes it pure torture keeping my hands away.

"What happened after Scourge?" she says, giving me a probing look over the top of her wine glass.

"Like you don't know? Jail happened. John got killed. My entire life circled the drain, and I've had to claw back a fraction of the respect that should've come naturally with the Randolph name. Dad's work ethic never recovered from the firm. He blamed me more than he ever did Taliban mortars for killing my brother and fucking up our family. He's an idiot for that, but for the broken heart that took down mom in the end?" I shrug because I don't know.

I never do.

"That wasn't me. His drinking and womanizing killed

her. He shut down and abandoned her after my brother's funeral. I could only do so much. Her heart attack came because he wasn't there for her."

Maddie reaches for my hand. I'm saying more than I have for years about the whole fucked up situation, and also not saying much at all.

"Cal, it's okay. I'm not out to hurt you. I *do* understand. Talk to me." Her eyes are huge, forgiving, beautiful. Can't stand them on me for more than a couple seconds before I throw more wine down my throat.

Another mistake. Each sip catalyzes the jittery mix of self-loathing and desire every look from those eyes brings.

I'm being tested. She wants to know if I'll stay honest, continue opening my heart and letting it spill out the same way it did earlier, guts and all.

"Talk changes nothing, doll. We can't erase seven years in a few kisses and a confession." I move closer, wrapping an arm around her neck, every fingertip igniting when her soft skin brushes mine.

How does she feel this good? It's beyond chemistry, the reaction that always starts the instant her body touches mine.

It's electric, magnetic, and a hundred other kinds of mystifying fuckery I can't describe without a science PhD. She puts me on edge in the best and worst ways, using some voodoo I'll never understand in ten lifetimes.

"I'm not trying to erase anything. I can't," she says, brushing my arm. Her hand massages my bicep, the same gentle touch she used on her father. "I want you to let me in so we can undo the damage. Have you ever wondered if the reason we're not making much progress with your father is because you're holding in so much venom?"

"No. It's too early to see results. We wowed the board and the senior managers. If we're able to win over Joe and Stefan, plus Mrs. Anders, odds are they'll look the other way if his will locks me out of ever having a stake in the company. Or at least they won't block a vote when Spence and Cade take their dads' places, and try to give me a hand." It's a longshot, but it's my last hope if the old bastard doesn't have a sudden and serious change of heart.

"I don't think it needs to be that complicated, or so risky," she whispers, twining her hand with mine. Fuck, the girl is pure black magic, button brown eyes and a soft smile built in kindness and shadowed in sexy. "Look, I'm not trying to make you re-visit anything you don't want to just because there's a lot I don't know. I'm trying to help. Cal...let me make this better. Give me details, take me through the years I missed. Then I'll be able to help the way I really want to."

We share a look. The only thing worse than going on a tour of the three year tragedy after I got yanked out of Maynard for a six by eight cell is ignoring this raging need to get my dick inside her by any means possible.

How does she do it? Shine on like the fucking sun itself, magnificent and brutal, without burning up in her own desire?

I don't know, but every man has his limit. She's touched mine several times over.

"Cal…" She says my name again, bringing a hand to my face, grazing my stubble.

Swallowing the last dreg of wine, I take her hand, pull her onto my lap, and stare into those soft, searching hazel eyes. "No. I owe you something, doll, but I'll be damned if I'm letting you under my skin under these conditions."

"Conditions? What —" I cut her off, grinding my hips into hers, pressing my hands to her ass. I push her down so she's able to feel how hard I am. "Oh. *Ohhh.*"

"Now you understand. You want under my skin. I'll let you in, but not while it's an unfair trade. You get my skin, I get your clothes, and then I take every inch of what I've wanted since the day you sauntered your sweet little ass back into my life. I take it until I've had my fill, as hard and deep and long as I want."

"Oh, God."

I stiffen when I hear her moan. Rocking my cock harder against her clit through our clothes, I give her a moment to swoon, to breathe, to say her prayers.

It's better to get it out now, while I'm digging my fingers into her hips, telling her with every rough imprint what's coming.

It's scorching, it's serious, and it's so fucking overdue.

IX: Unrelenting (Maddie)

"Cal, Cal, Cal...God!" Whimpering his name three more times doesn't save me from the fire in his kiss.

I hate what he's able to do to me. I hate that I can't resist. I hate that I'm about to give myself up without knowing if he's really changed, or if he's playing me one more time for his fake marriage con job.

Sex never cares about the tough questions, though.

My pussy tenses, aches, soaks itself in a flood of heat when his tongue enters my mouth. Growling, he sends one hand to the base of my neck, puts it there, and pulls me in. He won't let me go if I tried.

I'm caught in his power as much as my own desire. It's heart, it's soul, it's wanton need. My hand glides down, brushing his rough cock through his pants, and the raging need to feel it deep inside me expands tenfold.

"Come, doll," he says, pulling his teeth off my bottom lip. I think he means he wants me undone on the spot until he stands up, gesturing to the hall. "We can't do it here. I'm fucking my fiancée for the first time in a proper bed."

I don't resist as he picks me up, throws me over his

shoulder, and carries me to heaven. Even his hand burns its warmth on my skin, perched between the loose separation between my shorts and top.

Why do I want this so bad? Twenty-four hours ago, I thought he'd taken his lust out on another woman, the first time he acted like we were more than actors slaving under a suffocating sexual tension.

But when I think about our time on the yacht, on top of the Space Needle before it all went bad, and again at my parent's house, there isn't room for doubt.

I know perfectly well why I want him, why I'm desperate to believe he's turned over a new leaf.

It's more than that, doll. We both know it. It's a whole fucking mountain of more.

His words from the drive haunt me. They're as true as the lava foaming in my veins. True as my breath fading to short, quick gasps each time his fingers touch me in new places. True as the steady need for *more* beating its pulse in my heart, and this time, I want to scale the entire mountain.

He pushes his door open, carrying me into his room, and kicks the door shut behind him.

It's as immaculate in his inner sanctum as the rest of his place, a rich and decadent man cave with gold trim around the corners, fancy furniture, and a giant bed draped in ivory blankets, pillows, and sheets. The dim light doesn't hide a few strategically placed mirrors.

For some reason, they make me think of Tina, even though she was never here. I also trust he's told me the truth when he said he backed off before he stuck it in her. But how many others did he bring here before me?

How many women has he taken to screaming fits, watching them surrender to his cock from every angle? I don't know, but I hate them all.

It fills me with an irrational, seething jealousy. I bite him when he throws me down on the bed, and pushes his lips to mine again.

"Ah, fuck! Didn't think you had it in you to want it rough," he snarls, rubbing the tender middle of his lip with one finger a few times.

"I don't know what I want." I sigh, letting my legs fall apart, the better to make space for his big, strong body on top of me. He feels so incredible it's easy to forget I haven't *had* it with anyone before.

"What're you saying?" he says, silencing me with another kiss before I'm able to answer. "What don't you know?"

Shameful heat mingles with my lust. I'm thankful for the darkness because I know every inch of me is probably red by now, flushed with fire, confusion, and most of all, *doubt.*

Should I tell him the scary truth? What kind of hypocrite would I be if I didn't, after spending the last hour fighting to coax it out of him?

"Doll, answer me," he says, his face just inches from mine. His blue eyes are inquisitors when they're so bright, so demanding, driven by total lust.

"I've never done this, Cal." Each word sticks in my mouth like syrup.

"This?" He pauses, needing a moment for it to sink in. When it does, his face softens, and a new panicked intensity fills his eyes. "Oh. Fuck. You're telling me you've never...you're a virgin?"

It sounds like he can't believe it. I think I've made a dreadful mistake, and I'm probably going to melt under him before I get a chance to correct it.

"Sorry," I whisper. "I should have told you before. Figured I'd better spit it out than disappoint you with –"

"Doll, stop. Listen. If you think I'm disappointed because you've been waiting seven goddamned years for me to break you in...*Jesus*. You just told me the same cherry I thought about for years, pulled myself off to *hundreds* of times is still there, ripe for the taking, and it's all mine tonight? In what fucking universe would I ever be disappointed over my biggest wet dream's second coming? Or should I say your first?"

We stop and stare for several seconds. Long enough for my smile to recover. Reaching up, I put my fingers through his hair, open my body, and brace for the storm.

His lips miss my lips the next time they land. He has new targets in mind. They blaze a trail down my throat, sucking hard on tender skin.

Oh, God. Mercy! I'm moaning, writhing, tangling my hips into his.

Cal's fingers push between my thighs, pulling them apart, stroking a rough line of pleasure through my jeans. His nostrils flare and his breathing quickens. It's like my little confession sparks something primal, something I'm able to feel in his energy, the furious passion steaming out his lips and onto my skin.

I've waited forever, haven't I? And so has he.

I shouldn't have teased him putting my teeth into that kiss a few minutes ago. There's now a hundred percent certainty I'm about to have it rough, and there isn't any choice. Not when our sex is dynamite with a seven year fuse.

His hands catch my top and lift me up when he tears it off. He pulls me into his arms, practically shredding my bra strap when he jerks it loose, freeing my tender breasts.

"Seven fucking years, Maddie. That's how long I've waited to get to second base and put my mouth on these tits. Get ready."

Ready? I don't know what he means until his fingertips clamp around my nipples, seizing the pink pebble at the tip, a prelude to his wandering mouth.

Then comes the kiss, the teeth, the tongue, the love. My clit develops its own rogue ache when he sucks at my breasts. Each stroke of his tongue and needling drift of his teeth pushes me closer to a cliff I've only imagined, nearer to the ecstasy cascading in a dull, hot roaring waterfall.

I'm able to pinch his shirt with my hands, pulling it up, against his head. Somehow, I remember to breathe.

But when his hand climbs between my legs, plucks loose the metallic snap holding my shorts together, and stuffs his conquering fingers against my pussy, I'm done.

I'm so freaking done.

Cal rules me. Owns me. Strokes me to obsession's brink.

He only needs to tease my swollen, dripping labia once

before I'm bucking back.

Helplessly, frantically, unconditionally.

I want him inside me.

Wrong, I *need* him the hell inside me.

His mouth has moved to my other nipple, drawing it in with the heat of his breath, holding it prisoner while his tongue flicks it into rapid submission. I'm surprised my fingernails aren't carving a valley in his head with how hard they're holding on, the last thing grounding me before my virgin cunt folds to the pleasure.

"Doll, fuck yeah, give it up. Just like you've always wanted. Every breathless drop of pleasure I see on your face makes me harder." He rolls his hips against my thigh. Like I need any reminder.

Like I even need his fingers rubbing me senseless before the fireball building in my womb peaks, turns me to stone, and renders me completely his. That's when he shows me what his marvelous, experienced hands are really able to do.

His thumb never leaves my clit when my pussy tenses. Short, sharp, agonizing circles swarm me again and again, hypnotic and merciless.

His free arm slides under me, lifting me up, pressing my mouth to his as everything goes white.

Cal! I scream his own name into his mouth as release washes over me.

He groans, sucks in my breathless cries, drinks my own pleasure while his fingers hit my pussy again and again. I'm coming for what seems like forever, my brain ballooning with the steady hum of my own heartbeat, drunk and wet and delirious.

"Keep fucking coming. Give everything, doll. Everything we should've had when we were eighteen," he growls, sometime when I'm halfway through. His fingers quicken between my thighs, and it lifts me up higher, a parting kiss from nirvana before my body gives out, crashing me back to earth.

I'm so limp for the next few minutes I barely notice him tugging off the rest of my clothes. When he lifts me again, I'm naked, and he's lost his shirt somewhere in the storm.

"Wake up, love," he whispers, underscoring his words with a kiss. "The night is young, and you haven't even felt my tongue on your clit."

Imagining his face between my legs, strong and hungry, causes my eyes to fully open. Just in time for another sultry kiss, pulling me deeper into his magic, straight to the secret language our bodies use when our words fail us.

"God, yes," I hiss, running my nails along his naked chest. It's the first time I see his wall of muscle shirtless. It's hard, inked, and so, so strong.

"Like what you see?" he asks, swallowing my moan in his next kiss. "Fuck yeah, you do."

He answers for me. A small mercy because I'm coming undone. His skin on mine ignites new fire between my legs, hotter and deeper than before.

My pussy tingles when I feel the warmth in his shoulders while his muscles flex. If he wants, I'm sure he could pick me up and hold me mid-air while taking me as hard and deep as he'd like.

The black rose stamped on his hand crawls up his arms

in a tangle of vines and thorns, where it blooms again on his shoulder, a whole bouquet in darkness. Their needles drip black ink in thin lines, or maybe it's meant to be blood.

It's impossible not to remember the pain that brought us here even when my skin savors his.

But it doesn't blunt the pleasure. If anything, it brings us closer, and soon my mouth is on his skin, kissing a steady trail down his broad chest, into the valley of his chiseled abs. I trail to where his belt begins, tasting his earthy masculinity in every kiss, letting the primal craving it feeds inside me run rampant.

I'm tugging on his belt when he grabs my wrist. "Floor, doll. Get over there on your knees if you really want this cock in your mouth."

He takes me by the hand and guides me to a spot next to the bed. Landing on my knees, I look up, devoured by his deep blue eyes. His gaze never breaks.

Not while his huge hands go to his buckle, or when he pushes his trousers down.

Not while he presses my little hand to the massive bulge in his boxers, or when he helps pull them aside a second later.

Not even while his bare, gorgeous cock springs out, raging steel ready for my lips, or when my cheeks turn so red they glow like sister suns in the grey darkness.

"I'm sorry, I'm sorry," I whimper, shaking as my fingers close around him. "I've never done this…"

"Don't apologize, baby girl. Just suck. Open your sweet lips and take the head. Take as much as you can, inch by inch. Taste me. Your mouth will do the rest. It's in the blood, doll. Show me what you've wanted since the first day we locked lips at that party all those years ago…"

He's clueless how dangerous his invitation is. He doesn't even know it.

How many times I've imagined the scene before me…Jesus.

I'm a virgin, not a robot. I've had my dirty thoughts, maybe more than any woman who's getting it regularly. Seen myself on my knees with a swollen cock in hand a thousand times, and it was always Cal's. No exceptions. Not once whenever I turned in early, pressed my bullet vibrator against my clit, and let the relentless frustration sweep me away.

Tonight, it's not a fantasy anymore. There's nothing unreachable anymore when I finally break the spell of his sky blue eyes, moisten my lips, and engulf his furious tip.

"Oh. Fuck. Yeah!" He grunts each word quietly. His muscular cock jerks in my mouth, raging against my tongue, catching its pleasure as I learn to take his most intimate flesh on mine.

Closing my eyes, I find a new headspace, a zone where there's just his pleasure and mine.

I suck. I lick. I taste.

I roll my tongue up and down his steaming shaft, drinking the pre-come oozing out of him, focused on the cadence of his breath and harsh whispers. *Don't stop. Use me, Cal. Lose yourself in the flesh, the soul, the heart that's always been yours.*

"Sweet fuck, you're killing me, Madeline!" he calls my full name when my tongue digs into the soft line around his crown, drawing more sticky sap in reward.

His whole strong body seethes, bulges, threatens to explode. It's incredible how I'm able to massage his entire body just by having my mouth on the best muscle. I watch his blue eyes disappear in his lids. Cal's head rolls on his shoulders, divine face swaying gently, sweat beading on his brow.

Climax approaches, and I want to blow him to the moon and back. My fingers squeeze his thick base, nudging into his heavy balls. I open my mouth as wide as I can and swing low, taking a third of his length every time I push down deeper, all I can manage without doing damage.

Of course, his secret part matches the rest of him. It's huge, smooth, and totally resistant to being tamed.

I think my mouth can do it. His cock sputters more erratically when I dive down on it three more times. I'm bracing for the hot, fierce explosion flooding my mouth when his fingers dig into my hair, ripping my mouth off him.

"Enough," he grunts, the sexy energy returning to his eyes when I'm able to look up, wiping my mouth with one hand.

Fire returns to my helpless cheeks, too. I look up after a moment, afraid I've disappointed him, trying to find the words to ask. "Sorry. Was it…wrong?"

"Fuck no, you tease. You're a natural cocksucker, and your little mouth's begging to be trained long and hard later. Congratulations, doll." He smiles, staring into my questioning eyes. I don't understand why he stopped if I wasn't doing bad. "Much as I'd love finishing down your throat, I'd be out of my fucking mind after you told me there's something better."

Better? My eyes search his in the silence. He just takes me by the hands, pulls me up, and pushes me onto the bed, shoving my thighs apart.

"You're a virgin, doll. You're insane if you think I'm wasting this hard-on anywhere else before I've taken your cherry and stretched your little cunt to fit me like a glove."

Holy hell. I'm in a whole new round of panic, delight, and sweet anticipation when he drops to the floor.

Cal kisses into my thighs. He throws my legs over his shoulders, holds my legs open with his hands, and soon his breath adds its heat to the steaming mess in my core.

I'm squirming, whimpering, softly calling his name. He keeps my hips from sinking too low, stalls my aching pussy from reaching his face before he's good and ready.

"Cal, please. Please," I moan a few more times, shaking uncontrollably, losing myself in the strong warmth in his hands before he quits playing.

When his face sinks into my leaking pussy, it's the most brutal kind of bliss.

Fast, abrupt, and unbearably hot. Inescapable.

My clit steams against his kisses, soft wet lips fused to his tongue. He digs them apart with his chin, raking his stubble over tender flesh again and again. I'm ready to come before his tongue even dips into my quivering pink.

Cal knows what he's doing. *God, does he ever freaking know.*

My cunt throbs for release. His tongue smothers my clit and begins to make licks ten times softer than his fingers, and just as irresistible.

Throwing my hands above my head, I reach helplessly for the pillows, and see us in the huge mirror attached to the ceiling. Apparently, sex reflections aren't just an extra thrill for emotionally scarred rich men.

I'm just in time to see my own eyes roll back into my head as my entire body seizes. "Cal, Cal, Jesus!"

Pleasure rips through me in a wave cascading straight from his tongue through my soaked flesh. It screams, it resonates, it carries me halfway to heaven and drops me through the clouds. Hot white bliss soaks my brain, turning my clit into a steady, pulsing beacon for everything his mouth lashes into me.

I'm coming like I didn't know I could.

Ecstasy writes poetry on the fabric of my skin, shattering every shield I thought I had. His pleasure finds my heart, dips his enigma into it, and makes me more vulnerable, more confused, more addicted than ever.

When I'm able to open my eyes, it's his I see. Cal hovers, completely freed from his clothes and gloriously naked, his rigid cock pressed snug against the flesh it's eager to claim.

"You come so goddamned perfect, Maddie. Can't wait to see how you let go when I'm balls deep." He sweeps my loose hair aside, working his mouth down to mine for another kiss. It's slower, but so much hotter than before, like the wait has lifted his internal temperature several degrees. "How many times did you think about this over the years? Be honest, doll."

I'm too stunned to answer. I shake my head, hoping he's so horny he just forgets the question.

Whatever simple sex is supposed to be, it isn't this, is it?

Taking over my body isn't supposed to include hitting me with these questions aimed at my heart.

Oh, but he isn't letting up. The way his hips rock into mine, enough to make me moan, but not risk sinking in, tells me what kind of game this is.

"Cal, please. I want you," I whisper, the blood in my veins sprouting needles. They scratch, they tempt, they paint me all kinds of shameful red and lustful pink.

"Answer me, damn it," he snarls. Fisting my hair, he gives it a warning tug, turning my face to his, the better for his lips to ravage with another kiss. "I want to know, Maddie, how many times? How many times did you get yourself off imagining how hard I'd fuck you? How many times did you wish it'd been different, that you'd given yourself to me that night at Chelle's place because you were afraid you'd missed your chance to have *this* torturing your clit?"

Grunting, he pushes his full length against me. Coated in my wetness, his cock glides, evil friction pulling the answer out of me because *torturing* is right. And I'll do anything to end it.

"How many times, Maddie?" he whispers again, harsher than before, stroking his length against me again and again. I'm going to explode.

"All the time, ass! I must have dreamed it hundreds of times, lived it in my head over and over. Every time I had the gall and a little privacy to break out my vibrator or use my fingers. I pleasured myself to you, came to something I thought would never happen…" I despise the confession falling out as much as I love the controlling tease of his body on mine. My eyes are full of hate, frustration. Cal just eats it up, delighted to hear the awful truth, how bad I wanted him. "There, are you happy?"

He reaches behind him to something poised on the bed. I watch him lean back, rip the condom foil with his teeth, and then glide the oversized dark rubber sheath over his manhood with the world's slowest stroke.

When he finds his place between my legs again, I push my hand against his, trying to hold his cock away, even though my pussy is on fire. "You never answered me," I say, clenching my teeth.

"Don't fucking need to. After what's happened the last week, think we'd both agree talk is cheap. There's more than words to get a point across. Doll, let me *show* you why everything you've said makes me the happiest swinging dick this side of heaven."

My spine practically tilts into a crescent the first time he pushes into me, pressing my legs to his shoulders, thrusting to the hilt.

There's a rough tearing sensation as he takes what's left of my virginity. And then fire, fire, so much fire.

It burns in the goosebumps rising on my skin. Blazes in the sweat racing out my pores. Even shimmers, fierce and hot and endless as the stars outside his huge window, when I hear him grunt with satisfaction because I'm so full of him.

"So tight, so wet, and so fucking mine," Cal growls, bringing his teeth into my ankle. His cock shifts deeper on the second thrust, stretching me open.

Moaning, I try to move my hips to meet his, desperate to turn my first time discomfort into the pleasure rising behind his thrusts.

"Yes, yes, yes," I whimper, a slow staccato burst, each cry shriller than the last.

They're like sirens to his predator instincts. He bites my leg again before he tears his mouth off me, pinches my legs tighter to his shoulders, and brings it harder than I ever imagined.

The bed becomes an earthquake, and it ripples through me. I'm a shaking, screaming, ecstasy teased mess at the end of his next dozen thrusts. Chewing my lip and clenching the sheets for dear life is all I have, my one and only brace for this storm he's fucking into me with each passing second.

His free hand reaches down, finds my clit, and flicks maniacal circles. They're hypnotic, dizzying, and cruel in their intensity.

But it's the kind of cruelty that's mysterious, hinting at a higher pleasure, calling me back to it again and again.

So much like everything else involving this scary, powerful, soul stealing man.

"Going to break you, doll. Come for me. Come until you pull the fuck apart." His eyes are insane when he doubles his pace, thrusting into me harder, using the leverage on his knees to drive into me. His balls beat a frenzied rhythm on my ass, and it's their tempo making his commands impossible to ignore. Invincible to resistance.

My obedient body seizes a second later. I'm sweating through the next few seconds, keenly aware of what's coming.

The heatwave starts in my lower belly next to my loins before it surges, immersing my brain in the essential, confounding, and savage Cal Randolph. His cock drives deeper, harder, pushing me over the edge, off the face of the earth.

"Oh, Cal. Oh, holy, holy –"

Shit! Coming!

My mind finds words my upbringing always suppressed to keep itself from coming apart. It splinters, lost in a million lewd pieces, sex sparks showering through me like currents lit by raw, animal release.

"Fuck yes, doll. Give it. Every pulse. Every whimper. Love how you curl your everything when you come. I love it fucking *all.* Give me everything."

Oh, and I do.

My pussy convulses, flooding rampant pleasure through my body. My O reaches every nerve, deepening by the second, turning every muscle to stone before they melt to clay.

Cal barely gives me time to catch my breath. I'm loosening my grip on the sheets, letting the blood flow to my fingers, when he picks me up and flips me over.

"Ass up, Maddie," he whispers, nipping at my neck.

I should be all kinds of exhausted, ready to crash out face first. But his love bite fills me with a new energy, a manic need to serve him until he's found his release.

Pushing my face into the sheets, I stifle a whiny moan when he mounts me from behind. His fingers seize my ass, the same frantic tension I'm using to clutch the sheets.

He thrusts faster and harder than before. Bucking, grunting, relentless in his need to fuck.

His strokes lift me high and drop me on my knees.

He pushes with a force, a fury, and a passion I never imagined in my wettest, most secret fantasies.

This is no joke. No dream. It's the new reality, and it's deep inside me, beating its balls against my clit.

I can't hold on. Another O builds, making its presence known when the fire comes. My ears tune to his heavy breathing, his feral curses, his pleasure quickening in our race together.

"Breathe, breathe, breathe, Maddie, and don't fucking stop!" He says, fisting my hair, lifting my head so I'm forced to see the mirror over his leather headboard.

I see him behind me, owning my body in every stroke, my face crinkling with delight. My breasts swing like pendulums with every thrust, drunk on the same giddy numbness overwhelming every nerve.

His eyes...*God.* They're bright blue portals to the basest lust. His muscles bow, flex, bulging and dominating. When he comes, it's going to be with his entire soul on fire, and for the first time since we started, I'm afraid.

But there's no time for fear taking over. His cock

plunges into me faster, harder, and his fist jerks my neck prone, forcing my hips to tilt back into his endless pounding.

"Cal!" I call his name, eyelids fluttering shut, so close to pleasure's wave drowning me again. I don't want to face it alone.

"One more time, baby girl. Come for me again. One more, and I'll spill every damned drop."

He's either read my mind, or he's been controlling it the whole time.

My pussy pulses, pinching him at the base of his cock. Muscles I didn't know I had tense like springs, releasing their force with a violent relief when they've hit their limit.

I'm coming again.

Coming while his cock pistons, while he growls his imminent release, while every hard, tattooed inch of him owns me in the worst ways.

Actually, the *best* and worst.

"Fuck!" he screams it. Then his cock stiffens, swells, plunges to my depths, and finds its molten peace.

I lose the last thread of control I'm holding onto when I feel him jerk. Every magnificent inch he has throbs inside me, adding a vicious heat to my pussy's walls. My cunt sucks him harder, desperate to break the condom, wringing every twitch from his balls.

We're a two way conduit joined for one purpose. Orgasm fuses us in sweet release, and I swear our pulse and breathing match before it's over.

One heartbeat. One rhythm. Two souls.

It seems like forever before he pulls out, sliding off the bed to tie off the condom and throw it away. Gnawing my lip, I wonder what he'd feel like bare. I shudder. It's frightening to fathom the limitless pleasure this man can bring, and we've barely broken the surface.

"Goddamn, I needed that, doll," he says, flopping back onto the bed, taking me in his arms.

"Seven years is a long time to sit on that grenade." I place my hands on his chest for leverage, looking up with mischief hanging on my lips. "I'm glad I never settled for anyone else. No one except you would've shaken my world, much less rocked it."

"Same. Knowing my cock's the only one you've ever taken gives me fewer ungrateful assholes to hunt." He's smirking.

For the first time in awhile, it's adorable instead of infuriating. I slap my hand against his huge chest and he laughs. "Stop. We're fake married, remember? Until it's official, there might be more suitors. A girl's entitled to shop."

"Then they're entitled to meet my black rose," he says, his smile wilting, flexing his fist.

He can't be serious? Right?

What kind of psycho have I given my virginity to? And why does his crazy jealousy still excite me?

"Seriously, doll, I meant everything I said. Screw pretend. What we have here," he says, running his finger over the sunburst rose ring on my hand, "it's real. It's serious. And we've got a wedding to plan over the next few weeks. I want us good and legal, and I'm not waiting."

He's right. It's happening so fast it makes my vision blur. I need to ground myself, and tell him it'll be okay.

When I press my lips to his, they're warmer. Firmer. Different.

It must be my body's surrender to this man, or else the sudden forever approaching in my heart.

We do it two more times before I'm so exhausted I can't hold my eyes open. The last time, when he's on top of me, pressing his forehead into mine while his breath steams against my lips, I hear him whisper words I never expect.

"Love your body, doll. All of it. Love your heat, your cries, every time you lose it for me. Fuck, Maddie, I love you so much."

It's all he says before we go over the edge to heaven together. His cock pulses hard, twining our bodies once more, more inseparable with every O.

Before, our glue was tragedy. Tonight, it's become love, desire, and some otherworldly peace I can't quite pin down.

As bad as I want to accept it, enjoy it, and step into the future instead of bemoaning the past, there's a dark doubt. It keeps me hostage from the heaven in his bed when I finally fall asleep.

I dream about things best forgotten like they were yesterday.

Almost Seven Years Ago

I can't believe I forgot my German book. Mrs. Anders smiles when I sheepishly confess, and tells me to hurry up and bring it back. I don't even need a pass to go to my locker. She trusts me because it's never happened before.

I'm still embarrassed. Especially when Cal shoots me his patented smirk several desks over, as if he knows perfectly well where my head has been for the last few weeks since he walked me home from Chelle's party.

Okay, so we kissed.

I was weak, and I let him in. I may have enjoyed it.

Doesn't mean it changes anything. He hasn't made more than his usual token efforts to get my attention, teasing me with his jock posse when he walks past, or snickering at my little mistakes when I misplace a German word or two.

This wouldn't keep happening if I could just forget his constant, humiliating gaze.

I'm still kicking myself when I pick up my book, slam my locker shut, and get the scare of my life.

"What the fuck you doing out of class, Rags? It's the middle of the day." Scourge looks like he wants me dead.

His new nickname brings me close, a play on ragdoll, something he started after hearing doll stick.

Reason number one thousand and one I want to strangle Calvin: giving this loathsome idiot ideas.

"J-just getting my book and going back to class. Sorry," I sputter helplessly, noticing his locker hanging open for the first time.

He's hanging onto a backpack bursting at the seams, perched between his legs. Whatever gives it the weight looks heavy and illegal. I don't even want to know.

"Wait!" he snarls, pulling at my collar so hard it spins me around when I grab my stuff and try to walk away.

"Did you come out here to spy so you could fucking tattle? Thought maybe you'd bring something nice and juicy back to the kid you're blowing so he'd get my ass suspended, maybe fucking expelled?" He has me against the wall, breathing his fowl breath on me. It's sour, angry, and it makes my head squirm for fresh air. "Answer me, bitch. Hell of a coincidence if you just magically decided to dig through your shit *now,* while I'm around. I don't fucking buy it."

I don't say anything. I don't know what to say between his fish-eyed stare murdering me where I stand, and pondering my bad luck.

"Fuck it," he growls, pinning me against the wall by the shoulder, while his free hand goes to the zipper on his bag. "If you're gonna squeal, I want you to see what you're dealing with."

Don't look, don't look, don't –

"Look, damn you!" he whispers, pulling the flap on his bag aside, doing a quick check down both sides of the hall to make sure nobody else is around.

We're so alone, and I'm completely screwed.

He won't let me go. When I try to turn my eyes away, he grabs the back of my head and pushes my eyes to the floor, ignoring my stifled sobs.

Holding my breath, I open my eyes, and stare down at the black bag. There's something white inside. *A lot* of white stuff, wrapped up in plastic, like neat piles of bricks. It's an obvious drug pile I've never seen anywhere outside those crazy suspense shows dad glues himself to.

But this isn't TV. It's real.

My heart catches in my throat, pounding until it hurts. Scourge snorts and chuckles, releasing me, slowly closing the zipper. He doesn't need to keep his hand on me. I stand by helplessly as he rams the overflowing bag into his locker, and slams the door shut.

"Yeah, that's what I thought, Rags. Gift from my Uncle Match and his buddies. We're gonna make some sick profits real soon off the assholes in town who want something stronger than their crusty joints and cancer sticks. Now you know my secret. Heavy fucking bitch to hold onto, right?" He pins me down with his eyes. "Go the fuck to class. Pretend you never saw it. Because I swear to that shiny little cross you wear around your neck, you are fucking *fucked* if you breathe one word about this to anyone. You, Rags. Not me, not my friends, not even the asshole hankering to put his dick down your pretty little throat. I'll take you out with Cal watching if you flip, and I'll do it with a goddamned smile on my face."

It's a struggle not to scream when he reaches up, finds the chain around my neck, and rips it off with a force that would leave whiplash if it were any thicker.

"I'll keep this safe for a few days while I make sure you don't fuck me over. Fair?"

I nod. I'm completely numb. It hurts like he kicked me in the stomach to lose the only thing my grandmother left me, but I just keep bobbing my head. I nod until I'm dizzy.

"Good. Now, fucking scram, and maybe one day you'll get this back."

I turn around and speed to class, wiping the tears on my sleeve, hoping no one will notice. Mrs. Anders is in the middle of her lesson. She doesn't take much notice when I plop back into my seat, frantically paging through my book to the right lesson.

I make doubly sure I don't look back at Cal the entire time, which is probably my biggest mistake.

He knows there's something wrong. If only he'd never gotten his hopes up after that kiss, and decided it was an invitation to insert himself deeper into my life.

An hour later, I skip the bus to walk home. It's the best way to make sure I don't have a nervous breakdown in front of Chelle or the other girls.

Kat will be at her guitar lessons tonight, and dad is working overtime to pay down my tuition. That bodes well for some much needed alone time to screw my head back.

I have to think straight, clear, and fast. I'll need the night to decide whether I'll keep mum about Scourge's drugs, or beg my parents to call the police.

I'm mulling both miserable options when I hear the last words I need to know the universe has no mercy. "Doll, wait up!"

Cal charges me from behind, tugs on my shoulder, and shoves me against his broad chest when I refuse to slow down. So much for holding in those tears.

"What's wrong, Maddie? Talk to me!" It doesn't slow once his eyes are on me, wide and blue and searching as the sky. They lift me higher, sending me into the lonely ether when his brow creases, and he utters the words I fear most. "What the fuck did he do to you?"

"Cal, let go!" Twisting, I sever his grip, nearly dislocating my shoulder in the process. He staggers backwards, stunned by my energy, my need to get away before I say too much. I can't let him trigger the landmine that *will* wreck both of us. "Leave me alone. Please. I need to go home!"

My dire tone gets the message through. He doesn't follow.

I'm halfway down the block before I glance behind me. He's never looked fiercer in his gold lacrosse jersey and black shorts. His eyes dig into me from several yards away, clenched fists hanging at his sides.

That ice blue gaze is so cold, so sharp, so haunting. I can't handle it for more than a second.

Next time I turn, I run. My legs pump, filling my lungs with fire. I don't slow down until I'm at the last major street before my block.

That's when the chunky black Mercedes stops short of making my bad day my last. When I see who's inside, I wish I'd stepped right in front of it.

"Watch where you're going, you little bimbo!" An older

man with graying hair screams from the driver's window, shaking his fist, louder than the blaring horn his other hand activates.

Next to him, there's the most evil face I've ever seen. "Give her a break, dad. I know her. She's had a shitty day."

Scourge winks at me. His words do nothing to slow his father's rancor. Alex Palkovich Senior flips me the bird as the light turns green and he hits the accelerator, roaring away as fast as his taxpayer paid luxury wheels can carry him.

I should wish the councilman knew a fraction of what his screwed up son is into. But what I'd really like, more than anything else today, is some freaking peace and quiet.

My legs carry me home in a blinding, sad fury. I cross several more streets without looking, not caring if the next unlucky car I encounter plows into me. Apparently, that would be too easy because I'm able to get home without more interruptions.

And even when I'm safely in my room, face buried in my pillow, sobbing my pathetic life out, I still hear the silent words Cal only said with those eyes.

His gaze was proof he's about to do something stupid. It tells me, without doubt, it's only getting worse tomorrow, no matter what I do.

I won't let this go, doll.

If you won't tell me, then I'll figure it out myself. No one fucks you into a fit of tears and walks away.

X: Impassable (Cal)

I've spent seven years burying the day everything went to shit. Now, it's on my mind more than ever.

Guess that's the consequence of sharing a bed with an angel, having her tangled up in me, hammering the pussy I've wanted for years into sweet submission. We fuck so often it leaves my dick sore. It still doesn't keep me from coming back for more the next night.

Call it ritualistic. Pleasure at its purest. Salvaging a piece of my soul I thought I'd lost forever.

It's a thousand kinds of poetry, animal need and heart coming together in a sweltering, grunting, sheet-clenching dance.

Fuck yes, I do emphasize the *coming* part.

If doll wasn't in love with me before, she's smitten now. I've let her fall harder and deeper than anyone else. I've officially fucked her more times than I've let every woman combined stenciled into my little black book come back for seconds. My cock works its magic, but I didn't know it could curse me, too.

By the end of the week, I'm on the ferry to Bainbridge,

clenching my little black fuck book in my hand. I page through it, trying to place a face to the names and numbers.

Can't remember seventy percent of them, and the ones I do make me gag. I'm not much of a writer, but I do know when it's time to close out the darkest, loneliest chapter of my life.

"*Sayonara,*" I whisper, before flinging it off the ship's top deck, into the Puget Sound. It sinks below the waves with a splash.

There's no going back. I'm too far down the two-way street she's carved since I got her naked. Longer than our fucking, if I'm brutally honest.

I slump in the deck chair, pulling my sweater tight against the chill from the ocean, staring into its churning depths. If only I could toss the rest of our dirty past overboard as easily as I did my old hookups.

That's far too easy, especially when every time I'm in Maddie puts me more in tune with how I got there. Memories don't die so easy.

Today, I let them come. The second to worst day of my life returns for the first time in years, without creating a raging need to break my fist on the nearest surface.

Almost Seven Years Ago

I go straight from the street doll disappeared down back to school. If I'm quick, I might be able to catch the bully piece of shit before he's gone. Never any guarantees, knowing how often he skips out early with his crew.

There's no point wasting time to call for backup. Cade and Spence are out for the evening, both heading home for the long weekend we've got thanks to teachers' conferences. I'll be damned if I let this fester for four fucking days without finding out what's going on with Maddie.

I'm able to avoid the end of the day rush for the buses, the lockers, and then home as students flood out the main entrance. I find a couple kids I know and ask if they've seen him. They tell me he took off with his dad twenty minutes ago.

I'm too late. *Shit.*

Obviously, I don't give up that easy. I've seen him and his boys around town, know they like to spend their evenings around the community center not far from the Academy, where they can pass off weed to poorer kids in the parking lot for pocket change. I head home and do homework for a few hours before I grab my bike, praying he'll be where I think he is.

I'm in luck.

Scourge and his boys always leave out the back of the community center and cross the field sloppily fenced off for new construction, heading up the long hill behind the building. His black jeep with the chipped paint jumps out right away. Guess his politician daddy put a moratorium on buying him a new one after he totaled two brand new vehicles in the past year.

They're parked well away from any prying eyes at the end of the lot, next to overgrown brush. It's a perfect spot where they can smoke, jack each other off, or do whatever else these idiots get into alone.

Perched on the hill behind a bush, I wait five minutes before I see their black shapes moving across the field, coming toward me. There's no mistaking his idiots hanging on his every word, laughing, watching while he lights up a smoke.

I can't tell whether it's just a cig or something stronger. Hope it's weed. I'll get a better jump on him if he's out of it, and I need every advantage when it's three-to-one.

I'd kill for John's army chops right about now.

My fists tighten when he comes close enough to hear his voice. His smoke stinks like reefer, and he slows, clutching an overstuffed backpack slung around his shoulder. "...So the bitch pulls up her panties, gives me a look like I just kicked her dog, and asks me if I want to stay for dinner. Like, just sit down with her fucking family and pretend I'm not the jackass who just had his dick down her throat."

"No way!" his friend Reed says, doubling over with laughter. "Is she stupid? I thought you liked them fucking smarter than that."

"Hold it, I'm not done. Brains and pussy never mixed anyway. So, I smile, pull her in close, make her think I might be ready for a girlfriend instead of a hot hole to fill. Leave her in suspense for, oh, sixty seconds before I smack her across the forehead. Hard as I can." He pauses, grinning like he's accomplished something great, the two wing-men dipshits at his side laughing like hyenas.

"She goes off real predictable, spitting my name, asking

what the fuck. I throw her against the wall, push up that skirt, and dry hump some sense back into the cunt. She's too fuckin' dazed to even cry when I tell her she's out of her mind. Doesn't say shit when I remind her I've got my dick where it is because we know what a huge whore she is. All she'll ever stay."

"Ha ha, wow, man, where's the punchline?" Other kid in leather – Mike, I think – tries to force a smile, unable to override his inner cringe.

"Huh? You think this is a joke? I'm making a fucking point. You two wanna start getting your dicks wet, then start treating them with the same respect I do. My old man talks to a lot of assholes in finance, and they've got a good term: pump and dump. That's what you do. Drain your snake and leave them doe-eyed, always ready to bust their lip if they give you any."

Fuck listening to a second more of this. As soon as Scourge and his boys are past, just a few steps up the hill, it's time. I leap out, swinging a heavy branch I found in the brush.

"What the fuck!" The trio screams in unison.

I smash the pack leader across his shoulders, giving me the only three second opening I'll get. He goes down hard, that heavy looking black bag on him helping gravity. It snags on a couple rocks, and there's a ripping sound.

It's the look in his evil eyes that surprises me. Not rage, like I expected, but fear.

I don't know what to do with that. This isn't what I planned for, and there is no backup. So, I do the only thing

I can: push the sharp stick close to his face and stare down his cohorts, circling me like wolves. "Don't. You hit me, he gets it right through the eye. I'm not fucking around here, boys."

"Randolph," Scourge growls, recovering the same foul, fuck everybody look he always wears. "You even think about moving that thing another inch, I'll feed you your own balls. Back the fuck *off.*"

"No. Not before you tell me why Maddie went home in tears. I know you had a lot to do with it. Told you before, asshole; you mess with her, you get me."

He sits up, slumping against his bag. I can't tell what he's protecting, and honestly I could care less.

I just want an answer to my fucking question, before I'm forced to do something we'll regret.

I'm not a violent person. Never once thought of running off to Uncle Sam to play hero like my big brother, but we share the same blood. I can fight. Instinct understands how to do serious damage.

"Randolph –"

"Shut the fuck up! Just answer." I'm still trying, and I don't know why. The look on his face tells me it'll just be more crap out of his mouth.

"No need, asshole," he whispers. His hand goes for the lump in his pocket. It's probably the switch blade I've seen him with before, carving swastikas and nasty phrases into the desks and benches when he thinks no one's looking. He still thinks its funny to etch teacher's phone numbers into the walls, asking for 'a good time,' even though he's done it dozens of times. "You already know what's up, or you wouldn't be out here with a death wish."

His arm drops behind him, tugging on the bag, yanking the torn strap over his shoulder again. I motion to the bag for a split second with my stick. "What're you hiding, Alex?"

"Like you don't fucking know. Cut the shit, Randolph. You're making a huge mistake, getting in the middle. Can't believe you'd stick your dick out for that little nerd, and practically ask me to slice it off."

I can't stop him. He lurches to his feet, rather than drawing his knife. I fell for a feint. The assholes behind him shake off their daze, ready to hit me with everything they've got, as soon as Scourge says the word.

It's three on one, and I'm as ready as I'll ever be.

I swallow the nervous lump in my throat. *Whatever it takes.*

I'll suffer broken bones if it gets them suspended again, keeps them away from Maddie.

"Wait." He throws out his arms, blocking his friends before they make any moves, a poison smirk on his lips. "We don't need to settle this today. Not here. You don't want to jack my stash. I'm not the one you're dealing with, Randolph, if you're that fucking stupid. You squeal to the cops, you're settling score with every asshole West of Spokane who's counting on his fix."

This restraint from him is new. I hate it. He's gotten into countless fistfights over the years, ever since he was old enough to wear leather and chains, demolishing anybody who got in his way.

It's a classic standoff. The four of us are frozen, leering, adrenaline in the air so thick it burns my nostrils.

I know it's drugs, and he doesn't want to risk losing them. He knows they can break every bone in my body with three on one, but they'll pay a heavy price if I stab that black bag, or send somebody to the ER with contraband on them.

"Come on, guys. Leave this shithead to his last day on earth. Let it sink in how fucked he is before we've lightened our load, and we come back to deal with him." He should be laughing as he shoots me one more vicious look, turns, and starts heading up the hill with his boys at his side. Mike and Reed keep looking back, shaking their heads and grinning, like they're in on the big dirty secret I still don't fully understand.

A lot still doesn't make sense. What does that crap in the bag have to do with torturing Maddie?

I stand there like a fool for the next five minutes, watching their black jeep rumble out of the parking lot, trying to figure out what the hell I've gotten into.

Whatever it is, it's bad. Something I ought to go to the police about, before Maddie gets the chance, and puts a permanent target on her back.

Knocking him flat with that stick wasn't my biggest mistake.

It's hesitating.

I think I've bought more time. Another twenty-four hours, maybe. At least a good night's sleep to figure out what I'll say, before I skip over Principal Ross the coward, and go straight to the Seattle PD.

Trouble with assumptions is, they're worthless when they're wrong. Worse, they're fatal.

I never thought he'd strike back the very next day.

Just like I never thought he'd really skip over me, and go straight for her.

Present Day

Dad isn't answering my phone calls, and I can't get his nurse on the line either. I pull through the gate and head to the service entrance, which is always unlocked this time of day.

There's nobody upstairs to greet me when I reach his room, nudge the door open, and peer through the darkness.

What I see…it's a fucking mess.

There's a puddle on the floor. It's pooling underneath his withered hand hanging limply off the bed, something sticky, thick, and red. Then I notice his IV tubes. They're detached from his arm, adding their chemical drip to the floor's mess, the only sound breaking the eerie silence.

Holy shit.

Throwing the door open, I rush in, expecting him to be colder than deli meat when I finally get my hands on his shoulders, shaking him.

Wake up, wake up, please wake the fuck up!

It can't end like this.

He's warmer than I expect. His eyelids ripple, and a second later, they're wide open, bulging from his head. "No, no – stop! Let me die, you stupid ingrate!"

"Why won't you ever give me a chance?" It comes out explosive. I'm frustrated, angry, and yeah, a little scared shitless.

He ignores me as I stand up, furiously paging his nurse with the call button. It takes me a few seconds to figure out he's ripped out the wire connecting his intercom and vitals to the house. I whip out my cell phone.

"Yeah, Esther? Get up here. He's in trouble."

He sighs and rolls over, grunting in pain.

She's there almost instantly. I sit in the corner fuming while I watch her check his vitals. She reassures me there's no critical damage – no more than there should be for a dying man in his state. She fixes his IVs, straps everything carefully into place, and refills his morphine.

I'm trying to distract myself from the latest humiliation he's inflicted, searching the room. That's when I notice the messy stack of papers near his desk. Several have spilled over onto the floor, as if he's carelessly tossed them aside. Collecting the fallen papers in my hands, I stop and stare when I see the letter head.

Stefan Turnbladt, Partner, Randolph-Emerson-Turnbladt. It's too much to resist.

My eyes scan the note frantically. It's Stefan's elegant style, all right. The phrases my eyes pick out roil my blood.

A delightful dinner with your son and the future Mrs. Randolph...

It's been so long, Thomas...

Clearly, it isn't my place to say what the nature of your relationship should be. However, he's proven himself to this firm. Time and time again, he's proven himself to me.

Finally, I hit the end, bringing a wicked smile to my face. *Many on the board agree. I'm saying this as your colleague, and your friend. I can't reasonably assure we'll maintain Calvin's permanent divestment as agreed, and you have every right to know which way the wind is blowing. It's my duty as a friend and a business partner.*

Please, Thomas, before it's too late. Take one last look into your heart.

"You understand now?" dad says, watching me like a lizard from the bed. I look up just in time to see Esther shut the door behind her.

Suppressing my smile, I walk over to the bed, and take the familiar chair next to him. "Understand what, exactly? Offing yourself because you're not able to hold me hostage anymore makes you want to die?"

He doesn't answer. Just stares dead ahead, through the stack of letters I've gathered neatly on his desk. "I knew the risk this would happen, boy. The world never listens to dead men very long. You're too hard working...too god damned much like him..."

He can't mean John. But who else?

Fuck.

When it hits me, I get why he's avoiding me, eyes fixed on every infinity except the confused son next to him. "Why are you still here? You read the letter, Calvin. There's two more like it from others on the board. You'll get what you've always wanted when I'm gone, one way or another. Full partner, full stake, full responsibility. Congratulations."

It's too easy. I'm aware I should just shut up and accept the break life just handed out. It's not enough to stop the thoughts swirling violently in my head, going places I never imagined.

"I don't want it to go down like this. It's not too late to sort our crap out, to let go of bad blood." *To treat me like your son.* I keep that last line to myself.

"Pretend it never happened, you mean?" He snorts, turning toward me, skin stretched so thin on his face it's like paper. "Why should I waste more of my very limited time on the same thing I've tried to do every day since you shot my life to pieces?"

"Because maybe you'll stop handing out blame, and fucking deal," My hand grips the chair's arm. My fingers ache. I'm losing my patience. "Maybe it's not too late to see something different."

"Something for you, yes." It's disturbing how sharp and cruel his wit remains, imprisoned in his decaying body. "You always were a selfish little brat. I'm just sorry I didn't see it sooner, before you went to the schoolyard that day and –"

"Don't say it." I stand, sighing between my teeth, wondering why I'm wasting my time.

"No? And here I thought you wanted to trot down memory lane, and remember why I'll go to my grave hating everything like it was yesterday. Every stupid, impulsive thing you did, Calvin. Every way you tore the heart out of this family, and put a hole through your own mother's heart."

There's no reaching him.

He's right. If the board is leaning toward exoneration, giving me a proper stake in the firm after he's gone, I've won what I always wanted.

I don't need anything else.

Not even deathbed approval from my bitter dick of a father.

"I'm not the one who cheated on mom, chasing pussy and booze like it was water after John's death," I remind him. "Hell, I just *destroyed* the biggest bad habit I got from you, dad. Threw my black book with all the skirt I've chased into the Sound. Don't need that shit anymore. I love my fiancée. Long as I've got Maddie, there's no fucking way I'll ever need to look anywhere else. Sure, we're bound to take our punches because life is never roses. I swear, I'll handle them better than you."

His old knuckles go bone white when he presses his hands into the mattress, lifting himself up. I know the impotent fury on his face doesn't mean shit. It's the same look he's given me since he wound up in this bed, shedding weight and losing his mortal rancor, unable to project the cold-hearted tyrant he used to be.

He's lost his guilt-tripping power, too. He can't fucking stand it.

"Wait until you lose a son. *Two,* I should say, because the day you went out and became a murderer is the day I wrote you off forever. You've won your second chance from this world, Calvin, but you won't convince me. Never. Don't care if you get on your knees and recite sonnets to that stupid, flippant girl you frittered your life away for. Her love can't erase it. Now, get the hell out."

I stand my ground, unable to resist baring my teeth. "Call her stupid, flippant, or any wicked word again, and it'll be the last you see of me, asshole. Forever."

"Christ, *now* you tell me! If I'd known I just needed to insult your little urchin bride, I'd have done it to her face when she was here."

It's hard as hell to turn my back, march out, and slam the door on its hinges so hard it shakes the whole floor.

There's no other choice. I have to go.

If I spend another second staring at the devilish, hateful smile on his lips, I'd lose it. And then I might do something worse than the violent mistake that nearly cost me everything.

An hour later, I'm on the balcony with the last woman who'll ever matter. Wine in her hand, scotch in mine, my second of the evening.

"Just tell me one thing, Cal," she says, coming up behind me, wrapping her soft arms around my chest. "Was he always like this? Or did it just pick up after...you know."

I take a long pull from my drink before I answer. "Bastard was never perfect. You remember Principal Ross? How he pretended to be a paragon of virtue, while underneath he was a power-grubbing shit who let Scourge terrorize half the school?"

She nods. "How could I forget?"

"Same kind of asshole, my dad. We were trophies. Me and my brother both. Accessories to ambition, the same as mom. John gave him his hero, his upstanding citizen prize in flesh and blood, until bro went and got himself killed." I stare through the icy silence, the empathy in her eyes I didn't ask for. "I was his brains. He wanted me to go off to Stanford or MIT and make him proud. Put the summers of Calc, computer science, and field trips to Silicon Valley he paid for to good use. I was supposed to make RET the toughest firm on the coast, and double our billions."

"I'm sorry," she whispers, folding her hands tighter. With a sigh, I put my hands on hers, turn her around, and lock eyes. I love the heat in her skin, adore the sheen in her jet black hair. I'll never have enough.

"Why're we still talking about this doll? Long story short, he's been the same asshole to me in life he always was, and he'll die like one, too. What more do you want?"

"I don't know. I'm not a psychologist," she admits, shrugging in my arms. "Still, if we could just get to the root of his blame, his hate, maybe it'd be different. Maybe we could change him, before it's too late."

"We're too late now," I snap. "Look, I remember what it was like when John died. He barely tolerated me hanging around the house after I came home from juvy. When the soldiers showed up on our doorstep one evening with a letter from the President, I was already lower than dogshit. Taking blame for everything. I'll never forget it. Mom locked herself away, wailing herself hoarse for the next week. She couldn't even thank anyone at the funeral for coming, too sick to talk. Wasn't more than six months later before she died in her sleep."

"God, I can't imagine." Maddie presses her cheek into my chest, running her hand up my neck, gingerly massaging her fingers into my skin.

"You don't have to. I don't regret anything. Not the things I did, or the bullshit tragedies out of my hands, stacked on top of each other. I'd do my part the same, if I had a chance to do it all again." My thumb traces her jawline, skidding across her soft skin to her temple. I wait for her to look at me. "It led me to you, doll. For better or worse, through heaven and hell, even the days when I hit the gym after work, found the nearest punching bag, and beat my hands raw. It finally makes sense. It's not in vain. This is it, everything it was always meant to be."

I reach out my other hand to hers, clasp her ring finger, and run my hand along the huge rock clutched in gold. Swear it looks more beautiful every day it's on her. Before her, I never gave two thoughts to jewelry.

Now, when I see it, it's one more slice of everything wrong turned right.

"I love you, Cal," she whispers, folding into me, lacing her fingers through mine.

"Love you, doll. Always have, always will." I grip them like mad while we kiss. It's a long, slow, delicious dance of the lips. The kind I could never appreciate with anybody else, not since the first one we ever had at Chelle's party. I searched for it again and again when I thought I'd lost her. No girl ever came close.

They were hollow shells. Imitations. Ghosts.

This is authentic. It's a raw, exquisite storm we've barely begun exploring. I'm impatient as ever to find its beginning and end in all the years ahead.

Impatient as fuck to feel her hand on my face, brushing her warm gold ring of forever across my stubble. And it'll look even better when she's finally my wife, when she's carrying my kid, when the finger its wrapped around is older than sin.

Her lips drift off mine, only to return with a moan. I push my tongue to hers, taking what's mine, what's made everything I've suffered worth it. We melt into each other, and I'm about to haul her over my shoulder to bed when there's a noise I can't place.

I pull my lips off hers, looking to the distant ground below, wondering if some asshole's blown a tire on the city street next to my building.

No, it's the door. Someone's knocking. Pounding like a maniac at eight o'clock on a Sunday.

"You'd better get that," Maddie says nervously.

Whatever this is, it can't be good. She stays behind me as I head for the door, tearing it open. I never bother looking through the privacy hole. There's a better chance getting killed by a bad cup of coffee in this place than any of the well compensated security in the lobby letting anyone dangerous in.

"Spence?" I don't know why he's here, but he almost knocks me over in his rush to get in. "What the hell's happening?"

"Trouble. Cade had to fly out to New York this evening, like you know already, but he gave me this before he left." My friend shoves a manila folder into my hand, thick with papers. "Somebody's got it out for you, Cal. They're sending a message to Anders and Long. Started fucking around ever since your engagement hit the local news."

Shit. It hangs on my lips as I page through the bomb he's dropped on me.

They're documents sent over by the two members of the board, ever since Cade told them he'd get to the bottom of it. I see an impound notice for Mr. Long's yacht, something about the city claiming back dues on registry taxes he's always paid. The man is a boy scout, I know he'd never skimp on bills. Then the handwritten note from Mrs. Anders, describing the arson threats against her favorite church in Bavaria, the place she's supported for years with generous funds for restoration and maintenance.

"Who?" I say, wracking my brain. I'm afraid I already know the answer.

"One guess." He stops and stares awkwardly, noticing Maddie behind us. She's listening intently from the sofa.

I'm even more pissed than before, wondering if it'll ever end. No matter how far we come, it seems my past is destined to always find us, poisoning our moments big and small.

"I'll look at it tonight. Do some homework," I say, pressing the folder under my arm. "Are there hitmen, too, or what?"

Spence does a double-take, snorting under his breath.

"You joking, Cal? Because I'm not. Neither is Cade. The asshole behind this is way too careful for that."

Of course. And I've also decided he isn't stealing a minute more of my time with Maddie.

This hell already cost us seven years.

"I know," I say, pounding him on the back as I lead him to the door. "Give me a chance. I'll jump on it, but not tonight. Too busy spending quality time with my woman. See you at the wedding in a couple weeks."

"A couple weeks?!" He does a double take, grabbing my collar, pulling me into the hallway. "Holy shit. You're serious, aren't you?"

"Duh. Always was, but the time table's changed. I want us married before Labor Day, and I've got a lot of work to make that happen."

"Cal, I...Christ. I thought this was just a game to get your old man to let his guard down, or pull the right votes on the board. You know you've won, right? You're in, future partner, long as we don't let dirty laundry from a long time ago trip up the old farts with voting rights."

"Good luck. It's not going away unless we make it. He's waited to skewer me for years, Spence. Never got over what happened on the pavement at Maynard. He sees his chance. I'd do it, too, in his shoes. What better time to make a man's life a living hell than when it's finally worth living?"

"So you *want* to marry her? You're serious?" I want to wipe the disbelieving smile off his face. "Whatever, man. Congratulations I guess."

"Fuck you. Looks like you just came from a morgue.

Don't know if I ought to bother keeping you on the shortlist for best man."

"Hey, hey, hey!" Spence slams his hand into my shoulder, digging his fingers in. We lock eyes, and the skepticism in his face melts. "Don't do anything you'll regret. It's just, a couple weeks? Fuck, that's fast. You hadn't even seen her since the ugly times up until recently, yeah?"

I nod. "Yeah. I'm doing this, Spence, and I don't need anybody's approval. She's it. The only one. She always was."

"It's not a total shock. Hard to forget how you went after her before things got shitty. That time you hid her Euro history book in your bag, just to whip it out and look like a big hero when she was about to lose it in front of Mr. Gregorson…"

Does he have to remind me?

Obviously, I've had it bad forever for this girl. Played a dozen stupid tricks when I was just a horny, clueless little shit. Hard to believe she's mine at last. This time, without the hijinks.

Nothing, and I mean *nothing*, is ever taking that away.

I throw his hand off me. He stops laughing. "Save the good times for the toast at the reception, dick. Let me handle the rest. It's *my* wedding coming up, and I've got more incentive than anyone. Whenever you see Cade again, tell him not to worry. It'll be a load off his mind while he's on his mystery girl, whoever the fuck she is. Boy's starting to act as nuts as you, to be honest."

We share a smile. Mine, a little more knowing. Cade's bullshit cover story, going to New York on "business," doesn't seem half bad stacked against me knowing, beyond all reasonable doubt, that I've taken the last cherry I'll ever need to in my life.

"Fine. He'll be happy, I'm sure. But listen, before you make any moves, call us. We aren't leaving you to face this shit alone again. If we'd been there years ago, it could've been a hell of a lot different."

"Who knows." I'm too stuck on the future to replay the past a thousand different times. "Goodnight, Spence. Shake your ass. It's getting wet out there, and you never bring an umbrella."

We bump fists before he turns, straightening his collar. I watch him head for the elevator, leaning on the wall.

Where the fuck would I be without my friends?

Nowhere good. A man needs his blood brothers.

"Cal?" Maddie pokes her head out the door. "What's going on? Is everything okay?"

Tightening my hold on the folder tucked under my arm, I flash her a look, creasing my brow. "Nothing you ought to worry about, doll. Remind me where we left off."

I lead her inside with a kiss, careful to slip the folder behind me on the end table. What's in there is *my* problem. Not hers.

We're here together, after all these years, because I'm used to saving her. This is no different. No scheming fuckery gets to derail our wedding. Not when I've come so close to the future we're meant for, I can taste it, every time I take her lips, her tongue, press her face against me while her moans caress my ears.

We kiss, we suck, we lick until she can't help it. Love how she grinds against me. My face is on her throat, dipping into her cleavage, nipple rolled between my fingertips, when she stands up straight. "I need you," she whispers, giving my hand a vigorous tug.

We're only a few steps toward the bedroom when I change course. Forget the bed, it won't do for the fire burning me alive.

It's dark, rainy, and beautiful outside. I think this woman, this light, could make me a king anywhere when she's under me. Can't wait to prove myself right.

"Really? Here?" She questions the lust in my eyes, but there's no stopping it. Before she makes another sound, we're outside in the pouring rain, tearing off each other's clothes.

I help guide her into the recliner under the huge canopy. Peeling her top off, I free her breasts, crushing her softness through my fingertips, grunting when I see her swollen nipples bloom between my fingers.

They beg for my mouth. I surround them with my teeth, digging raw need into her while her hand goes to my cock, stroking it harder through my boxers. We pass the next few minutes in animal rapture, alive with anticipation, with want, with a glassy, sexual silence where our hearts become one with the rain beating down around us.

It's drumming enters my blood. I've never had my cock so roused in my life.

"You're fucking soaked for me, aren't you?" It shouldn't be a question.

Her breath catches in her throat when I smooth my hand between her legs, caressing her belly, thinking how I'll make it swell when I've planted my seed in her. I'll knock this woman up, one fine day, and then I'll be whole.

My fingers dip into her panties, pull her lips apart, feeling the wild heat inside her. Fuck yes, she's wet. She's ready.

I can't wait to bury every seething inch I've got in her pink.

We collide, and she grinds harder. Her mouth pulls to mine again and again, hungrier than ever, and I counter, attacking her tongue like it's the last kiss I've been waiting for.

Maddie whimpers in my mouth. I squeeze her ass harder with my free hand, pushing my thumb into her clit. Sweeping circles bring her off.

My cock hammers me blind, deaf, and dumb when she hitches, seizing up, coming on my fingers.

Growling, I push them in deeper, fucking her legs apart while my hand finds that spot inside her, owns it, and drowns her lace in a wetness that has nothing to do with the rain splashing down around us.

"Need you, doll. Right fucking now." It's all I'm able to get out when her high dissipates and I see her eyelids flutter open.

Then it's my hands' turn to do the talking. They lift her up, pry her panties away, and lower my boxers. She lays against me, serenading me with hot breath, while I reach for my wallet on the ground to get a condom.

"No." Her hand covers mine, and we lock eyes. "Cal, I'm on the pill. I want you to…"

The rosy blush on her cheeks needs no words. My cock jerks hard against her pussy, oozing on the trim strip of hair she keeps.

Bare? Sweet fuck.

Having her without the latex unchains the animal heat inside me already hanging by a thread. My eyes drill into hers while I take her hips, shove her legs apart, and lower her onto my bare cock for the first time.

"Goddamn! That's it, doll. There." The words are thunder in my throat when her heat surrounds me, drenching my cock in need.

Her whimper becomes a moan. I'm hellbent on turning the next few to screams as my hips push against hers. Rutting, working, fucking our way to the sunny calm this city's missing with its endless rain.

Maddie's cries turn shallow, shriller each time I thrust up in her. She glides against me like a piece of sky made for my rugged landscape. We tear our pleasure from the naked air, our steaming skin, every muscle in our bodies looking for fiery release.

"God, Cal!" she whimpers, right before I bring her over the edge again.

"Come for me!" I growl, grinding myself into her, the friction on my pubic bone ruling her little clit. "Come for the only cock you're meant for, woman. Only one that ever wanted to be in you, first and last you'll ever fuck. Just come, just come, just fucking come…"

Just come.

It echoes in my head, swift and relentless as the rain, picking up its tempo. It's like the sky is jealous, finding its release in the mysterious, lunatic fire arching her back and sweeping its fire in my balls.

Just come.

I can't fucking hold it. Not even for my fortune, my life, my soul. Seven years dreaming about having her bareback, hurling my seed inside her, are an unrelenting bitch when they catch up, grab me by the balls, and ignite the fuse at the base of my spine.

"Fuck, Maddie!" I'm afraid my hands hurt her when they dig into her ass, pulling her to me, fusing her like vices while the dynamite at the end of my cock explodes.

But there's only euphoria in her scream when she feels me, joining halfway through her O.

I let go, eyes rolling, shooting off in the most exquisite pussy I'll ever have.

There's fire in my spine, stars in my eyes, hot white shadows everywhere. Even the rain streaks like meteors as my eyes twitch, sockets surrounding them as electric as my spine. Every fucking bone in my body burns. There's nothing containing the furnace I've become with her except the *thud-thud-thud* of my own heart.

My cock thrusts balls deep. I unload like the speechless fuck I've become, grinding my teeth, surrendering to her greedy pussy pulling every drop from me.

I don't know how many times she comes. It's an eternity in the space of a few minutes as our bodies pulse together, slaves to the delight, the dark, and the primal.

Lucky me. I'm no stranger to darkness when it comes to this woman I want to keep forever.

I give myself over to it with a groan.

Her head rests on my shoulder when it's over. I'm still in her, holding my cock there like an animal in rut, so aroused I'm not sure I'll even lose my hardness and need my usual ninety seconds to rest before I take her again.

"Kiss me," I order, gently pushing her face to mine. My thumb rests on her cheek, and when I see those dark eyes of hers open, they're more beautiful than the most pristine Rainier sunrise.

It's getting darker. Colder. Wet to the point where it'd chill the bone, if we hadn't been so damned busy making our own heat.

"I love you, Cal," she whispers, before offering her lips to mine.

"Not like I love you," I say, pressing my forehead to hers, losing my sanity for the millionth time in those soft brown eyes. I reach for her hand, find the ring she's wearing, and run my thumb over the diamond until it hurts my skin. "But you will, doll. When all this is over, and we've got our wedding bands to join this thing, you'll know my madness. We'll love so fucking hard those years apart will seem like seconds. We'll go through three mattresses a year making up for what's lost."

"I don't care," she says, laughing, a wicked energy seizing her. "I just want you. Now and for the rest of my life."

Her mouth turns from angel to demon on mine when we kiss.

I take it long and hard, dipping her tongue into mine until I get a moan. My cock swells to full mast. She sighs, a smile surfacing underneath her kiss as I take her sweet cunt for the second time without pulling out.

Two down. Only a thousand more times to go before I'll consider letting up, and only fucking her to sleep a couple times some nights rather than to the brink of full collapse.

Later, when I'm drifting off next to her, letting my poor balls replenish themselves, I can't stop thinking how we got here.

I don't like dwelling on tragedy. That goes double when it still won't keep sticking its teeth into our life.

Maybe that's why I dream about the day it went to hell, and exiled me from paradise for seven evil years.

Almost Seven Years Ago

We're barely at Maynard through first period when the announcement comes over the speaker.

"Ladies and gentleman, this is Principal Ross speaking. Please ensure all students are evacuated through the fire escapes in a quick and orderly fashion. We've received a threat concerning an explosive device hidden somewhere in the building. While we believe this is a bluff, police and firefighters have been dispatched. All staff should follow the usual precautions."

"A bomb? Is he fucking serious?" Cade is the first one out of his seat. We're both slow to meld into the panicked throng of students flowing down the hall. Half look scared out of their wits. The others can't stop laughing, elbowing each other over the absurd notion anyone would want to blow this place up.

"So much for practice after school. Just our fucking luck." Spence crashes into my shoulder, looking deflated.

"Dude, Tina's about as easy as your mom. She'll still be wet for you next week. Relax." I wink at him, watching the fury clouding my friend's face before his fist smashes into my shoulder.

He's had his eye on the cheerleader since I brushed her off. The whole lacrosse team thinks I'm insane, dumping her before we were even official to pursue my crush on doll.

"Not half as big a slut as yours, Randolph," Spence snarls back. "You're lucky I respect your bro too much not to make a move. Between you and the old man being gone, she's home alone all day, just begging for every inch of the Spence Special…"

My turn to get pissed. He's in a headlock when we're stumbling outside, and all three of us crash outside together, clearing a path through our peers.

Cade thinks it's hilarious. He's laughing his beard off, a scruffy mess on his face like every boy who hits eighteen and gives it his first go growing hair on the chin. Somehow, it still gets him laid.

"Holy shit, look!" Cade's laughter dies in an instant and we stop screwing around as soon as we see the scene.

It's chaos. Police, SWAT vans, more firefighters than I've ever seen in one place. A few serious looking dudes in body armor who could probably give John a contest push their way through us, rushing inside, heavy weapons swaying on their backs.

I look for Maddie when we finally reach the curb, but I can't find her. Pisses me off.

I know Principal Ross is probably right. This whole thing will turn out to be someone's sick joke, but there's always that two second doubt making me wonder what happens if it's real.

What if something explodes inside our school, and the girl I'm losing it for doesn't make it out?

Teachers herd roughly three hundred pupils by the fences like sheep dogs, doing headcounts. I bite my cheek, arms folded, waiting impatiently for Gregorson to mark me present.

If I stare hard at the building several yards away, I can see some commotion happening through the big windows by the lockers. Cops are swarming, their dogs sniffing all over the place. I see several big men pull open lockers, throwing the contents on the ground, before more guys crowd around and I'm not able to make out anything.

A few more minutes tick by. Then I see the sight that makes my heart drop into my fucking guts.

Maddie, in her yellow sweater. Being led outside in handcuffs, stuffed into one of the waiting squad cars. Too stunned to wipe the tears rolling down her cheeks, even if they let her.

It's awhile longer before Ross appears at the front of the school, waves to the teachers around him, and we're all led inside. Cade notices I'm lagging behind everybody else first. "Hey, man, where're you going?"

"Ross," I say, going straight for the Principal's office. I don't care what Gregorson or anyone else thinks about the absence. He'll probably be in too big a huff to blow through his lesson to notice.

I don't know what the fuck's happening. I just know it's horrible, it can't be what it looks like, and the only ones missing before I noticed Maddie gone were Scourge and his idiots.

It's them, trying to land a kill shot.

I have to help her.

It takes forever to find out what's going on. I hear the receptionists talking it over while I wait almost an hour to see Ross.

"Oh my God. That poor girl. She must be sick in the head!"

"She wasn't cut out for this place anyway. I saw the financials, and her family...well, let's just say her father's a dock worker. They don't even clear sixty-thousand a year combined. She's smart, but she's clearly got problems. Poor thing."

I grip the armrests in the chair so hard they could snap.

That's the kind of shit I have to listen to, trying to decipher the useful bits, everything I hear about what went down near the lockers.

They all believe it's Maddie turned Unabomber. Say it was a young woman who called in the bomb threat. Didn't take the dogs long to find a stash of fireworks in her locker big enough for several Fourth of July barbecues.

I don't know how the fuck this happened, but I'm certain who's really behind it. Just can't decide who I want to strangle more: Scourge, or whatever soulless bitch he put up to calling in the threat.

"Calvin? Let's go," Ross sticks his head out, ushering me into his office. When we're both seated, he looks at me, fidgeting with the worn mouse pad in front of his desk. "I understand you've got some information about the threat today?"

"Yeah, you're holding the wrong girl," I tell him, refusing to hesitate on a single word.

The rest…well, it's harder. Especially when he gives me a skeptical look, leaning in his chair, folding his arms.

It's like he knows I want to throw Scourge under the bus. We both know there's no proof, as much as we also know there's a zero percent chance he'll ever expel the bastard.

Not while Alex Palkovich Senior controls the strings to his school board election next year.

"I don't have time for games," he warns me. "Who?"

"Me." I watch his jaw fall while I clear my throat. First thing's first – I have to get her free. Every second she spends at the police station, scared out of her wits, is too much for my fucked up heart to handle. "It was me, Principal. A prank. A really bad one. I didn't know it'd cause this much trouble…"

"Young man, you're in *very* serious trouble if what you're telling me is true. You do realize I have to report to the local authorities, possibly the FBI, right?"

Nodding, I never break eye contact, not even while he rubs his eyes. He's in disbelief, and honestly, so am I. But I never think twice when I let the rest out. "I put her up to it. Recorded her reading a silly little skit we came up with for German. She never knew the real purpose. Then I made the call from the bus station down the street, played her saying the words right off my phone."

"Jesus, Calvin. Why?"

"It's a stupid crush, sir. She wouldn't go to the dance with me a few months back. Obviously, I fucked up here and –"

"Language," he snaps, releasing a heavy sigh before he picks up the phone on his desk. "Jesus. I need to give your mother a courtesy call. It's the least I can do before you're taken in. It's the Seattle PD you'll have to deal with next."

"Wait, Principal. Maddie doesn't deserve this. Call the police first, and tell them to let her go. I swear, I'll confess to everything. *Please.*"

He twists his lips sourly, considering my request. I hold my breath until he dials, paces the room, and speaks into the receiver. "Hello, this is Harry Ross at Maynard

Academy. Yes, it's about Madeline Middleton, I've come across new information suggesting she isn't the prime suspect. Yes, yes, I *do* have a confession…"

XI: Once Upon a Tragedy (Maddie)

He takes me out for breakfast the next morning. It's another scrumptious spread like the one I've gotten used to, all the decadence and fewer of the carbs than I'd gotten used to with Beijing's street food.

I bite into a savory dish with fried chicken, waffles, and scallops glazed with a savory sauce. Sounds weird, tastes amazing.

But breakfast isn't half as incredible as the man with his arm in mine, sipping his black coffee while he looks over the stock summary on his phone.

"You know, I really thought I was done the day the bomb threat happened. My whole future would've gone up in smoke if you hadn't stepped in."

He slams his phone down on the table and gives me a hard look, softening it a second later with a smile. "Doll, I had to. I knew who did it. I wasn't going to sit by and let him screw you over because you saw his junkie cargo."

Remembering the big black bag busting at the seams

with packed cocaine still makes my heart pound after all these years. They never did find it, when all was said and done.

"I never understood how you talked your way out of it." I say, sipping my honey infused tea. It's comforting heat does little to soothe my curiosity. "When they first pulled me in, they wanted to keep me there without bail. It's funny, I didn't even think about jail. Who knows if it would've went that far…all I could imagine was how upset mom and daddy would be. Oh, and the stupid smile Kat would probably wear forever, becoming the family favorite."

I regret the last part as soon as it's out. How insensitive. The imaginary flip that never happened on my end is exactly what's put him under the gun with his father, ever since he was demoted for his hero brother.

"Sorry," I whisper, pulling away from him to stab into my breakfast again. I chew quietly, and feel his hand on mine a second later.

"Stop apologizing. What's done isn't our problem anymore." The calm in his voice surprises me. Normally, when we've talked about this before, he tries to shut me up, or push the subject aside as quickly as he can. Now, it's like there's a healthy acceptance, and the only reason we're still talking about it is to figure out how we want to define our future. "Principal Ross never would've thrown the book at me. No, I wasn't a political favorite like Scourge, but you forget the connections my parents had. My old man shit when he came to the police station. He got me out fast, though. They were never going to hold me like they did you. Got off with a stern talking to, a week long suspension, and a blemish on my perfect record when I missed the next game."

I try not to let the jealousy gnaw too deeply in my stomach. We both know full well what happened next.

"You didn't talk to me for days after you came back," I say, looking at him over the top of my tea cup.

"Couldn't. I was too pissed off and confused. Didn't want you staying a target until I figured out how I'd handle him." He snatches up his phone and starts sorting today's trades and prices, staring intently at the screen.

"Cal." I wait for him to look at me. "I just don't want anything like it *ever* happening again. If there's something going on, something for us to worry about, you'll tell me...won't you?"

He's silent for a moment. "Yeah, I will. Just not while we've got a wedding to plan. Excuse me," he adds, sliding out of the seat, heading for the men's room.

It's been magic the last week, ever since he brought me home from my parents' house, and made it clear the ring on my hand means something. I'm scared this can't last. It's too good. The last time he hid the truth, the results were horrific.

I want to believe it's kosher. Safe. On track for everything we were always meant for.

Want to believe it so badly, it's hard to confront him. I don't want to say anything before the wedding, nothing that threatens to ruin what's bound to be the happiest day of my life.

But what if he's doing it again? Avoiding me the way he did before his last mistake ripped us apart for years?

I can't stop thinking about it.

I remember the worst day of our lives like it was yesterday. It's been crystal clear in my head ever since I walked into his office, signed my name to the engagement contract, and let nature take its course all these weeks.

It makes me worry.

What if our paper love is paper thin?

Almost Seven Years Ago

No one ever thawed to him after he came back to school. Cal's one week absence was more like a decade. I noticed the change right away, how everyone kept their heads down when he came in, and sat in our history class. To everyone at Maynard except his two best friends, he'd become tainted.

Cade whispered a few words to his friend in a hurried tone. Cal barely responded.

I couldn't make out much, except the words that pricked my ears like needles. They quashed my urge to run up to him after class, throw my arms around him, and thank him for doing what he did – an act of brutal kindness I'm not sure I'll ever understand.

"He's a dead man, Cade. Scourge can't walk for this. First chance I get my hands on that motherfucker, I'll kill him."

I was with Chelle and Emily in the cafeteria a couple days later when I saw it.

Cal, Spence, and Cade passing Scourge and his posse, their eyes locked like two lion prides spying each other across the savannah. My eyes aren't the only ones on the boys. My friends go eerily silent, and the whole world comes to a halt, especially after Cal makes the first move.

We see Scourge on his feet, leering at his rival, his usual dead-eyed cruelty more smug than ever. Seconds later, he's off his feet, pinned to the wall. Cal's hands shake, pressing into the bully's collar, his fingers in a superhuman grip on the leather jacket.

"Not here. Not here, idiots," Scourge keeps saying. I realize he's talking to his guys, but I don't know why. It seems like a major blowup that will get Cal in even deeper crap, in front of everyone, should be exactly what he wants. "You want this bad, huh, Randolph?"

"You fucking know I do," Cal snarls, spit flying in a mist from his lips.

"God, I can't believe he's not punching back," Chelle says, leaning to us.

I can't believe it either. There's a terrible hole where my stomach used to be, filled with the bad that's certain to come from what's brewing.

"Track field. Three o'clock. You and me." Scourge smiles, his eyes more black and evil than I've ever seen them. "No weapons, numbnuts. Keep it fair."

"You're on, fuckhole. I've been waiting for this." A second later, Cal releases the prick. Scourge picks himself up, throws his arms around his friends, and leads them away.

Both groups of boys head for opposite sides to eat lunch. Cal won't even look at me when he walks by our table. Would my pleading eyes have made a difference?

I don't know, but they're on him the whole time. They're hanging in a constant state of begging, imploring him not to do something stupid, until I'm forced to get up when the bell rings for class.

By mid-afternoon, everybody knows. It'll be the biggest fight of the year, everyone says. Rich kids who can't wait to see a little blood spilled on the million dollar track and field facility paid for by their parents' tuition.

I'm going to be sick. But I can't just head home, leaving him to get destroyed because he stepped in, lied to Principal Ross and the police, and all for me.

I slip out of school after the last bell rings. I have a little under an hour before the fight starts. Kids are already loitering around the track and field facility, careful to watch for any teachers, or whatever else might disrupt their fun.

I buy a soda at the convenience store across the street. It's the kind that's clear, fizzy, and almost too sweet, the sort mom pours me when I have a stomach bug to keep some sugar in my system.

My reflection catches my eye in the window by the cashier. I look so drained, the corners of my eyes bloodshot with fear, a sickly match for my cream white dress peppered with soft pink roses.

I just want it to be over, and I want him to be okay.

I'm heading back to school, about to cross the street when my day gets worse. Scourge, Reed, and Mike are on a direct course for me. I want to run. It takes everything I can muster to avoid eye contact, but the bully sees me, and he isn't letting me go that easy.

"Nice fucking job, Rags," he says, wearing a wicked smile when he reaches out and pushes me so hard I almost lose my balance. "Make sure you land a front row seat. Best place you can get to watch me beat the shit out of your idiot boyfriend. Every tooth he loses is your fault, too."

Normally, I'd be too afraid to say anything. But before he completely blows past me, out of earshot, I drop my soda on the ground and scream. "Why are you doing this, Alex? Do you think it makes you stronger? Better? You're not a big man. You're a screwed up little coward, and you don't scare me, or anybody else."

Okay, that's a complete lie. But it gets his attention.

He isn't smiling anymore when he turns, stops, and stares at me like a nasty surprise stuck to his shoe. "You're full of shit. If it'd gone according to plan, you'd be on ice in juvy right now, bitch. I had to give my slut free dope just to dumb her up enough to make the call, pretending to be you. You've caused me a lot of fucking trouble since the day you decided to snoop, and I won't forget it. Don't worry, Rags. I'll deal with you soon, after I put your knight in shining dog shit in the hospital."

I stand my ground. It's times like this I wish my parents were rich enough to give me a better cell phone. One with a video recorder, so I could capture every word he just said. Not that I'd be brave enough to point it at his face and get away.

He heads into the gas station with his friends, probably looking to cob another pack of cigarettes before the showdown. It's just enough time to *run* to the track, wait for Cal, and beg him with every ounce of my being.

Please.

Please don't do this.

Present Day

The call sends him home early. Cal surprises me just as I'm about to nap on one of the plush sofas by the window. I know there's something wrong the instant I see him walk in, the placid calm on his face hiding a turmoil that doesn't lie.

"What is it?" I sit up, wide awake.

"Dad. His nurse called. Sounds like this might be the end."

We gather our things and go. One quick, hurried ride to Bainbridge later, and we're at the old man's side, staring down as he slides deeper into his coma.

"Is he…?" Cal looks on coldly, staring at his father, never bringing his eyes to the nurse as he asks the heavy question.

"Not quite yet, Mr. Randolph. His vitals aren't good, I'm afraid. He hasn't woken up since this morning. I can't say he ever will."

Cal nods. I squeeze his shoulder, trying to process the emotional tempest no doubt consuming him within. "Just let us be alone."

I sink into the seat next to my man while we listen to the nurse trot out on her heels, and shut the door behind her. Then, there's dead silence.

Emphasis on *dead.* I've never seen a human being breathe like the elder Randolph. His chest moves slow, haltingly, labored. It looks like he'll go any minute. When he does, there's nothing holding back the uncertainty. It scares me.

"I'm sorry. You're sure you want me here?" I ask, giving him a soft look. I'll do anything to ease the pained, scarcely hidden panic on his face.

"Obviously, doll. Wouldn't have brought you in if I didn't." He narrows his eyes, keeping them trained on the dying man in front of him the whole time. "What I'd really like is for this asshole to wake up, and see the future he'll never be a part of. I want him to look into the smiling face of the woman I'm about to marry, and know you were worth it. Helping you out years ago at Maynard fucked away whatever love and respect he pretended to have for me. And I'd do it again in a heartbeat."

He looks up, bathing me in his blue eyes. Today, they're ice. I can't look for more than a few seconds, or I know they'll leave frostbite somewhere on my heart.

His frank, brutal words tie knots in my stomach. He's completely entitled to feel how he does about his dying dad, of course, but the idealist in me doesn't give up so easily. I keep hoping for a miracle, like something from a fairy tale, where the elder Randolph sits up, opens his eyes, and tells his son he's sorry for everything. There won't be a contested inheritance. They hug, and the old man slips into the great beyond in peace.

Fantasy, I know. This is why I lost my mind the day he went out on that field with Scourge.

I've never been good at accepting the dark, awful things this world needs just to kindle light again.

"What's your favorite memory of him?" I reach for his hand, hooking my fingers through it. He looks at me like I've just lost my mind a second time. "I'm just curious."

"Curious, and nosy," he growls, letting out a heavy sigh as he turns, fixing his eyes on the old man's chest rising and falling under his blanket. "Fine. I guess the time he wasn't a complete ass to my brother. He really did love John, or respected him in a way he never did with me. He used to disappear every Thursday afternoon after the funeral. I thought it was to hit the bars around town or find more bimbos like the ones he started screwing before mom spent eighteen hours a day in bed. Pissed me off bad. One day, I followed him after work, a couple years before he was diagnosed and he was still coming into the office regularly. I'd just started at the firm. I was ready to rip into him as soon as I got the chance."

He's quiet. I squeeze his fingers tighter, whispering as I lean into him. "Where did he go?"

"He was visiting my brother's grave. I stalked him doing it for more than a month. Every Thursday, just like

227

clockwork. Far as I know, he kept up doing it for years, spending at least a solid hour there every week. Rain, sleet, or shine. He'd talk to that headstone like he never talked to anybody else. Told my dead brother shit about the family, about himself, about me…and that's how I know losing John fucked everything up. I would've been a disappointment, but not a walking curse, if only he'd been out of the Taliban's fucking way that day."

"You can't dwell on it," I tell him, running my fingers against his, feeling the angry tension in his hand. How am I ever going to soothe this madman? "Your father had secrets. Everybody does. He did the wrong thing, Cal, blaming you, walking away from your family, trying to heal in a screwed up way."

"Heal? He fucking gave himself cancer holding it in. Worse than anything that's in his cells, eating him up." He turns, giving the thin figure laying on the bed a furious look. "Why the fuck did it have to be like this, old man? Why couldn't you have at least *tried* after John?"

"John? Johnny?" It sounds like a death rattle underwater.

I stifle a gasp, trying not to jump when the old man shifts, ever so slightly, opening his eyes. Cal drops my hand, lunging off his chair, pulling his father's withered hand from the side of the bed, and gripping it between his palms.

"I'm here," he says. The words sound like dry leaves rustling.

"Oh, John. Thank God. You've come back to me." He talks slow, his wrinkled face crinkling with lines, clearly delirious.

Cal turns, giving me a terrible look. It's one I haven't seen before: resignation. Defeat. And it turns every vertebrae in my spine to ice.

"Yeah, dad. It's me," he says, turning around.

"Johnny, your little brother…where is he?" he licks his lips, straining to see the figure seated in front of him. "Where's Calvin?"

"Dunno."

"Well, just talk to him for me, okay? Tell him how much I regret treating him like a damned dog. Tell him I was a bastard…and I'm sorry. Sorry for how it all happened after you left. Tell him I'm sorry for his mom, sorry for the cheating, sorry for everything. Sorry I ran out, tortured this family, kicked him when he was down. And Johnny, tell him I won't let what's done catch up with him again. He tried to help that silly little girl. It was a *disgrace* for years. Now I want to let go. Want him to marry her. Want him to know I left him something to help. I left it for him. Left it right over…"

He trails off, his eyes closing, breathing heavier than ever. I'm holding my breath, trying my best not to become a bawling mess. It's heartrending and scary, especially when he mentions me.

"Left what, dad?" Cal keeps trying to maintain his stone cold pretense, but when the old man opens his eyes for the last time, it isn't working. I watch my fiancé crack, let out a loud sigh, and stand up to whisper in his father's ear. "I'm sorry, too. Never meant to make your life a living hell. Shit happened I never meant, and I guess you didn't mean it either. I love you, dad."

"Love you, Johnny," he says, the softest, most strained voice ever. "Love Christine. Hope she'll forgive me. And Calvin, I love Cal."

He slips off, his son's name the very last word. It hangs over us, an imaginary echo as dense as white noise. It takes another half hour, maybe more, for the monitor hooked up to the old man to flatline.

I'm standing at Cal's side, shaking, blotting my eyes. His hand tucked in mine, a grip so savage it hurts after awhile, but I don't care.

I'm not letting go. Not for anything.

Before the nurse comes in and we leave, I help him lift the edges of his father's blanket. Then we gently cover the old man's face. The rain pattering the windows makes an anxious, ticking backdrop to his grief. I find it uplifting. Here, in this moment, my hand in his, there's nowhere else I'd rather be.

We're leaving the mansion when he pulls me aside. We stop in front of a door in the hallway, on the opposite wing of the house, and Cal looks at me. "Hold up. I've got one more thing I want to do before I never see this place again."

I follow him into a dark room that looks more like a museum room than a proper living space. At first, I wonder if it's his brother's, but the Cold Play posters on the wall say otherwise. Their music was always on his iPod whenever I caught him working out at Maynard, a weirdly soft, sweet melody to the brutal attrition he inflicted on his body. Not at all what anyone would've expected from the school's star lacrosse player, oozing endless confidence and brash energy.

Music for sensitive artistic types and girls looking for a good cry didn't fit the Calvin Randolph I thought I knew. Maybe it's one of many reasons I always knew he hid more beneath his rough surface.

"Wow. It's simpler than I expected," I say, sitting on the old bed. "When we were kids, I used to think you lived in a palace. Always thought I'd find a cheetah sleeping in a hot tub, just like those rich kids on Instagram."

He smiles, shakes his head, and heads across the room. "Old man never let us have pets. He'd flip his shit if anything more exotic than a hummingbird wandered onto his property."

I watch him stop in front of an antique dresser. It takes him awhile to dig, so long it gets my attention when he isn't done after ten minutes, slowly working his way down the drawers, pushing aside old clothes and trinkets wrapped in newspaper.

"What's up? What are you looking for?"

He ignores me for another minute before he stops, reaches into the bottom drawer, and yanks out a stack of paper. "Shit, finally. Remember when you asked me awhile back about the letters you sent me in juvy?"

I nod, unsure why I'm blushing. I promptly forgot them when he brushed me off the first time. Just a few weeks ago, it was too easy to believe he meant what he said, that he'd tossed away each one. And with the cold, teasing circus he put me through, why would I ever think anything different?

Oh, but there's no doubt in the stack he carries toward

me. Cal's weight depresses the bed next to me, and he grabs my hand.

"They're here, doll. Sorry I lied. Didn't know how to tell you I saved every fucking one. Only company I had most nights, and a small miracle they all made it out intact. Too many rat bastards and straight up psychos locked up with me." His eyes pierce mine, brighter and more alive than they should be for a man whose estranged father just died. "I saved them, Maddie. Stuffed them into the same space I always meant for your panties. Always drooled over getting them off that year we met, having a trophy worth saving to prove I'd finally had you."

"Well, mission accomplished, I guess." I have to look away. I can't figure out whether I'm trying to hide the fresh fire on my cheeks, or the urge to blink away tears. "I can't believe you kept the letters. Kind of embarrassing, really."

No, not really. Not if I'm being fatally honest with myself. It hits me right in the feels, and that's a blow I don't need when I'm already falling hard for this grinning, enigmatic asshole next to me.

"Fuck embarrassing, doll. I'm the one who ought to be ashamed." He unfurls a page in his hands, scanning his eyes over it, and reads the phantom words I wrote years ago:

> *Sometimes I don't know why I keep writing when there's never a reply. I don't blame you for the silence. I'd be confused, hurt, probably a thousand other things if I was in your shoes, Cal.*

Remember Chelle? She got married last month. Absolutely beautiful wedding. Violets and irises everywhere – such a stunning contrast to bridal white. I want to get married someday. Settle down. Her wedding just made me think. I remembered, for the thousandth time, I only have a chance to do that thanks to you.

I can't repay your kindness, but I'll never stop hoping I do, one day. Being honest, everything still makes me think of that day and everything you did. I don't care how crazy it sounds or how many times you ball these letters up and throw them in the trash.

I'll keep telling you as long as I know you're out there. I don't care if you respond, as long as you read these words.

Yours, with my everlasting thanks,

Doll

"Only time you ever signed off with that name," he says, placing his palm on my cheek. I turn to meet his eyes, enveloped in his warmth and teasing smile.

"Only place I wasn't ashamed of it," I say. "Why didn't you ever write back?"

"Had to keep you away. Probably would've kept it that way, if I didn't have to come begging for a favor, and played on your guilt to get your name on the contract."

"Cal, *why*? If you'd just written back, you know, we might've found each other a lot sooner. We might've had this." I'm doing my best to hold his eyes. It isn't easy when I fly through all the lost years we could've had together, and all because of his stupid pride. I try not to let my emotions run away with me, for his sake, considering we covered up his lifeless father under an hour ago.

"Because I thought I was bad for you, Maddie." He thumbs my jawline, pushing goosebumps through my skin. "After everything that went down, I was fucking tainted. We both know it. I didn't save you just to crawl back years later, begging for a second chance, dripping my stain all over your life. I wanted you to have a normal life, good career, and forget every reason why I ever got into that stupid fight."

"I'm glad I don't do normal," I say, leaning into his hand. Those bright blue eyes burning his face are mirrors, and they make me self-conscious. "I wouldn't have wound up here."

"Yeah. Hope you ignore every word I say, doll, if it leads us to this. My old man making his amends before he breathed his last is the second happiest time I've ever been wrong in this life."

I push my arms around him, closing my eyes, plush against his broad chest. He doesn't need to mention the number one time because we're still living it.

The letters are the only thing he takes from the house. Then it's a long drive through the wrought iron gate for the last time, and an even longer wait in the soft, steady rain at the ferry terminal. We ride onto the massive ship together in the warmest silence I've ever known.

"What do you think he meant, anyway? About what he left for you?" I ask. I have to speak over the dull, comforting whir of the ferry's big engines.

"Don't know. I'll have the estate lawyer comb over any documents he's touched the last few weeks with tweezers, though. If there's a letter backing up the board's new attitude, or the trust has been changed, it'll make our lives a whole lot easier."

"He said he wouldn't let the past catch up with us. What did he mean?"

Cal looks at me. What I really want to say is, *what are you and everybody else hiding?*

I can't be mad at him right now. Not when his father just died. But it stings like a slow moving acid, knowing there's something I don't know, ever since Spence showed up for his surprise visit and their chit-chat in the hall.

"Doll, everything's fine. Dad's change of heart shocked the hell out of me. I never expected it in a million years. Chances are he's got a few more surprises left before he's buried. Leave them to me." He takes my hand by the wrist, brings it to his lips, and plants a reassuring kiss.

For a second, I hate his warmth. It melts me every time. The words he isn't saying might be concealing the truth, but the warmth when his mouth hits my skin never lies. It's

235

honest, addictive, and pulls me deeper into his sweet madness.

"You know this funeral isn't delaying anything on our end, right?" He gives me a look that makes my heart skip a beat, a smirk on his lips. "I still want us married by the Fourth. I want fireworks on the boat with my wife. Whatever happens with his funeral, get ready. We've got a lot of planning to do."

It isn't long before my lips join his. I'm still blinking back tears as the ferry pulls into the city's terminal, and we walk down to the lower deck to get our car ready to drive off it.

This impending marriage is like watching a comet streaking across the sky. It's either the most beautiful moment I'll ever experience, or it's going to explode in a reckless fireball.

XII: Seven Years Crazy (Cal)

It's a week and a half since dad died. The funeral is behind us. The weekend belongs to Maddie and me, and it's one of many reasons I'm working my ass off on a Friday, frantically tying up loose ends in my marketing campaigns.

They keep coming unraveled on the inheritance and estate ends, of course. It'll take months to iron out, and countless lawyers dipping into the enormous sum he left behind before I can call the whole affair a bitter memory. Last week, the funeral was somber, sparsely attended, and grey as the steel Seattle sky hanging over us the entire time.

I said goodbye to dad in front of distant relatives and the partners from the firm coming to pay their respects. Maddie stood at my side, dressed in black. Swear to almighty God she was the brightest thing there.

It's my turn to bring light this weekend, before the wedding hits at the end of the month. I also want to prove there's nothing to worry about, as soon as I'm able to un-fuck the latest wrenches Alex Palkovich Senior keeps jamming into my life.

At three o'clock, I turn off my computer and grab my

bag, but it isn't time to leave the office yet. I head for the old storage room with the shaky coffee table from the 1980s, a whiteboard, and nothing else on the auxiliary floor. Cade and Spence are right on time, swearing as they take their spots in the loose chairs, just as old and beat up as the table, a relic from the firm's grittier days after Black Monday hit in '87.

This is our war room. It's where we put out fires started by a bastard with a blood vendetta on my head.

When Cade looks up at me, his big blue eyes shiny as diamonds, I know today's news isn't good. "What the fuck is it now?" I ask, wanting to get the worst over with.

"It's Wilford Zephmyer this time. Found out late last night he's under the gun. Palkovich hired hackers threatening blackmail."

"Blackmail? Shit." Unbelievable. Shaking my head, I look both my boys in the eye. "Wilford's clean, even if he is a lecherous old fart. What do they even have to hold over his head" My fist taps the old table harder than I intend.

Threatening the board's sitting President is the biggest danger yet. If Palky throws a grenade into his life, it'll make the others panic. They'll drop me like hot lead, and bow to any nasty letters from anonymous strangers. Because if the RET curse, as they're starting to call it, can bring down the President, anyone is on the chopping block.

Cade shrugs. "Craigslist whores, Wilford says. Swears up and down he's always been an angel, and never did anything. But our hackers have sent him pictures of girls he hung with in Vegas when he went to check on his casino investments last year. Some of them look real cozy…like, pics that would make any woman wonder if they saw them. His wife will have conniptions if she sees the emails and the texts back and forth. All fake. Allegedly."

"Time to face the music: we're fucked." Spence's statement wins an icy glare from me. "He won't let up, Cal. We sort out city zoning issues with one board member's businesses one day, we have to prop up Mrs. Anders' charity the next. Now Zephmyer is in deep shit if this gets out, like we know it will. Then what do we do? Buy them a marriage counselor?"

"No. No," I say again. *Christ, I actually don't know.* "We have to go after the source, sooner or later. There's no other choice."

"Yeah, well good luck, Batman. The councilman's got his own security. We found that out real fast with those detectives we hired to do a little snooping. One walked away with a broken nose. The other got his tire blown out when he came too close to Alex's house one fine night." Spence drums his fingers on the table, eyes drifting to their sides while he thinks through our non-existent strategy. "He'd love a chance to put you away, Cal. For a second time. And unlike juvy, his brother's prison gangs can do a lot of damage if you wind up on their turf."

Cade nods, his deep voice rumbling. "Sweet revenge, in his eyes. Legal murder. He wants you gone for what happened to his kid."

For the first time in years, I want to hurt Scourge all over again. So what if he's dead? I don't regret it, even though it fucked up my life. They're both the same. Rotten father like bully son.

One was just a cruder thug, never evolving to cryptic bribes and city politics to get his way.

"If we're smart about it –"

"Smart? Man, we're fund managers and marketers. Not superheroes. This isn't a fucking action movie, Cal. Did you boys hear how Grant Shaw almost got himself killed trying to save his girl from a kidnapper?" Spence lets the nerve I've tapped go off.

"How could I forget? It was all over the news a few months ago. Billions didn't buy him a free pass from crazy, and we don't have his brother's connections." Cade puts his fists together, stretching his big arms out in front of him. He's just as frustrated, even if he's a lot more chill showing it.

Spence wipes his brow, leaning back in his chair. "Look, I'll do whatever I can for you, Cal, but I'm not getting chewed up by a German shepherd and then thrown behind bars over something stupid. Palkovich wants us to play dirty. He's baiting us to come at him with guys in black jumpsuits if not our own fists. We can't be dumbasses. We have to keep this legal, or we're not getting anywhere."

As much as I hate admitting it, he's right. I'm in a trance for the next minute, staring numbly at my phone. It's silenced, but the screen lights up with a Snap from Maddie. She loves sending me a new goofy pic every time those creative fucks add a new filter.

Amazing they haven't gotten hacked yet for all the

cringe-worthy data they're holding. The thought stops turning in my brain.

Wait.

"Guys, we're idiots right now," I say, sitting up in my chair. "The answer was right in front of us the whole time. If Palkovich wants to hire spooks from the deep web to air old Wilford's dirty laundry, we can play, too. We've scanned the pics they sent him, yeah?"

Cade looks at me thoughtfully. "Last I heard, that's right. Pretty sloppy, leaving their dicks hanging out in the meta-data. Palkovich is such a cheap fuck he probably found some kids to do his bidding, or else guys overseas who aren't up on top encryption."

"Also means it won't take us much work to track them down. Send them a message. Double team him with a double agent."

"Christ, Cal. You're really saying what I think you are?" Spence looks a lot more animated. Can't tell if he's about to endorse me or protest, but I don't give him the chance.

"There's dirt on Palky everywhere. Nobody's ever found it because he keeps it so well hidden. Hardly anybody's looking either when he does his yearly nice guy cover work, raising money for Seattle orphans or some shit. Who better to work the dirt on him than somebody he's already reached out to, and presumably paid?"

"You're heading into murky waters, bro." Cade gives me a serious look. "Any legal defense is null if we get hackers involved. There's a serious chance they'll bite us a second

241

time if our money isn't good enough, or Palkovich finds out and counters our offer."

"Fucking please. Lawyers were never pulling his balls out of the fire," Spence snaps. "I'd rather go hard than puss out. Put some smart teeth into Mr. Councilman's hide. Send him a very clear message when our guys find some bribes or women or whatever dirt he's hiding. Can't be hard considering he's got a brother in jail, and raised the nasty little shit who caused this mess. We find his hell, threaten to leak it, and give him one chance to stop fucking with Cal, and our company by default."

Cade still looks uneasy. He knows there isn't a better option. A risky plan is better than doing nothing.

"Fine. Let's just get this shit over. I've got enough on my plate." Cade relents, scratching the short, dark beard haloing his jaw. A nervous tick he's had since he was young, long before he had worthy facial hair, when he knows he's just agreed to a gamble.

"I'll reach out to the interns in IT. They're cool kids. Kept mum while I've had them analyzing the files. I'm sure they can find info on the hackers from those pics, too. A couple extra thousand will go a long way to college kids who already hit the deep web for free just to brag to their nerd friends." Spence's voice is a lot more upbeat, easing the fury in my pulse. "Give it a few days. We'll be set before the wedding. Extra time to spare for Cade to get his tongue on that mystery pussy worth crossing time zones for."

"Fuck you, Spencer. Mind your own business."

"What's bad for the boys at this table usually is for the

company, too. I'm just checking to make sure you're not letting your dick do the thinking these days."

"Least I've put mine to work, friend-o," Cade growls. "Must be quite a dry spell on your end. Or did you decide to throw your money after another useless IPO instead of those fucking hookers you chase with tits as big as watermelons?"

"Guys!" I throw my hands between them, before this gets physical. "Let's get rolling, and leave the locker room bullshit back in high school."

Spence is the first to nod, stand, and give me a fist bump before he leaves the room. It's incredible, really. The harder I try to put the academy days behind everyone, the more I realize they'll never go away.

It takes a week. The IT kids do their magic. One of them helps Spence reach out to the hackers using an encrypted protocol on the internet's darkest corners. They reply favorably, asking for their payment in Bitcoin, anonymous and untraceable. It's on.

They'll have something for us in another week. I barely notice the days ticking by because I'm having the time of my fucking life, the last days I'll ever spend as a bachelor.

It's mid-week when I see doll's text.

> **Maddie:** Let me know you're coming before you pick me up. I don't want surprises.

I snort, tucking my phone into my pocket. Hasn't she figured out by now there are some rules I'll always break?

Her sassy sister is the first person I see when I step into the bridal store. Highest quality shop in town, and also the most expensive place I'm confident she's set foot in her whole life. Probably why she looks like a bird out of its cage, her eyes scanning the luxuries while she waits by the dressing room.

"Where is she?" My question catches Kat Middleton off-guard.

"Nowhere you ought to be, Calvin." She stares me down, crossing her arms. "Did you not get the text? She asked for a heads up."

"Sorry, Maddie's hogging all the literacy. I only speak numbers."

"Ass!" I'm sure she wants to add more, but there isn't any time when an angel draped in white appears a second later. "Oh my God. I think that's the one, sis…if only this idiot weren't standing here in front of it."

Idiot? My dick makes me one when I look my woman up and down. My knees are stone. I'm frozen, staring at the sexiest Medusa I've ever seen, balls on fire. My eyes drink every beautiful fucking inch of her for fuel, from the ivory lace lining her peekaboo cleavage to the trim gown cradling her ass.

I wish I'd brought shears. Pretty as it is, I want it *gone*.

"Cal, what the heck?" Maddie lifts a hand to her mouth when she sees me.

"Hell," I correct her. Appropriate because I think I'm in

it, standing here with my jaw falling off every second I'm not inside her.

"You're ruining it! You're not supposed to see anything until the wedding!" She walks up to me and smacks my chest with her little hands."I finally found a good one, too."

"My bad," I say. No real apology whatsoever in my tone. "There's plenty more to choose from here."

"Yeah, so much it's taken us…what? Three hours just to nail down a shortlist?" Kat's looks grow harsher every time I bother looking at her. "I think this would've been the one."

"I should've known better with *him*." She smacks me again for good measure.

I'm not sure who's more sour. Maddie, Kat, or the attendant standing behind her, who'd been helping in the dressing room before she stepped out to watch me make an ass out of myself. "Well, it can't be this one now that he's seen it. We're back to square one. This is why we can't have nice things."

Kat lets out a huff of agreement, rolling her eyes.

I can't suppress my smirk when she pulls away. "Nothing's ruined if we put it to good use, doll."

Reaching into my wallet, I dig for my black charge card, and push it into the attendant's plump fingers as I take Maddie by the wrist. "Ring up double the cost. Everything she's wearing right now. When we're done, I want it cleaned, and donated to charity. Give us a minute, maybe ten."

Impossible to tell whose eyes are bigger, hers or Kat's. I

don't care as I lead my woman to the dressing room, slam the door shut behind us, and push her against the nearest wall.

She's beating my shoulders like mad until my lips find her throat. They caress, they suck, they bite, they taste what I can't wait another week to have on my wedding day.

"Cal…"

No talk. No names. No pleading.

I silence her with another kiss, grabbing the back of her neck, bringing her fully into it.

Then I put her down on the wooden bench, and my hand sweeps aside her gown. It takes every fiber of my discipline not to shred this expensive dress. I promised something to charity.

My teeth go into her skin instead. Small relief for the animal lust exploding outward. By the time I'm kissing a steady trail up her leg, the resistance is gone. She's melted, prone, her soft hands trembling at her sides as I shove her panties aside.

Her scent puts my tongue to work. I'm rock hard, rampant, fucking crazed to bring her off in this millionaire's boutique. She whimpers on the first few licks, still trying to fight, but it only takes seconds to make her lips buckle. My mouth digs in her, lips and tongue, taking as much pleasure as they give.

I've got a frantic urge to undo my belt and pull myself off while I'm buried in her cunt.

Too bad I'd miss the fireworks, grunting out my own hot pleasure. I resist, giving her my full attention, pleading with my eyes every time she looks down.

Her eyelids flutter. "God, Cal. You're insane. We shouldn't be –"

Oh, fuck, but we are.

My tongue finds her clit, melting her nervous words. More licks shut her up, making the need hammering in my blood ten times louder.

She's mine completely for the next few minutes. She meets her O up against the wall, legs splayed, biting the back of her hand so she doesn't scream.

Sweet fuck, yes. Take it, doll.

Then give it all to me.

I'm serious. I taste every supple tremor in her aching pussy. It's divine, an invigorating madness by the time I'm off my knees, grabbing her shoulders, staring into her eyes while she pants desire.

"Pull my cock out, Maddie." The words are raw anticipation.

I enjoy every second her hands come out, race to my zipper, and free my pounding hard-on from its prison in black wool. It springs out in her hand, oozing pre-come, too impatient to let me suffer through more than a couple quick strokes with her hungry fingers.

Doesn't help that her heels are off. I feel her toes on the backs of my thighs, urging me in, closer to the sweetness I'm desperate to fill, to fuck, to empty every ounce of myself in.

"You're a good wife," I whisper, clasping her face with both hands, before devouring her mouth. I mean every word.

"And you're getting ahead of yourself, Mr. Randolph. Last day to have me before the wedding fast we agreed to."

Shit, she's right. I knew there was a reason my balls twitched hot, vicious and molten. It's the last night before we start a seven day abstinence until our wedding night.

Undeniably the worst thing that's happened to me since juvy.

"Doll, don't tempt me. Not if you want to keep that thing you're wearing intact while I fuck your brains out." She isn't listening. The little minx squeezes my cock, this time harder, sending sweet, electric heat up my spine.

Enough, tease. I push her hand away and drop my pants, shoving her thighs apart. I don't tap the tip of my cock against her clit like I usually do because I'm that deep in crazy rut.

The end of my prick burns, screaming to have her wrapped around me, wedged up against the entrance to her womb. She hitches, moaning loud as sin when I make my first thrust.

Deeper, deeper, holy hell, *deeper.* Don't stop until my balls hit her ass. I hold myself in her for a moment, harsh breath sizzling between my teeth, taking one last long, good look at the woman I'm about to own.

"Cal, yes," she whimpers, her pleading eyes boring into me. "*Yes.*"

Like I need the encouragement. My cock edges back before slamming into her again, bringing me into my full fuck element. It's not long before she's clutching at my elbows, hanging on for dear life as she rides every wicked inch, each one hungrier than the last to mark her from the inside out.

We fuck with love. With lust. With tension.

We fuck like we haven't for seven years, and it's true because the hundred or so times I've mounted her still isn't making a dent in all the time I spent without her. We fuck through the unspoken secrets consuming us, everything putting us on edge, the Palkovich bullshit I'm afraid she'll back me into a corner over, or else learn some other way.

Everything is delicate. Fragile. Easy come, and easy go, just like the heat welling thick in my balls.

I want to tell her everything, of course. But only after it's ancient history, we're wearing our wedding bands, and this chaotic need to set the world right dies in a fire.

"Cal, Cal! I'm – oh, God!" She rarely brings herself to say it.

It's as adorable as it is infuriating. I want to hear more. Only cure is to pound my cock in harder, grind into her clit, slowing my strokes, leaving her on a ferocious precipice.

"Say it, doll. Say you want to come for me. Say your O belongs to this cock." I'll turn her into a dirty talker yet, by God.

Her eyes flutter open, angry and desperate. She can't believe I'm making her beg.

I can't believe she doesn't do it naturally because when she's this wound up, desperate for what's waiting on the other side of her O…fuck.

I keep my thrusts on a short leash while I wait for the magic words. Agonizing in the best way.

"Cal, please. I want to…want to come. Let me!"

"Not unless I hear the part about my cock, doll," I tell her, grinding my pubic bone harder into her clit.

Her eyes roll. I stop. She'll blow if I take it any further, digging her fingernails into my arms. My cock is completely soaked in her pink. It's impossible to stop moving, even when I'm still. It's torture for us both.

"End this, Maddie," I whisper. Reaching up, I fist her dark hair, pulling it tight, forcing her to look at me. "Tell me if you fucking want it."

She sucks her lip. Her chin twitches. I feel her hips shudder under mine, and then the sweetest words in the English language. Hell, maybe the global lexicon.

"I'm coming on your cock," she purrs, lifting her ass roughly off the bench. She slides into the renewed thrusts I give her, baring my teeth, counting in my head so I don't lose it, too. "Your cock, Cal, oh fuck, I'm coming!"

Her pussy convulses, shuddering around my length. I try like hell to keep pounding, but I can't hold it. Not when there's this molten sweetness tugging every inch of me, begging for my seed, pulling my release out of me.

"Fuck, Maddie!" My neck arches and I give the fuck in.

Lava bathes my blood, pours into my shaft, and seethes out of me. There's a force and a beauty I didn't know was possible in this release, losing it in the pussy I'm about to pledge my life to.

We're both a steaming, panting mess by the end. My cock roots itself deep, refusing to stop twitching until it's good and spent.

She's fine with that. My heat sets her off all over again. We enter the deep, find our ecstasy, it smothers our bodies like an invisible blanket. Goddamn, I feel good, and so does she. I can't even fathom how sweet, how *right*, her pussy feels. Finding its pleasure, delivering as much as it takes, and soon to be mine forever.

We're a sticky mess when our senses return. When she stands, I start laughing. Maddie turns around, hands on her freshly fucked hips, brow furrowed. "What's so funny?"

It takes her a second or two to see it in the mirror. Then her eyes fill with horror, noticing the long rip in the white fabric going up her ass.

So much for intact. Before she's able to hit me, or do something really insane like drop the good girl act and swear when she isn't coming her brains out, I pull her into my arms. She struggles, but only for a couple minutes before she's broken, laughing with me.

"A perfectly good dress – ruined! Calvin, I swear, if you do this to the one I pick for our wedding night, I'll –"

"You'll stop worrying because every fucking penny we've spent is worth it," I say, cutting her off with a kiss. She bites my lip at first, before giving in. I love it. "I'll pay for this one, plus a new dress for charity. I'm a man of my word."

"I can't believe I'm marrying you!" she says, playfully shaking her head.

"It'll be all too real in another week, beautiful. Then we get to sneak around making scenes like this forever to get off." I'm only half-joking, adjusting my tie as much as I can.

When she's back in her normal clothes, a sundress with

a powerful knack for making my cock hurt all over again, I lead her out. I get my card back from the horrified assistant manager after I tell her to run it a second time, and keep it on file for tomorrow, when Maddie should return to make her real choice. Kat disappeared while we were waiting. I can't say I blame her.

It's only later, in the car, when I see the text. Yet another cause for laughter.

> **Kat:** Jesus, sis. When I said get a room, I didn't mean the one in the back. What the hell is wrong with you guys?

"Seven years," I whisper, pushing her fingers through mine while my car splashes through puddles left by fresh summer rains. "That's what. Seven years can make a man crazy."

She gives me a knowing smile. I don't need any translation to understand this woman is the only other person on the planet who shares my breed of madness.

XIII: Hold Your Peace (Maddie)

Four days. That's how long I have left before I'm living every girl's dream.

In my case, marrying Cal Randolph is a dream I thought would never come true. I'm a lot more careful with my dress the second time, a beautiful cream colored gown I've picked out. I keep it at the store for a few last minute alterations, well away from his infectious desires.

And they're building by the day. Last night, I couldn't keep him off me. I decided to show him I'm serious about spending the next few nights back in the guest room I started in. Whatever it takes to keep up the fast for a few more days.

Heaven help me if it's any easier on my end. I'm thinking about the glimpse I saw of him in the shower this morning. He's started leaving the door wide open in the bathroom I always have to walk past. It's a strategically perfect view of his hard, wet body.

Lather. Steam. Muscles like steel and maddening ink drawn together like a kiss from a god, and just as dangerous. Just as tempting. Just as killing hard to resist.

I need to keep the distractions coming. I've thrown myself into reviewing a few new case files for work. I'm returning to China in a little under a month. Plenty of time for a lovely honeymoon, and for Cal to tie up a few loose ends related to his father. He's promised to go mobile with me for a few weeks, running his marketing campaigns overseas while we spend time together.

I can't wait for our first overseas trip as a married couple. I'm also wondering if I'll be able to tempt him into landing us a shiny new flat in Beijing for work and pleasure. Chances are this is far from my last trip there.

"Evening, doll." Cal steps through the door, shooting me a sultry look.

Wonderful timing. Always when I'm trying to forget Mr. Tall and Sexy. I flash him no more than a quick look and a smile before he walks over, placing a peck on my cheek, and heads upstairs to change out of his suit.

Thinking about his formal wear falling away piece by piece is another vision I don't need in my head. I tap my fingers not-so-gently on my laptop's keyboard, seeking grounding, focus. Whatever gets my mind off jumping the man who's going to be my husband in just a few more days.

The call from my boss' number comes out of nowhere. It's later than usual. I lift the phone to my ear, expecting something she's forgotten about when we talked yesterday. "Hello?"

"Madeline, I hope this is a good time because we need to talk. This isn't easy. I hate to be the bearer of bad news, however..."

I don't like the pause on the other end. She's an experienced woman, a Sterner veteran, and as much as she likes me, I've never heard her so flustered. "What is it, Pam? More account restructuring?"

"No, not exactly. Listen, there's no easy way to say this – cancel your plans for Beijing in August. We've had to rescind your clearance."

I can't believe what I'm hearing. I check the number on my screen, just to make sure some evil hacker hasn't spoofed her perfectly. The window on my laptop with Sterner Corp legal software locks, and doesn't open again when I input my password.

Jesus, it's for real. "What's going on? I don't understand."

"Some troubling associations we've found recently in routine security sweeps through our system, I'm afraid. Tech department takes its precautions to an extreme, as you know. Your computer shows signs of being compromised, and IT thinks it's deliberate."

"Deliberate? Jesus, Pam, I'd never –"

"No, no, certainly not! I don't believe you'd ever sabotage. Of course, you and *I* know you'd never risk sensitive information. I'm sure this is a misunderstanding, a mistake that'll sort itself out. Rest assured you're still on payroll. We can keep this leave going as long as we'd like."

As long as it takes to investigate, which will determine whether or not you're canned over nothing. It doesn't take much imagination to read between the lines, and hear what she's carefully not saying.

255

"Whatever you need from me. This is a *huge* mistake. I don't get how this happened."

"I don't either, to be honest. But I'm sure we'll work it out. You just worry about having an amazing time, Madeline. Congrats again on the big day."

"Oh, I will." I don't mean it to sound like a comeback to a challenge, but it does. "And thanks. I'd still like to know the minute anything changes. Call me, please."

"Absolutely. We'll sort it out quickly, I'm sure. Might have to shuffle a few flights around to catch up for the ones we've canceled, but we'll have you back in place roughly when we planned."

Yeah, and I'm not. I mumble another thanks and kill the call. That's when I hear Cal's footsteps pounding the staircase down to where I'm sitting.

"Maddie, what the hell? Did she give you a reason?" His eyes are furious. So bothered he could've only gotten that way eavesdropping from around the corner upstairs.

I'm not sure whether to be more offended, or alarmed that he cares so much over a baffling mistake. "I don't know any more than what you heard. You *seem* to already know something's up."

"Be serious, doll. I need answers. Couldn't make out every word. What did she say, after the part where you were compromised?"

No sooner than I throw my computer down next to me on the couch, his hands are on my shoulders. He lifts me up in a grip too tight to be more than a concerned lover's. "Talk to me," he orders.

First time in awhile I've wanted to slap the arrogance off his face. "No. Not unless you tell me what's going on, Cal. Why do you want to get up in my business so bad? It's like you *know* more than I do."

His face drops and he releases me. Another strike against my confidence.

"Shit!" he hisses a second later, pulling out his phone. "Excuse me. I have to call the boys."

"Oh, so you need to talk to Cade and Spence before the woman who'll be your freaking wife in just a few days?" My hands are on my hips. I can't believe I'm scolding him in the same voice mom used to give daddy when he came home after dropping too much money at the bar.

I wish it was something so forgivable. This is far more serious.

He turns, giving me a long, questioning look like I'm the one who's acting all mysterious. "Doll…"

"No, Calvin! No secrets. Tell me what's going on."

"God damn it, Maddie, there isn't time! Don't you understand I have to *move?* I can fix this for you, or we can chat. Already know which one I'd prefer. Give me time, please. Let me put my pieces where they belong, before I fuck up your life. I'll be home soon." He's heading for the door. He isn't giving me another second for questions.

He might as well have just walked over and slammed a dagger into my chest. When teary heat pricks at my eyes, it's so intense I'm shaking. A ragged breath fills my lungs, making a loud wheeze. It's loud enough to stop him by the door.

"Maddie, no. Don't hurt, and don't worry. Let me do my thing. I'll explain everything later, doll, I promise you that. I'm sorry, this can't wait." He stands there with a conflicted look on his face while I march to the couch, throw my laptop in my oversized purse, and march straight for the door. "Wait, wait, where the fuck are you –"

I'm just a few inches from his face when I lay into him. "Do it yourself, whatever *it* is, and forget about me. I'm a complete idiot. Nothing's changed. You're still taking matters into your own hands, and you won't talk to me about shit."

"Doll –"

I push through the door, kicking it shut behind me before he can follow. A vicious satisfaction ripples through my veins when I'm racing down the hall, heading for the elevator. I don't look back until I've got an Uber on the way.

It's less than sixty seconds before the tiny thrill of standing up to him burns itself out, just as I climb into my ride's backseat.

I'm disappointed. Betrayed. Hurt.

I don't know what to believe about the man I love.

Don't know who or what he really is in the double life he seems happy living, and covering up. After everything that's happened, I'll never understand how he still hasn't learned to trust, to open up, to throw me a simple bone so I can actually help.

I don't even know if I want to go through with this wedding anymore.

Is the ring on my finger real, or just one more lie hiding something terrible?

I don't know. There's so many blind spots.

To top it off, my sister almost takes the asshole prize away from him tonight as soon as I'm through the kitchen door, praying my parents aren't around. Kat looks up, holding a cup of that gross flowery tea she loves for reasons I'll never comprehend. "What did your idiot fiancé do this time?"

The absolute *worst* part of this rotten thing is, I can't even explain it because he's left me in the dark, and brought my heart a new ice age.

XIV: Count the Ways (Cal)

"Come the fuck on," I grunt through clenched teeth, waiting for my phone to connect.

Pick. Up.

"Cal?" Cade sounds like he just woke up from a nap. Then I hear the equally sleepy moan at his side, and I know he isn't alone.

"I need Palkovich's schedule, and I need it fucking *now.*"

"Whoa, holy shit. Calm down."

Okay, now I know he's gotten his rocks off *and* he's drunk. The sober Cade Turnbladt knows full well telling anyone to calm down never helps.

"Where are you?" he asks. "I'm not letting you downtown alone to do something stupid."

"There isn't time. I'm not asking for backup. Just want to talk. I'm not packing. I swear." I regret leaving the little Magnum I keep for personal protection at home, too distracted with other business. But it's for the best in this case. "Cade, fucking tell me. I need this."

"Yeah, you know this asshole doesn't do heart-to-heart chats, right? What do you think you're doing? Walking up to him with a smile and a handshake, thinking he'll magically sprout a conscience?"

"Cade." His name barely sounds human when it comes out. It's so raw it leaves my throat dry.

"Christ, Cal. Easy. Talk to me. Tell me what's happened, and maybe I'll think about revealing the asshole's location."

"They're going after Maddie. Somebody on his side is. She got a call from her boss, threatening to pull her career over some hacked bullshit. They're not letting her back in Beijing to work because they say she's been compromised. Too fucking big a coincidence, considering our situation." I leave out the part about how I let her storm out, tears and heartbreak oozing from every pore.

"Shit. That's tough."

I definitely don't mention how I rammed my fist into the tiled wall, cracking a section I'll need repaired, leaving soft bruises across my knuckles. It hurt like hell to let her go, walk out without giving chase.

But if I didn't, there wouldn't be a second chance to talk her down later. We won't have a future. I have to keep moving, and somehow stop my fist from meeting the councilman's face.

"Listen to me, I want you to call Spence," Cade says "Palkovich has a public meeting tonight. You might run him down there if you can get him alone afterward, but that still leaves us the big problem: he isn't going to listen. Especially not if he's bent on revenge. You can't just go in tongue blazing."

"I can, and I will. I'll make it *very* fucking clear what'll happen if he doesn't lay off us, if he doesn't get over the shit I've paid for a hundred times over. We'll make his life suffering. He has to know we've flipped his hackers."

"We have?" Cade sounds confused, sympathetic.

I'm not looking for emotions. I need the address. But he does have a point. "Someone's still messing with your girl, Cal. Maybe we've got a double agent on our hands in those idiots we bribed. That's what's worried me since the day you said 'go.' Dipping into sketchy shit guarantees we get burned."

"Too fucking late. And it's too late to talk to Spence, too. We can't back out. The address, Cade. Don't make me find yours, drag you out of that cushy bed, and embarrass you in front of your latest dick toy." My tone warns it's not an idle threat.

"Whatever, man. I'm trying to save you from yourself. If I let it drop, and you get yourself into serious trouble again, don't expect us to come running. We tried to help the sane way."

I don't need your fucking sanity right now. The cruel thought ripples through my brain, douses my blood in adrenaline, warning me how crazy this is about to become – especially if he won't give me what I'm after.

"Cade," I say his name one more time, slower and calmer.

"All right, already! Fuck. Cal, for the love of Christ, don't do something stupid. Here it is…"

I burn the address into my brain as he reads it, inputting the numbers and letters into my phone's GPS. It's the city convention center, not far from here. I should get there halfway through the meeting.

Plenty of time to find a spot to lurk while I figure out what comes next.

I end the call without a goodbye. Then I'm in my car, driving like a maniac through the windy streets, another God forsaken summer rain beating on my windows.

I can't let the past demolish everything I've worked for.

I have to make this right.

I'm sitting outside, listening to a man who could replace counting sheep with just his voice drone on about budgets and levies. I haven't heard Alex Palkovich Senior speak once, but I saw his silhouette when I peaked inside.

Same chiseled, arrogant face in a charcoal grey suit. Same hateful dark eyes as the ones that tried to kill me. Same dull mask, concealing the monster underneath, the thing that's willing to commit any evil to collect on my sins twice.

I don't know what the hell I'll say when he's out. Practicing a speech for your own worst enemy doesn't work.

Not when you're forced to lean on every instinct to avoid killing him in public.

I try to tell myself I don't mean it literally.

You're not like him, asshole, I remind myself. *You're better. You tried to move on.*

Tried, and failed miserably.

I can't imagine what happens if he ignores me. If I'm

not in handcuffs by the end of the night, I'll have to land on Maddie's doorstep with my tail tucked between my legs, spilling our malfunctioning scheme to use hackers to bring down a bastard who can't let the past stay buried.

Incidentally, the very same hackers who are probably fucking up her career beyond repair, none of which would be happening if she hadn't come back to me, and put her name on my fake fiancée contract.

There's no justice.

The happiest time of my life, due in under four days, is starting to feel like a curse.

I didn't throw away a whole decade just to ruin her life years later.

I can't. I won't. And Palkovich Senior isn't walking away intact if both can't and won't aren't soon reality.

I spend another half hour sitting outside the conference hall, quietly seething, when I hear them winding down. Lady Luck blesses me with an opening.

People stream past, eager to exit the stuffy old building. Palkovich is slow gathering up his things, pretending to care about some constituent's concerns while most of the room empties.

He doesn't notice me trailing him to the parking garage, which is mostly deserted by the time we're alone. He must've parked a couple levels higher. I see him head up the escalator. I choose a spot near a tight, dark corner to wait while his vehicle begins its slow descent a minute or two later.

I listen to the engine coming closer, my heart crawling

into my throat. *Okay, asshole. Now.*

Palky practically jumps out of his own skin when he sees me step in front of his car. His hand slams the horn, and he rolls down the window, screaming in a voice that's all too familiar. "Have you lost your fucking mind, homeless idiot?! Get out of my way!"

I do a slow, stern walk to his passenger window. He doesn't have time to hit the button to roll it up before my hands reach through, wrap around his collar, and pull his face up to mine. "Get out. Now."

He already thinks I'm a bum. Might as well let him think I'm dangerous, too.

Keeping my hand in my pocket, I let him wonder what's in it, moving my fingers ever-so-slightly. There's nothing, of course, but the imaginary gun tells him how serious this is. There's a spring in his step when his door pops open and he tumbles out. He leaves his car running while I corner him, standing in the dim orange light, facing the man whose rotten son shattered my life once.

"Do you know who I am?" I ask, tipping my face up to catch more light.

Recognition floods his wicked eyes. Recognition, hatred, and nothing else.

Slowly, he nods, his silvery hair reflecting in the shadows. "Calvin Randolph. Selfish, stupid murderer. Scum of the earth."

"Glad you're not senile yet, asshole. You ought to be able to guess why I'm here, then."

He's smiling. God damn, it's too much like Scourge's

old quirk of the lips. A smirk I thought I'd never see again outside my nightmares.

"You want your life back. You've come looking for peace," he says, a split second before his voice dips to a nastier tone. "How precious. You've got some balls, kid, asking me straight to my face after you took away what I'll *never* get back."

"Like I'm the unreasonable one? I'd say get over it, but I know you never will, Palky." There's a satisfying vein twitch in his forehead when I use the nickname. "Give it up, councilman. Get some help for your rage. Stop fucking with my life, and my woman's. Do it, while there's still time we can both walk away and forget this, before it gets worse."

"You took my own flesh and blood. So did she. I'll never quit, Randolph," he says, stepping up to me. "Not while you're still breathing. You don't deserve a happy fucking ending for what you did."

He's getting too close for his own damned good. It's hard to push my fist into my thigh, ensuring it doesn't wreck his jaw. "I'm not looking for an end. I'm after a new beginning. Last chance. I'm *done* letting everything that happened when I was a kid cut through the years like acid."

"Then you should've stayed home. Looked after her. Protected what you had, at least for a few more days, before we would've had some *real* fun together." He's almost in my face. I want to break his smug expression forever.

I don't understand. "What the hell are you talking about?"

"Why don't you go down to the police station and find

out?" He brushes past me, heading for his car.

No. I'm done playing nice with this cryptic piece of shit. Rage floods my knees, my hands, sends me heading toward him with full intent to strangle the bastard alive, but I never get the chance.

Another car comes flying in so close it nearly plows into him. Plants itself between me and Palkovich. It's disruption enough for him to scurry back to his driver's seat, and speed off a second later.

Rage rips me open. I'm screaming obscenities, still kicking like a mule hit by lightning when Spence grabs me. "Damn it, bro, you're lucky I got here when I did. Cade told me it'd go down like this. Stop fucking moving!"

Fuck him. I throw every punch reserved for Palkovich at my best friend, bellowing Maddie's name. It spills out into the vast garage and echoes like someone drifting out to sea.

I don't even know what the asshole who got away did to her, or how he did it – no thanks to my supposed friend rushing in to play white knight at the last second.

Doesn't he get this isn't about me anymore, but *her?*

Somehow, Spence opens his car, and shoves me inside. I put a few dents in his upholstery on the way. It's the best I'm able to do. Paralyzing anger makes me move like a drunken man, dumb and unfocused.

There's no point in fighting, screaming, slamming my foot into his seat like it'll end my woes. I sit up, realize we're in motion, and look at my friend's furious eyes in the rear view mirror. "You've got one chance to name a place before we drive down to Pike's and I let you find your way home."

"Take me across town. I need to see Maddie's parents, her sis, somebody. Have to know what's happened."

"Okay, dickhead. And then you're getting a driver home and paying my damages."

"Whatever," I grunt back. Obviously, I'll get us squared up, but right now I'm barely able to care what an unruly jackass I've been. Not while she's on my mind.

If Palkovich hurt her, or her family, so help me God.

I'll see the inside of a box shaped cell again before we're through.

When we get to the Middleton house, it's lit up. I'm not sure whether to be relieved or alarmed by the obvious activity signs.

Spence unlocks my door and waits in the car, pulling his phone out, probably to update Cade on my antics.

I don't care. I'm not even on the first step when the screen door flies open, and Kat Middleton storms toward me with a hate I thought I'd monopolized tonight.

"What the hell did you *do,* Calvin? It's your fucking fault she's in jail!"

"Jail? What?" Questions stick in my throat. So does a fresh new urge to break Spence's windshield for stopping me when I had a chance to bring that asshole down.

There isn't a chance to ask again. Her hand cracks across my cheek, leaving a burn as numbing as her words.

"They put her into handcuffs half an hour ago, idiot! Squad car and everything. Said she had the right to remain silent, wanted in connection with a major data-breach affecting several Seattle companies." Her speech comes hurried, breathless, harsh.

Shakes me to the core. Rattles my fucking bones. I'm speechless for the second time tonight. I can't even hold onto the anger anymore to keep my head straight.

"What did you do to her?" Kat stabs me with the question again. "What did you do? Answer me, goddammit!"

Another fiery strike to my face loosens my senses. I stagger backward, catching my breath, trying my best to throw her a damned bone. "Maddie's collateral damage from a man who's still pissed about his son. He's after me, Kat, and she's a secondary prize. Don't worry. I'm not letting him get anywhere."

"No? Really?" She laughs bitterly, rubbing anger and sadness from her eyes. They're so much like Maddie's soft eyes it stings deep. "So, where's your cape, superhero? You're lightning quick! Only an hour too late, dragging in here after the police picked her up over nothing. She was terrified."

Fuck. It curdles my stomach just looking at her, but I force myself to do it.

It's the least she deserves, knowing I'm sincere, that I won't let this go unless I'm dead. "Let me fix this, Kat. I know how to fight back. I'm leaving to do it right now."

"Whatever. Just get Maddie out of jail. Maybe if you're lucky, hero, she'll finally come to her senses and call off this shitty engagement. You've been bad for her since the day she had her first stupid crush. Do us all a favor, and stay out of her life."

There's nothing else to say. She's asking me to do the one thing I'll never touch.

Racing down the steps, I don't look back. There isn't any point.

Spence takes his sweet time unlocking my door. He grudgingly drives me into the city. We're heading for my condo when the defeat in my stomach opens up.

She was terrified. I keep hearing those three words in my head over and over, a funeral melody in my mind.

Every time I picture Palkovich smiling, knowing he had me fucked from the nano-second I cornered him, I want to explode. He let me stop him. He wanted to gloat. Showed me how deep the screws were going in.

And now he's hoping I'll lose my wits completely, go after him, do something completely suicidal.

A death wish doesn't faze him. I realize it now, when it's too fucking late.

He doesn't care what happens, as long as he's brought me to my knees, and sunk Maddie by association.

Seven years ago, I was able to help her.

Tonight, I don't know how.

I'm back in the darkest days after the incident. Sheer hopelessness throws me into the past, replays my sacrifice, and makes me wonder if the worst day of my life was for nothing.

Almost Seven Years Ago

Maddie's watching, her beautiful eyes glued to me behind her thick frames. The whole damned school is when I step outside, ready to meet asshole on the track and put an end to this.

It's amazing the teachers haven't caught on and interrupted. Guess Friday evening has a lot to do with it. The schoolyard is deserted, and even the parking lot has cleared out.

Scourge is waiting for me, leaning up against a wall by the bleachers with his crew, cigarette between his lips. He stubs it out when he sees me approaching. We cross the last few steps to each other and shake hands. For a second, it's like a friendly competition, and we're not ready to beat the living shit out of each other.

"You remember the rules, asshole?" he whispers.

"Duh. No weapons. You want to pat me down? Not sure you'll be able to jerk off to it later in your cast, but whatever."

The smirk on his face disappears. He lowers his arms, fists clenching, taking one last look across the field at the hundred or so students gathered around us. "You really are a fucking dog turd, Randolph. Least your little girlfriend won't have to worry about you knocking her up when we're done. I'm going to kick your fucking balls off."

Go ahead. Try. Honestly, I should be completely zen, focused, ready for him to throw the first punch any second. But my eyes keep scanning over the short fence behind us, and I see her there, dressed in her plush white blouse and black skirt, perfectly in line with school code.

Cal, no. Please no, her eyes whisper. Hard not to admire her spirit, trying to talk me out of this without saying a word. It's much too late for that.

The cheers and excitement erupting around us tell me it's time to duck. Just in time. It's on.

His fist goes over my head, exposing the bully's chest. I land two hard punches under his ribcage.

He goes down hard. Lucky strike. I'm beginning to wonder if this'll be easier than I thought when his next blow lands on my collarbone.

"Fuck!" I scream, punching back, kneeing him in the gut, trying to knock the wind out of his lungs. Fire rips through my body. I'll be nursing bruises into next week.

Scourge isn't built like me, but he has a nasty hook. He's thrown his weight around plenty of times intimidating others.

Today, if I'm lucky, I'll be able to end that by breaking his ego as well as a few bones.

Punching, kicking, rolling, the entire world tilts. I see a flash of Maddie's shoe, tapping nervously at the ground, right before he pounds me between the eyes. The bridge of my nose lights up, bathing my brain in fire. Those skull rings on his fingers break the skin. Blood flows down my face, threatening to blind me.

I see red. Literally.

It turns something crazy on inside me. A killer instinct, maybe. I don't even know how I'm able to throw him off me, slam him down, and grind him into the pavement, but I do.

It's happening too fast.

My body can't feel the pain anymore. There are no distractions. All that matters is hitting him as often and as hard as I fucking can.

Kids keep screaming, whistling, banging every surface next to them in the excitement. It's like a wind in the trees, drowned out by the deafening thud of my heart.

"Ass...hole!" Scourge kicks me square in the gut. I lean on all my weight. He comes so close to getting me off him, but not quite.

It also leaves him defenseless when I bring my fist into his throat. I swear I didn't mean to do any serious damage when this started. I just wanted to teach him a lesson, wanted him to learn to stop fucking with me, with Maddie, with everybody else.

Next thing I know, he's gagging. Basic human empathy overrides the animal urge flooding my veins. I'm able to stop myself from breaking every bone in his face. He rolls out from under me, struggles to his knees, holding out a hand. "Stop, you fuck...no more."

"You mean...you quit?" I'm almost as winded as he is. Disbelief is setting in.

The bastard doesn't say a word. Just hangs his head in shame, total shock, probably a dozen other new emotions.

It's over. I won.

I make sure my knees are working properly before I start moving away.

I'm heading for the opening behind the fence, ready to sweep Maddie up in my arms first chance I get, when the world explodes behind me. I turn around, wondering if somebody in the bleachers lit off firecrackers to celebrate the end of the most excitement Maynard is bound to see for awhile.

No. I should've recognized the noise sooner.

How many times have I heard it on those war documentaries John watches when he's home?

"Holy shit!" A couple dozen guys behind the fence scream in unison, before they take off running, starting the mass panic as everyone leaves the field.

The gun in Scourge's hand leaves no room for doubt about what I heard. Blood drains from my face, and I run my hands over my waist, checking to make sure I haven't been shot in the shock.

Not yet, thank Christ.

"What the fuck? You said no weapons," I whisper.

"Fuck you and your little rules, Randolph. You're dead." He fires three more times.

I go down, hit the ground, trying to claw my way through the pavement and failing. There's nowhere to run. Somehow, I remember it's important to keep moving. I lunge toward him with my head down. He wasn't as far as I'd feared.

He's also an incredibly bad shot. Seems like he empties half a clip, maybe more, none of the bullets finding their mark in my flesh.

My eyes are closed when I grab his knees, throw my

weight into him, and scream like a maniac as the gun goes off again. This time, it's right next to my ear, a few inches away from ending me.

It's life or death now. I sink my teeth into his hand, desperate to pry the gun out, kicking him as hard as I can. The asshole won't stop moving, flinging his hand into my face, trying to point the gun just right so it digs into my temple.

"No!" It's the last sound I make before another bullet explodes next to me. I know I'm still alive because I sense movement, his arm giving way as I twist it back toward him.

No arm wrestling match has ever meant so much. If I can just get the gun away, knock it out of his hand and away from his face, I just might be able to –

Everything explodes as it goes off again. He isn't fighting anymore. He's suddenly very, very weak.

What the hell? That's the question I keep asking myself as I struggle to my knees, stare down at Alex Palkovich slumping over, and see the raw gouge where the right side of his face used to be.

It finally makes sense.

I'm alive. He isn't.

I've accidentally fucking killed a man.

Hell was only starting. I don't know how long I curled up on the ground, shocked and horrified, covering my eyes because I couldn't stand looking at the blood anymore.

Then came the sirens, loud and everywhere, and two big

cops grabbing my arms. They pushed my hands together, locked the cold steel around them, and shoved me to my feet without any words.

Maddie was on the curb before they loaded me in the squad car. I'll never forget her words, her tears, the frenzied regret gushing from her throat like a howling wolf. I watched her fall, slapping the pavement with her hands, dark hair a frazzled mess laying over her rose speckled dress, and just as beautiful as ever.

"Wait, wait! Don't take him away. Please, you can't, this is wrong!" It has to be emotion pouring out. The cops aren't listening to her young reasoning after I murdered a man.

She realizes it after a few frenzied seconds. Then her eyes turn to me, big and pleading, alive with more love and desperation than I've ever seen on another human being. "It's not over, Cal. It can't end like this. I'll be here. I'll do *anything* to help. *Anything!*"

Poetic words and promises don't slow down the officer in the driver's seat. Last look I get, I see her crying harder, mouthing something I can barely hear over the distance growing between us. But it's louder than my own dying pulse in my ears.

"I'll never forget this, Cal. Just wait. I'll never, *ever* let you down!"

And she never did.

Everything else is a blur after my intake behind bars. And juvy is the biggest reprieve I'm given. If I'd come from the wrong side of the tracks instead of a billionaire family, I'd have probably gone straight to adult jail, heaped in with hardened cons and killers.

Some days in here, I wonder if it's what I deserve.

I remember seeing dad's brutal disappointment the first time he sat across the table in the visiting area. John was there, too, sent home on emergency leave to help my parents cope with my fatal fuck up. It was the last time I'd see my brother alive.

"Hang the fuck in there, bro," John tells me, reaching across the table to grip my hand. "You'll be out by the time I come home again. We'll run to Pike's Place and pick up fish to fry. Celebrate your homecoming, and mine. Give everybody who said you were finished the middle finger."

"Johnathon, please. Language." Dad wags his finger, giving me a sour look. He doesn't completely hate me yet. He has his favorite, sure, and as long as John meets expectations, he'll tolerate having a murderer for a son.

"Aw, dad, come on. We need to build him up. Give the kid something to live for while he's in this miserable fucking place, and a future once he's home. Sorry." John adds the apology almost as an afterthought, when our father's eyes won't get off him.

I smile for the first time since I wound up in here. Maybe the next three years in here won't destroy me.

"Appreciate the encouragement." I say, slapping his hand. The clock overhead tells us our time is running out, leaving me to another evening doing laundry in the hot, grimy warehouse-like atmosphere in the facility's basement. "We'll have our fish fry."

"Hell yeah, we will, little bro. Just stay strong. Listen to the guards. Listen to me and dad, too. You'll make it. Time heals all. Give it a few years, and this'll all be just a bad memory."

His words are prophetic.

Over the next few months, I manage.

Lawyers work their magic, chipping away at my sentence. Months, and then more than a year are shaved off. My parents throw money at the firm like strippers. It helps. Their expertise and the lenient state laws reduce me to a year in juvenile detention on involuntary manslaughter when it's done.

I finish my diploma a month later, handwriting my answers to the final exam, wearing an orange jumpsuit, wondering why the fuck I'm bothering if no good college will accept me with a felony record.

Maddie's final tears haunt me through the year I spend in prison after the plea deal. Her letters keep me company, tell me this wasn't for nothing, that there's still somebody who cares on the outside, despite the gruesome mistakes.

Assholes are everywhere. I have to work twice as hard as the ordinary inmate to stay safe, since they know my family's kid. They discover fast I'm not easy prey after a few fist fights. The black roses I adopt in ink help round out my hard ass creed, and so does the lifting, bulking young muscle to masculine perfection.

Of course, the rose tattoos aren't for the deranged shits

I deal with in jail. They're for her, always her, and I carry them around like a dirty secret after I promise I'll never reply to any of Maddie's letters.

I exit juvy a different man, resigned to my fate. Too resigned, maybe, because my black heart almost expects John's death when it hits, shredding what little chance at normalcy and rehabilitation I ever had.

My brother dies a hero. My father's conscience goes with him on a rugged hill in Afghanistan.

It makes a fucked up situation irredeemable.

I can't believe he's gone.

John, I miss like the part of my soul I lost for her, killing that piece of shit behind Maynard. Losing him makes me wonder if John dying is some fucked up sense of karma, coming to collect for what I've done.

I learn to close myself off after the funeral. Just focus on business, even when Cade and Spence reach out to me, offering to show me the ropes at the family firm I should've worked at already for years.

Closed. That's my heart, soul, and mind.

Incredible it took a fake engagement and my old man's funeral to make me open them again.

Worst part is, it hasn't changed a fucking thing. Not if Alex Palkovich succeeds in gutting me like his son never did.

It's all for nothing if I can't save my girl a second time.

Present Day

Listen to me and dad. I can't pin down why those words from John echo louder than any others until it hits heavy in my mind.

One memory strikes another, hot fusion filling my brain. *Eureka.*

Next thing I know, I'm shaking Spence's damaged seat, yelling in his ear. "Turn the car around! Take me to the terminal. I've got to get the fuck over to that storage place on Bainbridge."

"Bainbridge? What –"

"Spence, just do it. Trust me. I'll buy you a whole new car, whatever the hell you want, when this is through. Help me."

I've stretched my friend's patience thin, but he doesn't just turn me loose when we're at the ferry terminal. He drives his car onto the ship, and we cruise across the Sound together, silent brotherly support at my side.

When we're on the island, we drive straight up to the storage facility with dad's stuff. I've let the cleaners and realtors work like a whirlwind since his funeral. The mansion is gutted, empty except for the essentials, several prospective buyers mulling offers.

Spence helps me open the small hanger-sized unit containing the old stuff I plan to auction off at an estate sale in a few weeks. Everything except the files in the 'keep' corner, which I haven't had time to go through yet.

"Come on, man. You really think we've got time to find

anything in that heap?" Spence asks, as soon as he sees the small library there is to sift through.

"Dad left something behind to help. He told me to my face before he died," I say, remembering the old man's words.

His doubt doesn't slow my hands. I flip through old faded folders and tabs with chicken scratch like a man on a mission. Spence sets to work on the other side after awhile, knowing this will go a hell of a lot faster if we both hit it. We're in the thick of it for over an hour before I have to rest, before I stop myself from flinging the trash I'm finding to the winds.

Where the fuck is it? There has to be something about Palkovich here. Dad was notorious for keeping tabs on his enemies, crafting back up plans and last resorts. He couldn't do much to the bastard councilman in life, but now that he doesn't have a reputation or a company to worry him...

"Hey, don't puss out yet. This looks recent," Spence says, holding up a grey stack of folders pulled from a separate box. I run over, just in time for him to hiss through his teeth, flipping through the thick pages. "Jesus. Palky's dirtier than we thought, or your old man got his whole life story before he passed."

I rip the papers out of his hands. Spence gives me an annoyed look I ignore, too busy drilling my eyes into our discovery.

It's too much to read in one night, but what I see is plenty. I flip through it, remembering how to smile. There are so many words, so many records, so many ways to bend this evil asshole over.

Swiss banks. Embezzlement. Fraud. Campaign slush fund. Blackmail. Cryptography. DDOS attacks.

I'm not technical enough to know what all the jargon is in some of these reports. But I recognize the companies he's hit. The attacks were all over the local news. Dad's list tells me he's been doing it for at least the last five years.

Last campaign season, Palkovich's opponent went down hard, his goofy nudes conveniently hacked off his phone and dropped for public mockery just days before the election.

There's also money going everywhere. I see copied checks and ledgers written out to motorcycle gangs, mafias, and an alphabet soup of sketchy groups overseas, including a few wire transfers to Chinese investment firms I'm fairly certain don't really exist.

"Damn," Spence whispers for the second time behind me, standing over my shoulder, his arms folded. "Your old man didn't leave a fucking stone unturned. We've got him."

"By the balls," I whisper, secretly wondering how long my father compiled this information, and sat on it. What's here had to have taken months, well before I ever tried to sell him on my fake engagement.

Was his sour, unforgiving bullshit just an act from the time I brought Maddie to meet him that day? Hell, maybe longer?

I don't know.

Don't particularly care.

There isn't any time for the big questions until she's free.

"Come on. We've got fifteen minutes before the next

ferry," I tell Spence, throwing the files into a box and heading for his car. I save my questions until the ship pulls up, just minutes away from opening its gates for the tiny trickle of cars stacked behind us, waiting to board for Seattle.

"Where's Palkovich due next?"

Spence does a slow turn, his eyes wide. "Cal, we're going to the police with everything we've gathered here. Don't tell me you're asking because you want to…fuck."

He knows. We both do.

"You know it'll take time to turn this shit over to an investigator. I'm not letting my woman sit in a damned cell while the officials sort it out."

Spence looks at the clock on his dashboard, tapping it once. "Considering it's after midnight, there's nowhere the man ought to be except home."

"Then it's time we paid him a visit." I slap him on the shoulder, giving it a brotherly squeeze. "You're a good man, braving the fire with me. Whatever happens tonight, rest easy. You're not getting burned."

"I'd better have your word on that. Can not fucking believe I'm considering this." His lips are still twisted in doubt as we drive onto the ferry.

There's a solid half hour or more to reconsider before we're back in the city. But when Spence heads toward the ritzy ocean front neighborhoods, I know he'll never let me down. Someday, somehow I'll repay him big.

I'm scaling a goddamned vine, just like in an action movie or something. It's been thirty minutes since we pulled up as close to the Palkovich place as we can possibly get without alerting his security detail.

He's got a gate, a guard shack, and a few guys in dark camo patrolling the perimeter. It's more than my old man had, despite less need for it among Bainbridge's everlasting peace and quiet. Also far more elaborate security than a jackoff city councilman who inherited a few million should be able to afford.

Spence helps me over the fence, and we run for the back of the mansion, staggering through an overgrown garden area. It's too fucking noisy on our way inside. A small miracle we don't trip any cameras, sensors, or men with dogs. I've stuffed several pages from the files we recovered into the pocket of my suit, enough to make a threat, assuming he doesn't have us arrested at first glance for trespassing.

It's another miracle we make it onto the balcony. Spence scuttles behind me, and I pull him over the ledge. Then we creep to the huge French doors, stooped over, peering inside. It's easy to see the master bedroom through the glass. There's a dim light on inside, a lone figure propped up in the bed, reading on a glowing tablet screen.

I instantly recognize the asshole who got away just hours ago. My hand reaches for my pocket, the one without the papers, clenching the big, smooth rock I picked up from his landscaped garden.

Spence gives me a look. "Ready?"

"No. But it's not like we've got another choice." Smashing the stone into his thick glass door is almost as satisfying as driving my fist into the asshole's jaw.

There's a noise like the world shattering, and we leap in through the opening, careful not to get cut on any jagged edges still clinging to the frame. The councilman is on his feet, staring in disbelief, his face whiter than the permanent frost on Mount Rainier.

"You again!" Palkovich growls, as soon as I'm in his face. "I knew you'd learned nothing from the parking garage. Simple-minded thuggery is all you know, you cowardly little –"

I cut him off, wrapping my hands around his throat, hoisting him high.

"Cal, no!" Spence yells, but I ignore him, slamming the monster who's got my girl locked away into his handcrafted wooden wall. One of the brittle panels splits. "We need him in one piece."

"I'll show you simple-minded thuggery, asshole," I whisper. My lungs are lava. Two flesh bags gone volcanic, and it's impossible to keep them from exploding. I make a bigger mistake when I peer into my enemy's eyes.

The fear I'm hoping to see on the Senior Palkovich isn't there. It's raw, arrogant hate.

Spence may be right about our need to keep this miserable creep intact, but I don't know how to do it.

"Show me, Randolph. Go ahead, skin me alive in my own home. I'll have you locked up for life, just like the bitch who got my son killed. You'll never see her again."

"You'll die behind bars one way or another. Same fate that always should've belonged to your screwed up son." A brutal hurt sparks in his eyes when I mention Alex Jr. I fucking love it.

But I don't want to kill again.

Not by accident. Not by intent. Not even if the jackass in front of me with my hands around his throat fully deserves it.

"You have no leverage. What did you hope to achieve, barging in here like this?" he asks, defiant as ever. His arms tremble, the fight burning through him, but he's too small, too weak, to lift a single finger of mine off him. "Go ahead, do what you will. Make my broken corpse the evidence this city needs to lock you away like the rabid animal you are, Randolph."

"Cal, don't. Let him breathe. Please, brother." Spence is next to me, his eyes pleading, one more reminder the monster who's neck I want to snap is speaking nothing but the truth.

"Find it out of my pocket, Spence. Show this fuckwit the truth." I wait while my friend does as he's told, retrieving the documents, one of many silver bullets we've got locked and loaded.

"Please," Palkovich spits, rolling his eyes when he sees the paper. "Do you really think I'll be strong armed into whatever impotent threat you've brought from your lawyer? You're an even bigger fool than I –"

"Shut the fuck up." My fingers press into his throat, making him think twice about trying to talk while Spence holds the papers close. "Just read."

I watch the bastard's eyes move over the papers. His face turns red, and then white, the resistance in his eyes sinking like a drowning insect. It's miraculous I keep the same steady hold, letting his defeat soak through him, without doing the world a favor by wringing the life from his bones.

Spence is right. I can't kill him. I can't even fuck him up like I want.

Not if I want doll back in my arms ASAP.

"Shit, Cal, let him talk already. He's had enough time to read it," Spence says, squeezing my shoulder.

I release Palkovich, and let his feet hit the floor. He's gasping, backing toward his bed slowly, less from my hands than the headlong panic setting in.

"You going to come with us peacefully, or do we have to drag you?" I ask, flexing my fists at my side. They hope like nothing else he'll give them good reason to do the second option.

"Do the smart thing, Palky," Spence says, carefully positioning himself between us. "We covered our bases. Sent copies of these pages to friends. They've got orders to turn it over to the Seattle police if there's no word from us in a few more hours. Fucking with us here won't save you. It'll just make this worse."

Thank God for Cade. The texts we sent him are insurance. Just in case the stubborn fuck in front of us with his vicious eyes and frazzled silver hair doesn't play nice.

"You can't do this to me," he says, backing into his nightstand. I watch the old man's hand wrap around a small gold reading lamp, lifting it like a dagger behind his back. "You can't put me away! You know who I am! Do you have any clue how many goddamned *years* I worked to avenge my son? How long I waited to bury you, destroy her, butcher everyone who had a hand in his murder?"

"You waited too long," I say, stepping up. "And I mean seven fucking years too late. Alex Jr. would be here today if he hadn't brought a gun to a fistfight between stupid kids. Things got out of hand, and I paid the price. Never meant to kill him. The time to save your bully son was years ago, and you missed it."

No more fucking around. He pulls the lamp from the wall and swings it at my face, easily missing. A wounded animal sound escapes his lips when I knock it out of his hand, snatching it off the ground before he can try a second time.

It's heavier than I thought. Perfect for caving his skull in, if I really want to.

"No, no, you idiot...you can't do this. You can't...oh, Alex!" He doubles over, knees breaking his fall. I watch the asshole collapse next to his bed, his shadow twitching as he weeps.

Then I notice mine next to it.

It's scary how much I look like the monster, hovering over him with a weight in my hand that could easily end him. There's also something I never, ever expected – a hideous sympathy for this broken demon on the ground next to me, grieving his lost son.

I didn't ask for this shit. I hate it even more that I still have a soul, and maybe he does, too.

"This is insane. I'm calling the cops." Spence comes up next to me, brushing his hand against the lamp. He's trying to get it away from me before I do something incredibly stupid.

I rip it away, pass it to my other hand, and give him a dirty look. "No. He's still got his guards out there. We don't need more confusion, or anybody else getting hurt."

I let go. The lamp hits the floor with a heavy thud, and I'm down on my knees next to this pile of human hate, clutching at his shoulders. "Give up. Come with us to the station. Confess, and do your time. You've lived a shitty life, councilman. Someone has to pay. Honor your son, your family, by doing the right thing for once in your life."

"You lecture me about...morals? What the *hell* do you know, killer?" He stiffens in my grip, but he isn't fighting anymore.

What do I know? I close my eyes for a split second, and wonder.

I see Maddie in my head. Feel the love that's always caused me grief, but never any regret.

For her, I'd do it all again, except better. I wouldn't betray her. Wouldn't hold my secrets so close, waiting for them to slip and come down on us like an avalanche. Definitely wouldn't wait so many years to clear my name, delaying what we were always meant for, and what we're still bound to become in the deepest part of our hearts.

"I've faced my mistakes, Alex. That's what I know," I tell him, looking square into his cold, judging eyes. "I've confronted them, paid their toll, and made some new ones along the way. It's not too late for you. There's always time to –"

"Just get the hell off me," he growls, pushing my hands away. Spence reaches out cautiously, helping him up, while I get on my feet. One more look, and I see the change in his eyes, before the words are even out of his mouth. "I'll go. I'll give them a statement. It's not like there's any other choice. I'd rather spend the rest of my life behind bars than suffer another minute of this."

I don't know what's come over him. We're suspicious when he grabs his robe and we lead him out. But he has his guards stand down as soon as they see him crossing the estate grounds. He gets into Spence's car, and doesn't say a word until we're helping him into the police station.

I think he's accepted his fate. And I've accepted mine.

Now, I just have to convince Maddie how sorry I am for tearing her heart out a second time with my silence. I'll spend my whole life chasing her, too, if it means I finally get the *I do* I've waited my whole life to hear.

XV: Nearer Our Forever (Maddie)

Whenever I imagined him sitting in a tiny bland cell, I thought time would be a special torture.

Now that I'm living a small slice of what Cal went through, I *know* it is, but not for the reasons I expect.

I can't tell how long I've sat on this bench, staring through the narrow bars of my holding pen. It's a slow night, and there aren't many others locked up here. Just a woman with obvious issues a few cells down, and a drunk, murmuring the same thing over and over again in his dazed sleep.

Why? Why, why, why why?

He says it so many times it doesn't make any sense. It's like the world wants to give voice to the same question echoing inside me, the only clear thing piercing the confusion Cal left.

Why did he have to hide his trouble?

Why did he wait until it came to my family's doorstep?

Why did I ever fall for a man who's the same trouble he always was?

Why?

There are no easy answers. And none harder than the cold hard fact that I can't stop loving him even though he's locked away, cost me my career, and possibly my freedom, too.

Hours had to have passed since I was pulled into the squad car and life as I knew it ended. I'm tired, so tired, I don't know how to think. My brain can't take more shock. I'm starting to drift off for some badly needed sleep when a figure appears behind my cell, twisting the heavy lock.

"Ms. Middleton?" the man says, flashing his badge.

"It's Randolph soon," I say, catching myself and letting the anger heat my blood only after it's out.

"Well, whatever, I need you to come with me. There's been a mistake."

"What mistake?" I rub my eyes, wide awake by the time I'm on my feet.

The warden tells me nothing. He just takes me into a waiting area I haven't seen before, probably because they sent me through the back entrance reserved for processing future convicts.

I'm expecting the absolute worst: another group of cops, another police vehicle waiting to take me off to a real jail, rather than this police station. I'm sure I'll have a court date soon.

Oh, if only it were so simple.

Seeing Calvin in front of me, leaning on the wall the same way he used to when he lurked Maynard's halls, complicates everything.

"What's going on?" I'm afraid to put two and two

together, turning to face the warden again.

"Honest mix up, ma'am. Happens often in these digital security cases. Another suspect confessed this morning to the cyber-attacks. You're no longer under investigation. Our sincerest apologies for the inconvenience."

"Doll." Cal lays a hand on my shoulder.

I close my eyes, taking a deep, filling breath before I turn. My already unsettled blood heats several degrees. I'm on fire by the time I look into his handsome, searching face. He's looking for a forgiveness I'm not quite ready to give.

"Fuck you," I say, a split second before my palm crashes across his cheek so hard it makes me gasp. "Don't you *ever* 'doll' me again if you're going to keep secrets this hurtful."

He reaches up, his smile gone, touching the tender red sunburst I've blasted on his cheek. "I deserved that. I'm fucking sorry, Maddie. It was wrong to keep a lid on Palkovich coming after us. Lesson learned, and I'll never forget how hard it was."

He sounds so sincere. I look over his shoulder, desperate to catch a glimpse of my parents, Kat, anyone who might understand, and offer advice. I just see his friend, Spencer, sitting in a chair and pretending not to watch us over his phone, unable to resist the insane fireworks between us.

"You almost ruined my life," I say, every muscle in my body tensing when he tries to approach. I put out my hand, trying to preserve my space. "Then you went and saved me again, didn't you? This *was* you, right? I don't suppose I'd be walking out of here so quickly, if it wasn't."

"It's a long story," he says. No, I won't let his infamous

smirk save him this time. "I'll explain everything, if you'll just give me a chance. Danger's over now. We've won our peace. We'll never have to worry about anybody derailing us again."

"Jesus Christ, Cal," I whisper, shaking my head. I feel my exhaustion in every heartbeat, a lethal cocktail mixed with the adrenaline prickling my blood. "What do I do here? You're everything that's wrong for me and…and…" I'm tearing up, or maybe I've got brain freeze. I don't know which.

"I'm the best thing that ever happened to you," he finishes for me. "At least, that's how it is on my end. I think we share it. I've done my time thinking, Maddie. Couldn't stop my brain from galloping if I tried when I went crazy to get you out. Every tragedy, every tear, every fuck up just brings me to the same conclusion: I'll always love you, doll. Always. Everything I've ever done, righteous or wicked, it's all been for you."

What do I say to a man telling me he's staked the weight of his life on love? Words aren't enough.

"Think this through. Please. But I need a damned answer by the end of the day," he says, closing the gap between us to just a few more inches, his blue eyes an ocean storming through me. "I can't live not knowing. I –"

"Shut up," I tell him, wrapping my arms around his neck. "Here's your answer."

My fingernails press into his skin when we kiss. It's the subtlety of lightning, just as strong and unpredictable, and it doesn't end until our mouths have pulled everything from each other.

This man may be the death of me yet. But I'd rather face it, and forgive, rather than ever contemplate a life without him.

One Week Later

"He'll always be a bit of a bastard, Maddie, I don't care what anyone says." Dad gives me a look, adjusting his bow tie. It's attached to the most expensive outfit he's ever worn in his life. "But if you're certain he's good for you, then I am, too. Also can't say I'm sad about the fact he put that maniac behind bars. Our own city council…Jesus. Don't want to imagine what would've happened if he'd tried to screw you over without Cal in the way."

"Yeah, and I guess he *did* promise you a lifetime of great pizzas for ruining several dinners." I jab my father playfully in the side. "It's a little late for second thoughts. Guess I'd rather have you getting them out now, before the 'forever hold your peace' part."

We both laugh. His thick, carefree chuckle is the last thing I hear before the music swells behind the door.

That's our cue. We step outside the church and walk into a pristine mid-summer day. The white flowers lead us to the aisle by the shore, bright and airy white, a perfect match for the shade of dress I've chosen.

I didn't think I'd find anything more stunning than the dress we destroyed together at the bridal shop – especially not with Kat being so on edge after my short-lived prison stint. But a single look across the gown tells me we did.

And we did good.

I never teared up during the rehearsal. Now, it's all too real, the piping notes of *Here Comes the Bride* chiming in my ears as my father leads me down the aisle, through our smiling guests.

Mom looks me square in the face when we pass. Kat flashes me a quick thumbs up, and the relief floods in when I see a smile replacing the nervous doubt on her face.

It's only been days since Cal saved me a second time. Not enough time to sell my family a hundred percent on his heroics, but there'll be plenty of time for that in the years to come.

Despite his mistakes, despite his doubts, he always ends up in the right place.

So much like the chaotic love that's led me straight to the gorgeous sight ahead.

My man looks stunning. That's a given most days, but at our wedding? He's like a god who's decided to grace mere mortals with his superhuman presence for an afternoon.

I can't take my eyes off him. The navy hued suit hugs his tall, muscular edges, forming a splendidly dark blue contrast to our ocean backdrop. His red tie gives him another splash of color, but it's not enough to pull my eyes off his. Today, his blue-eyed gaze shines so strong, so steady, so bright, I couldn't break it in a thousand years.

"He's all yours," dad tells me, planting a quick peck on my forehead before he takes his seat next to my mom and little sister.

Then I'm at the altar, standing face to face with the man I love. I lay my hands in his, forgetting there's even a minister behind us until the man speaks.

"Dearly beloved, we're gathered here today to join this man and this woman…"

It begins so slow, but it's incredible how quickly the words drift by. My mind tries lingering on every phrase, reliving our joys and sorrows, wondering how many more there'll be ahead. Big, deep words tumble through my soul.

Holy matrimony…

Our entire relationship has been pretty unholy, hasn't it? But here we are. Free, in love, and defiant as ever.

In sickness and in health…

After the darkness we've lived, what's a sniffle or two?

Lawfully wedded husband…

It's like we were married since our fake engagement began. Making it official gives it a heavier air, but it lightens the load in my heart, grown heavy on the mischievous spark in his blue eyes.

Until death do you part?

I take a second to gather my words, squeezing his fingers with mine. "I do."

Two words. So simple and powerful for two strumming hearts. I know I'm not the only one feeling it because Cal's pulse quickens against my skin, faster when the minister gives him his turn.

"And do you, Calvin Randolph, take this woman…"

In plenty and want…

We've had ours in spades.

In joy and in sorrow...

What sense would one ever make without the other?

As long as you both shall live?

For the first time, when I hear those words, I think I finally get infinity.

And I'm in love with it, as sure as it stares at me through his chiseled jaw and sky blue eyes.

I expect Cal to repeat the lines exactly. But that's not what my ears hear when he opens his lips, pulling my hand closer, fully surrounding my fingers in his. "Yeah, I do. Because this woman's the only one ever meant to tie me down, and make me love it. Because I can't believe it took seven years to get here, and because I'd live seven hundred to do it again. Because I love you, Maddie, and I'll swear in front of our family, our city, and God himself that I'll do whatever it takes to make you the happiest wife a man ever had. I do, because it's finally real. *Finally.*"

I'm too teared up to move, hot droplets rolling down my cheeks. Thankfully, I don't have to.

Cal's gone off script with his vow, and the results are beautiful. No different from how he breaks protocol before the minister says the infamous words, pulling me into his arms, our lips colliding.

Kiss the bride. It sounds like a whisper, somewhere that's a hundred miles away, just like the cheers and laughter breaking out among our guests.

I'm not sure whose lips come harder. Oh, but it's all too real, just like he said.

Achingly, intensely, forever real.

"Okay, I'm still not sold, but I've heard a lot of chatter going around. Palk-a-what's-his-face was bad news. I'll be a good sister-in-law. I'll give Cal a *little* credit for knocking him down." Kat sits in the chair next to me at the reception, our first break as a married couple.

"I hope you'll give him more in good time," I tell my sister, lifting my drink.

I take a long sip from the champagne flute, watching Cal in the corner across the huge reception hall, making the quick round with all the high profile people who've shown up on the extended guest list for one of the biggest weddings in Seattle this year. I let him do his thing, watching with a smile. It comes easy when I see the new found respect in people's eyes, finally freed from the same past that haunted us. That's what everybody knowing the truth about the councilman gives us.

Freedom.

"Yeah, well, he has to earn it. I want to see him treat you like a lady, Mads. Like, it'd go a long way if he ever let up on that silly 'doll' talk." Kat knocks back her champagne like it's a whiskey shot. Five seconds later, a horrified looking waiter refills her glass for the third time.

"Nope. That's our thing."

Sis takes another pull from her glass. It clatters when she sets it on the table. "Your thing is letting him talk to you like a toy? Hmm, kinky."

Normally, I'd be annoyed. Today is far too happy for something so petty.

"It's the old nickname he gave me at Maynard. Hard as it's been to shake the past, there's a part of me that'll always want to remember. We didn't get here with roses and candy, Kat. Our love is a warpath."

She's quiet, listening to the soft, happy people around us. I think we're actually having a moment before my sister leans over, grabs my ear, and pulls it open so she can whisper. "Don't tell anybody, but I think *maybe* you actually made the right choice for a hubby. And if you didn't, I'll find a way to hide the body."

"Stop!" We're both laughing when I push her away.

My sister loves me in her own weird way, and it's good to know it. I also think she'll be a great sister-in-law to Cal in time. Also a wonderfully eccentric aunt to our future kids.

I mentally make a note to give her hell if she ever winds up married.

"What joke did I miss, ladies?" Cal appears behind me, laying his firm hands on my shoulders. His touch sends instant lightning through my skin, and I look up into the blue eyes I'm eager to spend my life falling into.

"It's nothing. Just old secrets between sisters."

"Yes, very serious ones," Kat says, sighing sadly into her almost empty champagne glass. "Thanks for the good taste in drinks here, Cal. I think I'm in love."

"Seriously, you'd better slow down. You're going to limp home sick. Mom and daddy really don't need that." My big sister instinct kicks in. I can't resist wagging a warning finger at her.

Kat smiles, rolling her eyes as she looks from me to Cal. "When do you guys leave for Beijing again?"

"Next week for the second leg of our honeymoon. Then it's back to work for both of us." Cal brings his hand lower, rubbing the spot between my shoulders. It's secretive, suggestive, and way too sexy for our own good. "Speaking of honeymoon, doll, our ride'll be here in twenty minutes. Yacht is almost fueled up and ready, according to the guy at the dock."

I wish my sister well and stand up, pushing my hand into his. I'd be lying if I said I wasn't excited to see what kind of surprises he has waiting for us later on his ship.

On our way out, we pay our respects to my parents one more time. Mom seems to be warming to him, which thrills me, and dad always gives a man another chance. I'm certain the worst of the drama is just a memory.

We're almost to the door, saying our goodbyes to the myriad guests along the way, when a big arm reaches out and slaps Cal on his other shoulder. "Heading out already, my man? Seems like the fun just started."

"That's because you've been through at least five thousand shots of scotch," Cal tells Cade. Spence appears on my other side, offering his congratulations.

"Welcome to babysitting him full time, Mrs. Randolph," he says with a smile. "And seriously – congratu-fucking-lations."

Cal swears off flinging their crap back at him long enough to share a brotherly hug. I step aside for a second or two and let them have their fun, touched by the bond between these three men. If it hadn't been for their help, I'm not sure he'd have gotten me out of jail as quickly as he did.

"You heard anything from Turner?" Cade asks. "Told me last week he was covering Palky's trial, about to kick up anytime."

"Life sentence," Spence growls, more than a little happiness shining in his eyes. "Not that he's too long for this world. Bastards like him who've thrived too long on riches never take to prison easy."

"He'll pay, whether he likes it or not," Cal says, more serious than I've heard him since we did our vows. "Justice is being done right this time, like it always should've been. I don't care about the case, boys. If I never have to see that snake's name in front of me again, I'll live happy. It's good timing we're heading off to China while he goes in front of the judge." He looks at me.

"Yeah, just perfect." I'm smiling, but part of me is morbidly curious.

There's no forgiveness on my end for the man who tried to frame me for a hack attack I had nothing to do with. I want him to pay, and I want to know how. But not if it poisons our future.

"We're going away. We're very happy. That's all that matters, right?" I look at the three men. His friends give me friendly smiles, nodding.

He's lucky he claimed me when he did. Spence and Cade are too easy on the eyes, even if they're missing the patented Calvin Randolph charm. I'm not sure what I should wonder about more – how long it'll take his friends to get hitched, or how the hell three insanely handsome men ended up rocking their family firm?

"Damned right." Cal answers my question, raising my hand to his lips. The kiss he leaves on my skin fuels the steady, quickening burn between my thighs.

"Bro, take care of yourself on the water, and in China, too." Spence says, slapping his back one more time. "We'll hold down the fort until you're back."

"Yeah," Cade agrees. "Can't wait to hear there's another Randolph on deck next time you're home."

"The day will come. Enjoy yourselves, boys. I'll check in later this week." Cal's grip on my hand tightens. It's hard, suppressing the urge in my ovaries to do what his friend suggested.

Babymaking time isn't here, not quite yet, but it will be soon. I know it.

As he walks me to the limo, all I think about is how much it doesn't matter tonight on our honeymoon. My body doesn't need a baby now to know it's going to savor every drop of pleasure he spills into me tonight.

Cal doesn't do anything small, or half-assed. I'll never forget our wedding night.

It's breezy, cool, and peaceful when I step onto the ship's upper deck. I take a seat next to him at the controls, admiring the black rose ink shifting on his arms as he steers us out of the harbor, into the sound and the Salish sea.

The ship sails into the night as the very last embers of sun slink below the horizon. My arms hug tight to his waist. He's never been warmer. I'm so cozy, so turned on, my hand drifts down his muscular abs, tracing every edge.

Cal stops me with a smile before I'm able to take my hand to the bulge I know I'll find just a little lower. "Patience, doll. I'm not that kind of man."

I burst out laughing it's so ridiculous. "No? Then what sort are you?"

"The type who can't fuck his wife proper until she's more in love with him. Give me a couple more minutes." It's then I realize he's put the ship on a deliberate course.

We're rounding Bainbridge Island's northern edge, and I see a familiar dark silhouette on the horizon. There's no reason for the detour since we're heading for the Orcas more than another hour north. Not unless...

"Wow!" I squeeze him tighter when the first blue sunburst streaks high and explodes in the sky.

Fireworks. Bright, numerous, and beautiful.

"But how? The Fourth isn't for a couple more days..." I lay my hand on his face, savoring his stubble against my skin, staring into his smiling eyes.

"Told you awhile back I'd make the whole city know our love. Dad's old place is still technically in my hands for a few more days. Didn't take much to find a crew and load up on the best rockets a man can buy. Going to give the city a serious need to step up their game, though."

He isn't joking. I'm touched, as surely as the sky lights up like Independence Day has come early.

For us, embarking on our new lives, I suppose it has.

I see orange, red, and lily white. They flare wide in brilliant rings before flaming out, just in time for new ones to take their place, each spark brighter than the stars. Every explosion illuminates the sad old house on the shore, more distant than ever as the yacht rolls by its shore.

"Better take a good, long look," I say, trailing his father's old place with my eyes. I catch a quick glimpse of the crew and their equipment on a hill near the water, launching the amazing display skyward. "Probably won't see it again while it's still yours."

"I'd rather look ahead, doll," he whispers, grabbing my hand. "Fuck the past. I'm glad dad and I came to terms before he died, but that place will never be anything except a black hole for me. Closing day can't come soon enough."

He's right.

The weight lifting off him leaves him so light and vibrant it echoes in his pulse. I feel it when I run my fingers through his, laying my head on his shoulder, perfectly poised so I can enjoy our wedding fireworks up close and personal.

We're silent as the ship passes on. Even when the sky bursts are almost too small to see, I hear them booming in the distance, a grand finale left to the city to enjoy. For some reason, that makes me smile even more.

I'm sure most of the people watching from the shores who know why it's happening think I'm some spoiled, high maintenance rich girl. They'll never know how hard it was to get to our happy place, here on the tranquil sea, the ring on my finger sitting *right* in a way it never was before.

I'll take his advice about the past. I don't care anymore. It'll be in our history forever, sure, but it doesn't have to define us. Neither does what anyone in the present thinks.

We're sailing peacefully up the coast for another hour, enjoying our first drink alone as man and wife. The Dom flows freely, bubbly and delightful. I think about Kat at the reception, and hope she isn't blackout drunk by now.

We sip ours slowly, tasting its decadent richness.

It's good, but nothing like the lips I've been staring into all night. Nothing can ever drown the need building inside me except him.

"It's not polite to stare," he says, narrowing his eyes. His grip on my hand tightens. "Especially when you won't tell your husband what you really want."

Damn. A single tease is all it takes tonight to make my nipples pebble. "Whatever do you mean?" I tease back. "Cal, I really couldn't be happier. You've knocked about half the dreams off my bucket list tonight with this awesome wedding, the yacht ride, the fireworks —"

"Only half? Good." He leans in, forcing me to feel his breath, torturing me every second he refuses to close with a kiss. "That means your other dreams must be filthy, doll. Let me teach you a thing or two about that."

At last, his lips touch down on mine. I let go of the moan I've been holding in for the last twenty minutes. My hands are ravenous. They pull at his collar, but he bats my greedy hands away when they try to slip to his buttons, eager to pop them off.

Not fair.

Still, it doesn't stop me from taking everything I can get when his mouth attacks mine. Lust swarms my blood in waves, vicious and stifling, forcing my thighs together for fractional relief as I take his tongue again and again.

Somehow, he manages to steer us into port on the first stop of our honeymoon. It's a small, exclusive tourist spot with a private dock. There's a light on in the cabin, and a servant waiting to tend to our every need. We may not bother tonight, considering everything I'll ever need is in front of me.

"We have to go. Now," I whisper, pinching his hand.

Cal helps me up, pushing his palm into the small of my back, and then a little lower to the ridge of my ass. My hips fold into his like a flower bending toward the light.

"No, doll. This ship has a perfectly good cabin. I'd like to put it to good use before we turn in for the night on land."

No protest here. I follow him down the narrow marble stairs, trying not to trip on the edge of my skirt. I never thought I'd want to shed something so beautiful clinging to my skin so quickly.

But that's the power this man has over me on our wedding night. That's the strength, the beauty, and the prowess my eyes admire from every edge of his body.

He pushes through a small door on the lower level. It opens a master suite with all the amenities, a massive plush bed anchored in the middle. His foot kicks the door shut behind him. We don't say another word, just fall into each other, lost in our heartbeats, our breath, and tearing off our clothes.

I'm afraid he'll rip my wedding dress to shreds when he starts pulling it apart, but he's surprisingly gentle, never lowering the need throbbing in his eyes as he stares into me. "Do you have any clue how hard I'm about to fuck my wife for the first time?"

"Show me," I whisper. My voice trembles, a dead giveaway for how bad I want him to.

Another push, and the elegant fabric falls, pooling at my feet. I shimmy out of my panties when his thumbs hook around them. His hands clasp my shoulders, digging his fingers in, bringing me down on my knees.

I'm face-to-face with his immaculate cock. Pre-come rolls out the tip when I grasp his base, rolling the smooth skin up and down, trying not to let my imagination overwhelm me. It's far too easy to imagine this inside me, doing everything I know it's so good at.

Has it really only been days since the last time we had sex? My heart drums, insisting it must be years, and holy hell, how I've missed stroking his cock with my tongue.

"Fuck, Maddie," he growls, fisting my hair when I open my mouth and draw him in. "It's been an eternity."

Yes, it has.

My mouth helps put a dent in the lost time we need to make up. Every inch I take is warm, pulsing, furious in the denial it's suffered. He finds his rhythm, thrusting into my mouth, helping my head each time he pulls on my hair.

Why didn't anyone tell me those pulls could feel almost

as good as his kiss? My pussy drips between my legs, melting like a candle under a torch. Desire makes me dizzy, but I ground myself, sucking him faster, gliding my fingers to his base, pushing gently into his heavy balls.

His eyes are on me the entire time. I realize he's watching my hand. Whenever the dim light catches the ring just right, he sighs, his chest bulging, and he lets out tortured grunt. "Just fucking end me, doll. Seeing your hand like that wrapped around my cock...it's goddamned beautiful. Best sight I'll ever see."

I moan into him, sucking faster. He growls louder. I know I've hit the mark when he twitches, throbbing faster, harder, grinding his hips into my face. I want to make him lose it, but it's no big surprise when he tugs my face off him by the hair, another rugged growl escaping his throat.

"All fours, Maddie. On the bed. Right fucking now."

My pussy tenses more than I thought possible. I love how he's almost speechless, his brain a little closer to the caveman whiles of his body.

We're married now. This is how it is, how it was always meant to be.

No more thinking. That comes later.

This is sex built for emotion, for flesh, for souls. Not earthly intellects.

"Calvin, please," I whisper, face down on the bed, lifting my hips to him, waiting for the heat of his fingers digging into my skin.

"Please what, beautiful?" He gives my hair another rough tug. His swollen cock tilts against my hips, holding me back with his knees so I can't grind into him. "Tell me, doll, is *this* what you want?"

His full length presses into my labia, catching the wetness leaking out of me.

Holy hell. I'm dying.

"You know it, hubby," I whisper, throat turning into cotton because I *know* what he wants to hear. "Fuck me."

God, it still feels dirty saying it. But, oh, when doesn't dirty feel good?

"Finally. Only took until our wedding night to hear you let go," he rumbles, planting his arms on the bed, against my shoulders, bearing down. His hot whisper fills my ear, so warm and lush, I tremble. "Good girl, Maddie. And good girls get presents on their wedding night. Here's yours: I will mount you, I will fuck you, I will flood your sweet cunt until my balls can't anymore. Let's fuck like man and wife."

No words. He sinks into me with a feral grunt. My pussy hugs his cock, tightening around him, a shrill whimper escaping my throat as I realize how good I'm making him feel.

"Fuck me," I whisper again, raising my ass to meet his strokes.

There's a savage energy in his thrusts. A longing, even though he's balls deep. I'm close to coming, my eyes fluttering shut, when he reaches between my legs, thumbing my clit.

His friction pushes me into the sun.

"Come for me, doll. Come like the hot little wife you always wanted to be." His words are thunder in my ear.

They shake me to my core, bring me into meltdown.

His hips move like pistons, pinning me against the bed. Slamming his cock deep, he holds it while my body convulses. I scream so loud I'm certain it leaves the ship, heading for any ears on the shore.

Orgasm consumes me. I don't know how he's still holding up when my legs stop shaking and he flips me over. There's a single, slow kiss to catch my breath, his forehead against mine, and then I see new fire in his eyes.

When he sinks into me again, I swear he's even harder than before. My nails rake his open shirt, finding his perfect abs, admiring the strength he's about to make me feel in my bones.

He pushes it off his body, leaning backward just long enough to lose his last clothing, giving me a magnificent view of his naked body.

It's inked. It's hard. It's about to be mine.

"Cal…" I still tense like it's our very first time when he's nude.

"Maddie, fuck, you're tighter than ever tonight. Very dangerous." I lick my lips, opening my eyes, wondering what he means. A familiar smirk lights the space below his blue eyes, beaming down. "Makes me want to fuck you harder. Fuck you with the insane longing I've always had for this night, when I knew I'd own this pussy for good."

"Do it," I whisper, forgetting to be careful what I wish for.

I raise my legs. He hugs them to his shoulders and thrusts in, sliding deeper, pushing his tip until I'm achingly full.

We move. We collide. We join bodies in a primal rut, searching for release.

My body works for his seed. I move in ways I didn't even know I could, throwing myself into him, lacing my fingers with his when he reaches his full manic pace. I'm pinching him so hard my knuckles turn white.

"Cal, fuck, yes!" Words come without thinking. Pleasure overrides everything each time his cock strokes deep, wedding my flesh to his. I want to hold back, to keep control, to wait until he's found release before I let myself drift into storming bliss again.

"Fucking come! Come with me," he commands, a split second before the swelling deep inside me begins.

His cock throbs, bursts, pours his heat into me. My pussy surrenders the second his seed hits my flesh.

We come together. So hot, so hard, so frantic. I see stars in the whites of my eyes, pure burning lust forged from heartbreak and shattered lives reborn. We beat the odds.

It's still hard to believe my husband's seed is filling me while I thrash underneath him like an animal, setting me off again. He drags my fingers into his, stretching the very bones in my fingers, growling his release while his cock hurls fire.

So much for control.

My soul feels lighter when I exit heaven, emptied like a cloth wrung dry. Then he lowers himself into a new sultry kiss, and I let my mouth frolic on his for what seems like another eternity.

"Best I ever had," he growls, breaking away, catching his

breath. "Fuck, Maddie. Knew I chose you for a reason."

I flash him a dirty look and sink my teeth lightly into his ear. "Shut up, Mr. Romantic. You, with your seven year yearning for our wedding night. We've arrived, and it's so much better than sex."

"Guilty. But the chemistry when we fuck is one hell of a perk."

"Yes, well…" I run my palm across his face as he pulls out of me, crashing down on the bed next to me. "There's sex, and a thousand other reasons."

"Better start counting, doll. You've got a couple minutes tops before I'm hard again, and too fucking horny for the flowery stuff." He gives me another kiss, pressing my hand to his face when I graze his stubble against my fingers.

Oh, if I had the time to live seven years in an instant. I'd have never let him go, tragedy be damned. I'd seize every flirtatious word, every missed opportunity, and every tragic outcome. I'd re-live them all, experiencing the myriad what-ifs, just to lay here with him like this again, looking toward our long, happy future.

I'm not with a playground crush, or a fake fiancé who just happens to be amazing in bed.

I'm with my husband; my finer, inevitable half.

And until the day I die, I'll wear his ring, taste his lips, and call myself Mrs. Madeline Randolph. Happiest, luckiest, and most cherished woman on earth.

Thanks!

Want more Nicole Snow? Sign up for my newsletter to hear about new releases, subscriber only goodies, and other fun stuff!

JOIN THE NICOLE SNOW NEWSLETTER! - http://eepurl.com/HwFW1

Thank you so much for buying this book. I hope my romances will brighten your mornings and darken your evenings with total pleasure. Sensuality makes everything more vivid, doesn't it?

If you liked this book, please consider leaving a review and checking out my other erotic romance tales.

Got a comment on my work? Email me at nicolesnowerotica@gmail.com. I love hearing from my fans!

Kisses,
Nicole Snow

More Intense Romance
by Nicole Snow

FIGHT FOR HER HEART

BIG BAD DARE: TATTOOS AND SUBMISSION

MERCILESS LOVE: A DARK ROMANCE

LOVE SCARS: BAD BOY'S BRIDE

RECKLESSLY HIS: A BAD BOY MAFIA ROMANCE

STEPBROTHER CHARMING:
A BILLIONAIRE BAD BOY ROMANCE

STEPBROTHER UNSEALED:
A BAD BOY MILITARY ROMANCE

PRINCE WITH BENEFITS:
A BILLIONAIRE ROYAL ROMANCE

MARRY ME AGAIN:
A BILLIONAIRE SECOND CHANCE ROMANCE

Prairie Devils MC Books

OUTLAW KIND OF LOVE

NOMAD KIND OF LOVE

SAVAGE KIND OF LOVE

WICKED KIND OF LOVE

BITTER KIND OF LOVE

Grizzlies MC Books

OUTLAW'S KISS

OUTLAW'S OBSESSION

OUTLAW'S BRIDE

OUTLAW'S VOW

Deadly Pistols MC Books

NEVER LOVE AN OUTLAW

NEVER KISS AN OUTLAW

NEVER HAVE AN OUTLAW'S BABY

NEVER WED AN OUTLAW

Baby Fever Books

BABY FEVER BRIDE

BABY FEVER PROMISE

BABY FEVER SECRETS

SEXY SAMPLES:
BABY FEVER BRIDE

I: Tick-Tock (Penny)

It's only ten o'clock in the morning, and I'm completely boned.

No, not in the way I want to be. There's nothing handsome, alpha, or inked about the middle aged doctor rattling off my lab results, and they're not pretty.

I'm sitting in his office, trying to listen to what he's saying, before I ask if there's been a horrible screw up.

Wishful thinking. Dr. Potter, a thin balding man who can't stop giving me the most sympathetic look in the world, doesn't make mistakes.

"Just to confirm, we ran your blood test three times before reporting the results to the CDC, as required under Federal law. There's no mistaking it." He holds a finger up, as if he's read my mind. "I'm sincerely sorry to deliver the bad news, Ms. Silvers. The fever and sweats you've been complaining about should have already diminished. They won't be back. As for the long-term consequences –"

He stops when I choke up. *Long-term…that's really what he wants to call it?*

He's just told me my blood test came back positive for the fucking Zeno virus. I'm never going to be a mom.

Not unless I get pregnant next month, which seems about as likely as the wiry old doctor ripping off his face and

319

revealing an Adonis underneath. One who'll wink at me and volunteer to be a donor.

Yeah, nobody's that lucky. And if there's anything I'm sure about today, it's my luck running out.

It's my fault for taking that humanitarian trip to Cuba, where one bad mosquito bite was waiting to change my life forever. I can feel the spot under my elbow where the hot red welt used to be. Biting my lip, I reach down and scratch it, even though there's nothing there anymore.

Hot blood races through my cheeks. I'm shaking. Sixty seconds away from breaking down.

Another embarrassment I don't need while I'm glued to this chair, unable to put as many miles as I can between myself and this hellish consultation.

"Ms. Silvers, please…it's going to be all right," he says in his best dad voice, reaching over, pressing a reassuring hand down on my shoulder. It's not helping. "If you'll allow me, I'd like to review the positives in your situation: infertility is the only clinically known side effect of Zeno syndrome. You won't suffer anything more dire. Plus everything I've read in the journals lately sounds promising. They're working on a treatment. There's a real chance Zeno induced infertility may be reversible with good time, if the research pays off."

If? Until now, I've held in the tears. Now, they're coming, wet and ugly and full of angst.

"Easy for you to say!" I sputter. "I never should've taken that trip. I wouldn't have even thought about it if I'd known it meant giving up my chances to ever be a mom. God, if

I'd just stuck to Miami for the beaches, gave myself a normal getaway like most people…"

"No. You can't beat yourself up. Besides, Zeno has been working its way into our coastal communities, Ms. Silvers. The CDC report on my desk says as much. A hundred cases in Florida this week alone." He's still rubbing my shoulder, as if the most boring, detached man in the world can comfort me. "Listen, if you'd like, we can explore what the university has to offer in terms of egg preservation. There's no guarantees, of course, but it's entirely possible –"

"That *what?*" My voice shakes. "I'll magically find a way to pay a bunch of quacks to stab me with needles, and then pay them ten times more to keep my unborn children in test tubes? I'm a secretary for a third rate company, Doctor. I make fifteen bucks an hour. You might as well tell me I'm about to meet Mr. Right when I walk out this door, have him propose tomorrow, and knock me up by next Friday."

Potter looks nervously at the wall. His hand drifts off me. Well, at least I'm not the only one here who's embarrassed, not that it's much satisfaction.

He clears his throat, and folds his hands, leaning toward me over the desk. It takes me a second to realize he's eyeing the medical degree on the wall behind me. Okay, maybe I regret throwing the quack word around in front of him. I'm sure he'll forgive me.

"You do have eighteen months before the full effects of Zeno in your reproductive system make the odds of conceiving virtually zero."

A year and a half. Lovely.

Not even enough time to build up a serious relationship from coffee dates or – God forbid – Tinder. Much less rest assured I've really met the one, the man I want to have a baby with.

And that's assuming I'd have better prospects than the usual idiots I've met before. Like the boy a couple weeks ago, who showed up late to our dinner at an overpriced French place, bearing gifts. Gifts, in this case, being the cheap purple dildo he buried in a bouquet of plastic roses.

It takes real talent to embarrass a girl in public, plus insult her intelligence in one go.

I'm shaking my head, pushing away date nights I wish I could forget, holding in the verbal sting I want to unleash on the entire world, using the doctor as a proxy.

But it isn't his fault, or his problem. Dr. Potter isn't here to listen to my disasters in dating, or fix my non-existent sex life.

He's a general practitioner, not a psychologist, and having an incurable tropical disease means he can't even help with that.

I want to leave. But there's another horrible question on the tip of my tongue. "So, does this virus affect anything else downstairs? Like my chances of enjoying…you know."

As if sex should even be on the radar. I've been celibate for so long it shouldn't matter, twenty-three years. Maybe the disease will give me one more reason to keep my V-card.

Dr. Oblivious takes a few seconds to get what I mean. Then his eyebrows shift up. "Uh, no, not at all. You're free to involve yourself with any partner using the usual precautions. There's no risk of human-to-human transmission, Ms. Silvers. Your partners can't catch the disease unless they walk through the wrong mosquito-infested areas at the wrong time, just as you did, and the odds of that happening are exceedingly low."

Low. Yeah, just like me.

Lucky, lucky me, with my dead love life, boring job, and distant family. Add shattered dreams to the list.

There's nothing to celebrate here. The only place I ever beat the odds was contracting a rare Caribbean virus, destroying my future without even knowing it at first bite.

Why couldn't it have been the lottery instead?

I need to get out of here. I just want to go back to work, punch in my last few hours, and then go home and pull the blanket over my head.

When I'm in my cocoon, I can pretend I never ignored all the half-assed CDC warnings to have a great time in an amazing country that's just opened up to Americans again. I can pretend my junk hasn't just been trashed by a thumb-sized vampire bite, that I'm going to get my shit together, and be an amazing wife and mother whenever the right boy comes along and proves to me he's a man. I can pretend I still have time, more than eighteen months before the sword falls, obliterating the future I always imagined.

And I can pretend the holidays aren't coming, that I won't cry over the dinner table when mom taps my foot with her cane, and asks me why the hell I haven't found myself a boyfriend yet.

"Ms. Silvers?"

"Jesus, just call me Penny, Doctor! That's what everybody else says," I tell him, giving into the sarcasm pulling me deep into the black pit in my gut. "I read you loud and clear. I get how screwed I am. There's nothing you can do for me, right? Can we be done?"

He doesn't say anything, just turns his face to the small tablet in his hands, and begins scrawling a sloppy signature with his finger. A second later, he hits a button, and the device prints out a tiny prescription slip, which he tears off and hands to me.

"This will make you feel better in the interim," he says. "Simple pain relievers, on the off chance your fever returns. Until then, it should help minimize your discomfort from our talk today. While your viral load is dropping to acceptable levels, it could be lower. Please be sure to rest, and drink plenty of water."

If only guzzling water like a desert explorer would flush it all out of my system. I'd drink Lake Michigan dry. It's visible outside his window, behind the Chicago skyline, rippling in grey and gloomy November shadows.

"Thanks," I mutter, crinkling the paper in my fist as the doctor stands, ushering me out the door.

If I were him, I'd be relieved to see the last of me, too. I'm sure I'm about to become the latest statistic in a medical journal, one more faceless person tracked by the outbreak that's been making inroads in the country thanks to people like me. I should be grateful tropical mosquitoes are the only way it spreads, and so far they haven't found any in the Midwest that can carry it.

At least I won't have to worry about infecting anybody else. Small comfort when I'm out the door, heading for the train so I can get across town, back to the office. Frankly, no one else deserves to have this curse inflicted on them if they can avoid it.

But I'm not thinking about them, the lucky ones. I'm being selfish, focusing on myself, and quietly hating every healthy woman in America who will never have to worry about their biological clock going up in a fireball.

The worst day of my life gets predictably worse.

By afternoon, my right heel comes apart. I'm distracted, lost in my own head, mourning the babies I'll never hold in my arms because there's not enough time to make them happen. I don't see the small break in the marble floor that trips me, threatens to send me crashing down face first, or worse.

It's a small miracle I catch myself against the banister overlooking the twenty second floor of the Shaw Glass Tower where I work. I just wanted some fresh air and people watching, staring down at the ants in the lobby, anything to take my mind off the bad news, not to mention the mountain of work I still have left for today's clients at Franklin, Harrison, and Hitch.

Spinning, I grip the banister tightly, catching myself before I go over it. I'm crushed by the news about my childless future, but I'm not suicidal.

The pivot turns the small fissure cutting through my

heel into a break. I see the end snap off, and go rolling across the floor, coming to a stop against the wall. I swear, walk over, and throw it into my pocket. At least I'm able to hide the damage for the rest of the afternoon, screening calls for the firm, stuffing envelopes, and responding to last minute requests when Mr. Franklin himself walks up and bangs his fist on my desk.

I'm so distracted, I've lost track of time.

"Hey, you're twenty minutes past quitting time. Go home and get some rest, Penny." My normally gruff boss flashes me a softer look, before he turns around and heads back into his office. "Looks like you need it."

Ugh. Finding out I'm Zeno positive is the last thing I need. The second to last is sympathy from a sixty year old partner, especially one whose manners typically match his bulldog appearance. If Mr. Franklin sees how worn down I am, then I must *really* look like hell.

I gather my things and shut down my computer, dropping a few last envelopes in the mail on the way out. I'm careful heading out onto the windy streets, wrapping my coat tight against the late autumn chill.

I can't wait to get home, curl up on the couch with my cat, Murphy, and watch something that will put Zeno and the babies I'll never have far, far away. Then it hits me that the overfed little lion I call my pet will probably be the *only* baby I ever have.

I'm wiping my eyes, waiting for the train, trying to hide the hurt. My luck doesn't improve when the doors slide open. Of course, it's more crowded than usual for rush hour.

I'm so angry on the way in, I only catch a glimpse of the man in the corner, but I feel his eyes. They're on me, hard and searching, glued to my back until the inevitable chill courses up my spine. I tuck myself deeper in the standing crowd, gripping the steel pole, hiding from his gaze.

I don't notice him again until he's right behind me. He wastes no time. His fingers graze the back of my coat, just above my butt.

I've always been creeped out by the pervs I've run into in the city's transit system, but they've never *scared* me like this man.

I'm also pissed. I spin around and shoot him a death glare, lashing out with my fear.

"What the fuck do you think you're doing?" I turn my nose up. I'm not sorry about it when I see him.

He's probably twice my age. Unshaven. Liquor rolls off his breath when he cracks a half-toothless grin. My hand forms a fist that wants to wipe it off his disgusting face.

"Thought you looked lonely, baby. It's a full house here today. Come a little closer. Let's be friends. You're cold, and I've got all the fucking warmth you're ever gonna need."

His hand reaches for my wrist. Now, I'm really worried.

Run of the mill pervs aren't this persistent. I don't have time to think, or enough space to punch, kick, or scream. I'm stunned by his aggressive, pawing hands. He catches me around the waist, and pulls me against a tiny open space in the wall, away from the steel pole I'd been hanging onto for my life.

Shit. I don't know what to do. I need to make up my mind *fast*.

This man could be the city's next serial killer for all I know. He's already eyeballing the door, like he's ready to drag me off, into the unknown, threatening to make my crap day so much worse.

Two choices: I can either kick, bite, and scratch with everything I've got, or I can scream bloody murder and hope one of the fellow sardines packed into this metal box will actually help me.

"What'sa matter, baby? You a fighter? My boys like that," he rumbles, studying my eyes, drunker than I thought. "Don't fret. Don't move. Just listen. Stick with me just a little while longer, girlie, and I'll help you find your way to the perfect —"

"Love! I've been looking all over for you," another male voice interrupts.

An arm crashes into the bastard whispering weird threats in my ear a second later, knocking him through the crowd. Several people curse and grumble. My perv is gone, replaced by the handsomest six and a half feet of masculinity I've ever seen packed into a suit, a tie, and a long dark jacket.

Eyes as bright and blue as oceans engulf me, set in a determined face with a jaw that looks like it could break fists. Mr. Strange and Sexy replaces the creeper's hand on my wrist with his own, and leads me through the crowd, leaning into my ear with his lips.

"Play along. I caught him eyeing you the second you stepped on," he whispers. "Follow me. We've got to put some space between us and that man."

Tingles rush up my back. There's certainty in his voice,

like he knows a lot more than I do, and none of it's good. He lays his free hand gently on my back, and doesn't take it off until he has me settled in the only free seat in this car. He stands next to me, hanging onto the pole. He's smiling down at me with his strong jaw and brash blue eyes, utterly unaffected by the restless crowd around us as the train jerks away from its latest stop and resumes its journey.

I don't know whether to breathe, or start sweating all over again. There's no time to decide. I'm paralyzed an instant later, when I hear the familiar slurred voice ring out behind my hero.

"What's your problem, buddy? Butting in like you've got some business with her? Don't think you got any goddamn clue who you're dealing with, and you don't wanna find out." His voice drops another octave with every sentence, evil and furious.

Oh, no. I grip the stranger's hand tighter, begging with my eyes. *Please. Don't let go.*

I'll handle this. That's what his eyes say to mine, before he turns to face the perv, speaks a few words, and pats a spot on his hip barely covered by the end of his jacket.

My heart won't stop pounding. I'm afraid because the creeper keeps coming, growling words in the stranger's face, so persistent on a train this crowded.

Who *are* we dealing with? I don't want to find out. I just want him gone.

An announcement comes through the speaker and a couple next to us squeeze by, laughing loudly. I can't hear a thing between the two men. My savior says something, and it must be big, because the older man's eyes go wide. Creeper does a quick turn, barreling through several people toward the door, who give him dirty looks the whole way.

We don't say anything until the train slows at its next stop. His suit feels so soft beneath my fingertips. The sheer quality hits me through my frightened haze.

I have about sixty seconds to wonder what a man like him is doing here, when he looks like he could easily have his own driver.

His suit has more stitches than the ones the partners at the firm wear, and they're millionaires. The man underneath is even better. He's seductively tall, built, and refined. Strength and sophistication brought together in one Adonis. My eyes go to his like magnets when he looks at me again, and he gives me a reassuring nod.

"He's gone."

I look down, heat flushing my cheeks, ashamed of the sudden attraction I'm fighting. I should just be glad for his kindness, and get ready to go. "Good thing you were here. I didn't like the way he moved on me. Did you really tell him you had a…"

I stop myself, look around, and whisper the last word low underneath my breath. "A gun?"

The stranger smiles. He reaches into his pocket, plucks out a fancy new phone in a leather case that looks like it's lined with honest-to-God platinum trim. Smiling, he holds it up, and taps the screen.

"Worse. I've got a reputation. The man was probably

mafia, just so you know. It's satisfying when they run like the bitches they are."

"Mafia?!" I say it too loudly, and I feel several eyes on me. I'm covering my mouth as more red shame brushes my cheeks.

Strange and Sexy looks up, freezing my eyes in his stark blue stare. "You were about ten seconds from having a syringe stabbed in your thigh so you could be dragged off to the highest bidder. I told him he'd back the hell off my wife, or he'd be seeing the sheriff with a few broken bones. Didn't have to say much to make him believe me. He took off as soon as I said my name."

Mafia? Sheriff? His name?

Who the hell am I dealing with? I'm reeling so hard, I can't force the question out.

It's just as well. He's looking at his phone, firing off a text message to someone, which dings a second later.

"Is that your wife?" I ask. "The real one, I mean?"

He smirks, looking up over his phone. "I'm blissfully unmarried. Not looking to settle down anytime soon, as a matter of fact. I'm a very busy man."

Yes, of course he is. His jackass streak is starting to show through his five thousand dollar suit. I don't know whether to be relieved or irked he hasn't suggested I owe him yet for helping me out with some lewd remark.

Then again, if he's really as rich and powerful as he looks, he probably has his pick of high class women lined up each and every night. I hate that I'm wearing my cheapest work dress, grey and black, boring as the office itself. Plus the stupid bandage from my blood test at the clinic is still stuck to my arm.

"What do you do?" I ask, wondering if I'll regret making this small talk.

"Real estate. I'm on my way to a board meeting in the 'burbs right now. Can't beat the train for cutting through rush hour." He ignores me again, tapping away at his phone.

I have to clear my throat before he looks up again, bathing me in those bright blue eyes. "Funny, you look like you're a few years older than me, but it seems like you can't put that thing down. What's so important? Hot Tinder match?"

I've pegged him in his late twenties, at least. His eyes meet mine, more amused than before, and his kissable lips turn up at my challenge. "Business, love. I'm not done until around midnight most days, but this makes it easier. Thank God for technology, right? There's plenty of time over my late night snack to talk to the next girl I'm going to bang."

Eye roll time. I remember he's saved my life, though, and hold my sarcasm in check.

"It must get exhausting," I say, letting my eyes sweep down his massive chest.

Sweet Jesus, that body. It looks like he could hold up his Tinder dates along with half the world on his washboard frame, without breaking a sweat.

My mind goes places it shouldn't. Places off limits. I'm forced to imagine planting my hands on his tree trunk chest, underneath his princely exterior, and riding the patronizing smirk off his lips with everything my hips are worth.

"You get used to it," he says, narrowing his eyes. He holds out his phone. "Here, I'll let you hold this. Now, tell me all about what was on your mind when you almost wound up a missing person."

The fun is over. Today's rotten news comes bounding back. I'm biting my tongue, hating he noticed how distracted I was.

Hating it even more that I have to think about the most tragic day of my life. Somehow, a future without kids and a broken heel doesn't seem half bad when I think about the terrible things that could've happened if the perv had done what Strange and Sexy warned me about.

"You know, it looks like you're a fan of keeping your business to yourself. I think I'll do the same." It comes out more harsh than it should.

"Wow. I didn't mean to pry into your business if it's going to upset you," he says, holding his hands up. "All right. Quick, let's play twenty questions on safe mode before our stops. Mine's coming up in about five minutes. Let's keep the focus on me."

I don't want to ask him anything. I want to be done, but his firm, mysterious smile has a strange way of disarming me. Sighing, I fidget with his phone in my hands, my finger tracing its cool metal edge.

Holy shit, I think it really might be platinum. I look up, gazing into his eyes, wondering if I'm dealing with the President's nephew, or something.

"You said that man was mafia. How can you possibly know?"

"Told you I'm in real estate, city and 'burbs. Cockroaches are everywhere. Tough negotiators. Boys who hide their dirty money in legit businesses. It'd freak you out to know how far old money, blood, and crime gets you in my industry." The look on his face says he's completely serious. "Don't worry. I'm not a criminal myself. These hands are squeaky clean."

He holds them up again so I can see. They're refined, but thick and strong, just like the rest of him. Heat flares between my legs when I think about what they'd feel like all over me. After everything that's happened today, it's wrong on so many levels I can't even count them.

"And where do those hands go when they're not stuck to your phone?" I ask, digging my teeth gently into my lower lip, hoping he won't see.

Fine. If I'm going to lose my head to this silly crush, I might as well go all the way.

He doesn't answer right away. His smile grows wider, and he leans down, reaching above my ear. He pushes a loose lock of hair away so there's nothing blocking his whisper. "These hands are explorers, love. They've been places. Everywhere that makes desperate, redheaded angels like yourself scream."

Holy hell.

"Desperate?" I'm taken aback, breathlessly forcing it out, failing miserably to hide my reaction. "What gives you *that* idea?"

He isn't wrong, but I can't fathom why. No man can read my mind. Or did I also put on a sticker that reads

'VIRGIN' in screaming neon caps sometime today? Like, sometime in between colliding with this sexy freak, and finding out any sex I have is probably going to be emotionally and biologically empty, despite waiting my whole life for the right package?

"You want me, love. You want it bad when you've just pulled yourself out of some seriously fucked up shit. If I wasn't on my way to a board meeting, for real, I'd get us a ride at the next stop, bring you back to my penthouse, and eat your pussy until that other heel you're wearing snaps like a twig."

Oh.

Fuck.

I don't realize my eyes are closed until his hand slowly winds down my neck. When they're open, I'm looking into raw temptation. A man with a face and body offering to take away all my heinous problems for one night.

A man who won't disappoint. I know in every word, every glance, and every breath he delivers.

My fingers tighten on the strange phone still in my hands. "Should we swap numbers?"

"It's only proper when I've saved my damsel in distress, obviously."

His arrogance doesn't put me off frantically digging through my purse, searching for mine. I don't trust that he isn't instantly going to delete anything I put into my phone the instant he's off this train.

I don't know this man. He could be toying with me. I've heard the way the partners talk about women when they think their doors are closed. The rich, boisterous, bragging talk involving their latest conquests – especially the poor, clueless girls half their ages, totally in the dark about getting fucked behind their wives' backs.

I realize I'm not thinking right now. I'm going to follow through on trading digits, but I need to mull this over. I'm looking for a happy distraction from my problems – not another big fat mistake. Not even a big, dark, and muscular one.

"You mentioned your name…" I say, ripping open my purse and pushing my phone into his hands with the contacts screen open.

"It's Hayden." He types quickly, staring at the screen.

My lips purse. It's a fitting name, powerful and seductive. I'm amazed there's no lock screen on his phone, allowing me to go straight for the contacts.

"Oh, shit," he mouths, handing my phone back to me. We share a look, and realize a second later the train is stopped. People bolt down the aisle, brushing past us.

"You've got my number. Sorry, love, I really have to run." Before I can stop him, he reaches for the little black object laying on top of everything else in my purse.

As luck would have it, the one that isn't his phone.

Nope. He's got my personal diary.

"Hey!" I stand up, wobbling on my busted heel, panic crashing over me before I rush after.

There are too many people talking for him to hear me. He's already stuffed my little black notebook into his pocket, thinking it's his phone. And I'm left holding the speedy bastard's unit in what feels like a ten thousand dollar case.

He's gone.

I've just bought myself another problem. I'm gritting my teeth as I stumble around the seat, struggling to pick everything up I can reach, making sure I don't lose his phone.

I want to kick myself for jumping at the only good thing that's happened to me today, and causing more grief.

But kicking or jumping anything is out of the question. Not until I get myself another pair of shoes.

GET *BABY FEVER BRIDE*
AT YOUR FAVORITE RETAILER!

Made in the USA
Lexington, KY
10 January 2018